Praise fo
He Gets That F

‹‹‹‹‹‹‹‹‹‹‹‹

"A piercing, mesmerizing look into the fragility and resiliency of the human experience . . . a bold page-turner that will leave you breathless with anticipation. With *He Gets That From Me*, Friedland invites you to ask yourself the questions you didn't even know you needed to answer—about family, forgiveness, sacrifice, and love. An absolute home run."
—AMY IMPELLIZZERI, award-winning author of *Lemongrass Hope* and *I Know How This Ends*

"*He Gets That from Me* takes on timeless questions about parenthood and our presumptions about birth, biology, and family. Describing a modern-day arrangement between two dads and a surrogate, the story opens our eyes to the many ways a family can be created while also telling a suspenseful narrative full of unexpected thrills that keep the reader wanting more. A moving story throughout, it ends with a twist that will leave you thinking about the book long after you've finished reading it."
—MELISSA BRISMAN, ESQ., reproductive attorney

"Jacqueline Friedland creates a host of complex characters in this nuanced, compelling exploration of what it really means to be a family, and why we should maybe think twice before heading to ancestry.com."
—LAURA HANKIN, author of *Happy & You Know It* and *A Special Place for Women*

He Gets That From Me

He Gets That From Me

Jacqueline Friedland

SparkPress

Published by SparkPress, a BookSparks imprint,
A division of SparkPoint Studio, LLC
Phoenix, Arizona, USA, 85007
www.gosparkpress.com

Published 2021
Printed in the United States of America
Print ISBN: 978-1-68463-097-4
E-ISBN: 978-1-68463-098-1

Library of Congress Control Number: 2021906583

Interior design by Tabitha Lahr

*For my father,
with love*

Chapter 1

MAGGIE
JANUARY 2007

I'm just wrapping a towel around my wet body when I hear Wyatt calling for me on the baby monitor. I should have expected this, should have planned better or moved faster. Wyatt's been waking earlier from his naps with each passing day. He clearly no longer needs the marathon midday snooze that was a staple of his first year of life. I'll have to figure out how to keep him occupied for another few minutes if I want any chance of making it to work on time.

As I hurry to his room, I ignore the mess of mail that's been sitting on the hallway table for the past three days. At the top of the stack is an unopened invitation from the one and only high school friend who still condescends to keep in touch with me.

Instead of thinking about a trip back to New York for a bridal shower that I don't want to attend, and can't afford to get to anyway, I focus on the large plastic jar of rubber fish resting near the laundry basket at my feet. I scoop up the jar, and one of Wyatt's blankies from the pile of dirty laundry, and scurry down the hallway.

He's standing at the edge of his crib, his brown curls pointing in every direction as he shakes at the bars like a jailbird.

"Here, sweetie." I unscrew the large lid from the jar and pull out a squishy red fish. He reaches for it, looks at it curiously, and promptly brings it to his mouth. The fish is much too big to fit past his lips—a fact that will hopefully puzzle him long enough to allow me to finish dressing.

"Mommy has to get ready for work. I'll be back in just a few minutes." I place the jar in the corner of the crib so he can extract additional fish to manipulate as necessary, and then I dash back to my room.

I realize I'm still holding the blankie. It's the one Nick's aunt and uncle sent, a soft chenille square with Wyatt's Hebrew name embroidered along one side. I know that the white threading spells out "Yehuda," a name we chose in an effort to honor my deceased grandfather, but I never learned how to actually read the boxy Hebrew letters. I toss the blankie onto my dresser and quickly towel-dry my hair, hoping my own curls won't resemble Wyatt's ridiculous bedhead after this hasty personal grooming session. I have twenty-five minutes to get to Bed, Bath & Beyond on the other side of town, and if Nick doesn't get home within the next five minutes, my manager is going to chew me out six ways to Sacramento.

I pull on a pair of black jeans, my last clean pair, and rummage in the next drawer to see if I can find a tunic long enough to cover the small hole at the top of one of the pant legs. I hear myself sigh as I run the numbers in my head again. At nine dollars an hour, it's delusional to think about saving up money, to imagine returning to college. It's a joke to have any dreams at all.

Wyatt suddenly lets out a frustrated wail.

"Mommy's coming, Wyatt," I shout into the air. "Just one more second!" I slip on my black sneakers and scurry back into the nursery.

Wyatt's diaper is bulging against his tight little pajama pants. At the sound of keys jingling in the front door of the apartment, I scoop him out of the crib, grab my purse from where it's sitting on our coffee table, and meet Nick as he walks in the door.

"Sorry for the stinky welcome," I offer as I hold Wyatt out in his direction.

"Hey, kid." Nick smiles and reaches for our son with one hand, a bag full of takeout containers hanging from the other. "Oh," he adds, wrinkling his nose.

"Gotta go!" My keys are in my hand, and I'm placing a brisk kiss on Nick's cheek. The scent of garlic and cilantro is strong as I push past him and out the front door. Then I'm flying down the concrete steps toward the parking lot below our building, heading toward my '92 Honda, rushing against the clock, racing against luck.

⸺⸺⸺⸺⸺

When I come skidding through the doorway of BB&B at exactly 4:01 p.m., my co-workers, Kim and Dougie, are chatting across their registers, and they don't even look up. The store is unusually empty for a Thursday afternoon. I set my tote bag beneath the register at my station and punch in a few numbers to awaken the machine. Cynthia, my manager, is nowhere to be seen.

"Why is it so quiet?" I call across to Kim, whose register is three stations over from my own. The ones between us are always empty at this time of day.

"Post-holiday lull," Dougie answers from the register beyond Kim's. Dougie is in his early thirties and is the most senior employee among us, having worked here for three years, ever since he moved to Arizona from Tulsa.

An elderly woman walks into the store with a list in her hand. We stop our chatting and watch silently as she makes her way toward the first aisle, where a wealth of toasters and smaller kitchen gadgets await. We're still quiet when Cynthia appears from behind the displays of holiday-themed wrapping paper and gift bags, now all on sale, and begins making her way toward me.

"So dead today," she says by way of greeting, and she glances around the store for emphasis.

I stand a little taller as she approaches me, noting that her bleached hair looks freshly blown. If I'm lucky, that means she has somewhere else to be and won't spend the whole night breathing down my neck.

"What's dinner?" She tips her chin toward my stowed tote.

"Pulled beef burritos and Mexican street corn," I answer, remembering what Nick told me last night as he was cramming the takeout containers from the restaurant into the fridge.

Cynthia has so many self-imposed dietary restrictions that she won't touch anything unless she can read all the ingredients before digging in, but she likes hearing about the dishes Nick creates at work. She nods pensively in response and then continues down the row of registers toward Dougie. They quickly get involved in a detailed discussion about the placement of makeup mirrors in the stock room.

Standing here without customers to ring up is about as interesting as watching a cactus grow, and I miss the busier days of the holiday season. I resist the temptation to pick at my cuticles, if just for something to do, and instead, I study the displays of impulse-buy items placed throughout the front portion of the store. There are economy-size jars full of candies and colorful popcorn, kitschy potholders, hair accessories and curling irons, all piled in precarious pyramids meant to entice the customers.

My gaze travels to the back portion of my station, where there's a dog-eared copy of *Arizona Parenting Magazine* resting on top of the stack of store bags. It's an outdated issue that I assume was left behind by a customer. I reach for the magazine and start flipping through the pages, trying to entertain myself by reading the Thanksgiving recipes.

A customer finally appears, pushing a shopping cart full of turquoise-colored bath towels, but she walks towards Kim's register, so I turn my attention back to the magazine. After the recipes, there is a final section full of advertisements and coupons, and I'm annoyed that this diversion has lasted only a few minutes. There are still more than three hours left of my shift, and after a long morning trying to entertain Wyatt at home, I'm already dragging. I wonder if I should walk over to Kim's station and let her fill me in on the latest drama she's having with her mother-in-law, or if I could possibly close my eyes and steal a little cat nap while I'm standing up.

I'm just closing the magazine when I notice an ad that says, "Compensation of $35,000+." I stop the page from turning and pull it closer to read the ad in its entirety.

> *Can you help create a family? Become a Surrogate Mother! Satisfaction Beyond Words! Generous Compensation! You can make a beautiful dream come true!!*

My excitement dissipates as quickly as it had arrived. I wonder if these ads actually work, if there are really women out there who read these quarter-page displays and then raise their hands, screaming, "Pick me, pick me!" I suspect that most of these advertisements are the basis of one nefarious scheme or another, a way to get people to release personal information about themselves so that some lowlife can steal their identities. I can't imagine that fertility clinics would truly find their baby carriers this way. I snort to myself as I notice that the requirements for carrying someone else's baby seem to be even less rigorous than the prerequisites for my cashier job. They want a US citizen between the ages of twenty-one and thirty-eight who has previously birthed at least one child. That's it.

Since I'm so clearly qualified, based on these conditions, I actually consider it for a few seconds, fantasizing about handing over a baby to a formerly childless mother and then skipping off to an education course at a local university. A nagging thought about my parents creeps up on me then—the idea that I could reach out and ask them for tuition money—but I tamp it down like always, unable to stomach the notion. I am not going back to good old Gail and Leon with my tail between my legs and proving that they were right all along.

I close the magazine and push it back to the corner where I found it, shaking my head at myself for daydreaming, for imaging that my prior fuckups might ever stop standing in my way.

Chapter 2

DONOVAN
JUNE 2018

According to the paperwork in front of me, I am a thief and a fool. I should be shaved and dressed already. Instead, I'm still staring at the four genealogy reports I've got spread out across the kitchen table. My morning coffee languishes beside them, now cold, in a mug that reads, "Fab Dad."

I'm feeling anything but "fab" as I study the data in front of me. I lean closer, rubbing my hand against my rough chin, as I examine the colorful charts and diagrams, trying to make sense of what I'm seeing.

The information seems to indicate that my ten-year-old son might not be my son at all.

I read everything over again from left to right. The results confirm that Teddy is the biological son of my husband, Chip, just like we've always thought. Their genetic connection has long been perfectly obvious from their matching blond widows' peaks, their nearly photographic memories, and so many other conspicuous similarities.

Kai, on the other hand, has always resembled me. With his dark eyes and even darker hair, we figured that our second-born twin came from the egg that was fertilized by my sperm.

We ordered these genetic testing kits from Relativity as a follow-up to our kids' school project on family trees, thinking it'd be interesting to learn more about our genetic histories, but none of us imagined results like these.

Based on the Relativity reports, it seems that Kai shares no genetic material with me. And none with Chip, either. Even worse, there is no way, based on these results, that Kai and Teddy could possibly be genetic half-brothers.

I race to our small office at the back end of the apartment and search for the thick file from the fertility clinic, an overstuffed folder that's been left undisturbed for more than a decade. The papers have been packed away in a drawer ever since we brought our babies home, all of us exhausted from the cross-country drive. We kept subfolders on the woman who carried the babies, and on egg donor #2674, a college student with so many of the genetic traits that Chip and I had decided were important when we filled out our wish lists— strong health history, exceedingly high intelligence verified through SAT scores and IQ tests, demonstrable athleticism, so on and so forth.

I flip frantically through the pages until I find the report on the egg donor's ancestry. My heart sinks as I see that the results are just as I remembered. Our donor's workup shows a genetic origin that is 75 percent Mediterranean, a combination of Greek, Northern Italian, and Turkish. The remainder of her blood was deemed to have trickled down from various Scandinavian countries. That was part of why we liked her—genes that might produce children with olive complexions like my own, but might just as likely result in a blond-haired blue-eyed child resembling Chip. Why, then, does Kai's report show lineage only from eastern European countries like Hungary, Poland, and Romania?

At the sound of commotion outside the apartment door, I hurry to return the papers to their folder and shove everything back into place in the metal file drawer. As I'm racing back toward the kitchen, the door opens and Chip bursts in with Teddy and Kai.

The boys dump their dusty baseball bags beside the door, hidden metal bats clattering against the floor, and start scrambling toward the kitchen.

"Cleats!" Chip and I shout the word simultaneously and then smile at each other, applauding our own predictability.

The boys groan and drop to the floor in tandem, unlacing their muddy, spike-covered shoes and sparing our parquet floors.

Chip is still smiling at me from his post by the door, the layer of sweat coating his temples proof of his two hours coaching fifth grade Little League in the June sunshine. I want to lose myself in the picture he creates—a satisfied athlete, lingering in the doorway with his cap on backwards and a baseball Henley taut across his chest, a half-full Gatorade in hand—but the reports are sitting on the table in the kitchen. I never imagined there would be anything to keep secret when I downloaded the results and printed them off the Relativity website. I thought I'd be so cute, putting the boys' reports in separate envelopes for them each to open with glee—but now it feels like I've left live grenades unattended in the other room.

"One sec!" I pivot, bolt back to the table, and snatch up the papers and envelopes. I have everything in a stack, ready to stash in some high-up cabinet, when a now-barefoot Chip makes his way into the kitchen, the boys following closely behind. Panicking at their presence, I freeze.

Chip finishes the remainder of his blue sports drink and walks over to the recycling bin behind me to discard the bottle.

"What's all that?" he asks casually, glancing over my shoulder.

"No, nothing." I open my eyes extra wide at him, indicating there is definitely an issue here, but it's not something we can discuss at the current moment with the boys underfoot. "Just work stuff." I jam the papers into the outside pocket of my messenger bag, trying to appear nonchalant. One thing I've learned from raising children is how frustratingly perceptive even the littlest people can be.

Chip shrugs and heads to the open refrigerator, where Kai and Teddy are already standing inside the door, making a mess of my cheese drawer. Chip reaches above their heads for the bowl of champagne grapes on the top shelf.

I wait for the boys to find what they want but then grow impatient as they keep opening containers, peering inside this one and that one and then returning everything back to the shelves, all now in haphazard disarray.

"Guys, move," I finally bark, my tone angrier than I intended.

Teddy, who is shoving one of those horrible processed cheese slices into his mouth, shoots me a questioning look, but Kai is still struggling to pull a yogurt drink from its six-pack on one of the shelves.

"Leave it, Kai!" I demand, my voice rising.

Kai backs away from the stainless-steel door of the fridge, his dark eyes darting quickly to Chip and then back to me.

"Sorry," he says quietly, a look of confusion on his still-flushed face.

I don't answer as a I stare back at him, this child with his chocolate brown eyes and slick, dark hair, the boy who I always believed resembled my older sister. Of the two babies we brought home at the end of our long and winding journey with surrogacy, he is the one I always thought was my own flesh and blood.

"Pa?" he asks me, blinking rapidly as he begins to realize that something else is wrong.

I feel heat rising to the sides of my face, spreading across my temples—a sudden, deep anger, the sensation of confusion coupled with despair.

"Papa?" he says again, and my heart splinters as I try to process the impossible idea that I might not be his father at all.

"It's okay. Sorry, sorry." I rush back at them all, regretting the way I've extinguished everyone's Saturday afternoon buzz. "I just got frazzled by work stuff. Look"—I motion down to my sweats—"I didn't even have a chance to get dressed yet. But I shouldn't have let the work blitz influence my behavior. Completely my fault. If you guys go hit the shower, I'll have lunch on the table in ten minutes."

They hesitate, unsure if they've really been dismissed.

"And a smile on my face," I add. "Promise."

"I call first!" Kai shouts in response, running past me toward the small bathroom the boys share, clearly prepared to forget what just happened.

"No way—you went first yesterday!" Teddy is darting after him, a second piece of cheese still in his hand, oblivious to the tension that remains in the kitchen behind him.

As the boys' voices get farther away, Chip looks back at me and leans against the fridge. "You want to tell me what that was about?" he asks gently.

I glance back over my shoulder, nervous to be overheard.

The distant whirr of the shower starts up, and a second later, a door slams. I poke my head out from the kitchen and see Teddy still standing in the hallway outside the bathroom, a look of defeat on his chiseled face.

"You can use ours, Ted," I call to him, offering up this forbidden fruit, even though I know that bottles of conditioner will end up abandoned in all states of disarray—tops askew and shimmery liquid dripping helplessly into Rorschach images on the tile below. Towels will be strewn on the floor, left for dead, as though a magic gnome might hang them back.

Teddy's eyes light up at the offer.

"Just *please* don't make a mess." As if there's any point.

"Got it!" He nods and scurries toward the master bedroom, lifting his shirt over his head as he goes.

I sigh, sorry that he and I have very different definitions of the word "mess."

"Our shower?" Chip raises a golden eyebrow. "This must be serious." He's all light-heartedness and smiles, clearly not expecting the magnitude of what I'm about to tell him.

"The Relativity results came back. The DNA tests." The words rush out in a hushed whisper. "Kai's results don't match any of ours. There's no overlap. Not with either of us, and not with Teddy."

Chip is silent for a beat, impassive, almost as if I haven't said anything at all. I can see the moment that the information registers, and suddenly he springs into action.

"What? What do you mean?" he demands. He's scanning the kitchen counters. "Where are the reports? That's not possible."

I scuttle around him and pull them from the canvas bag. "Look."

He grabs the papers from my outstretched hand and places them on the kitchen island. I read the results again from over his shoulder as he studies them. First he examines Kai's, then Teddy's. He doesn't even look at mine or his.

"This doesn't make sense. The boys have the same mother. How could they not share a single origin country in common?" he asks me, as though I'm the one who has come up with the incomprehensible results he's reading. He looks back at the reports for a moment longer and then reaches for the paper with his own results, his eyes scanning quickly over the information. "Well, this at least makes sense."

I know he's seeing information he would have expected on his own report. Chip is more or less "Mayflower stock," even though he can't fully trace his lineage back to a literal pilgrim, much to his family's dismay. Still, the report confirms that he is 94 percent of European descent, with an emphasis on England, France, and Scandinavia. The remaining 6 percent is listed as "unassigned," which we were told to expect as a normal part of the results.

He glances quickly at the report with my information, which reads mostly as we'd expect. I am 97 percent European, with the greatest connections showing me to be Italian and Iberian. The results also allege that I am 3 percent Native American. I don't have time to focus on that unexpected bit of trivia, though.

"Well, clearly this is wrong," Chip says, flinging the pages back onto the kitchen island beside us as if they're worthless. "What a hoax." His lip curls as he prepares to write off this whole experiment as hogwash.

I don't respond, and his features slowly slacken as he registers that I believe there might be veracity to these results—that the horrific implications contained on these pages might be truth.

"Stop it," he says gently, putting a hand on my shoulder, as if to steady me. "Don't. What are you thinking? That the fertility clinic screwed something up? That the kid was switched at birth? You're not serious." He tilts his head as he regards me, like he can't believe the ridiculousness of my reaction.

And in that horrible moment, I suddenly realize that this mistake may have gone beyond the fertility lab. Here I was wondering if they had implanted the wrong embryo in the surrogate. But it could be so much worse. If the results are correct, if Kai is not my son, then I might have another son out there in the world—a ten-year-old child who has been living for a decade with the wrong parents.

Chip is watching me. His eyes narrow as though he can hear my thoughts. "No." His voice is firm. "That's preposterous, Donny. 'Switched at birth' isn't something that happens in real life. And anyway, it couldn't possibly be more obvious that Kai is the fruit of your loins. All you have to do is take one look at him."

But now I'm wondering if everyone's always thought Kai looks so much like me simply because he looks so different from Chip. "Well, then, how do you explain these?" I wave the papers in the air.

He steps closer to me and puts his hands on either side of my face, his palms cradling my chin, and it's as if he's trying to control the direction of my thoughts through his grasp, holding tight to keep me from getting hysterical. He lowers his head slightly so our gazes are level, our faces only inches apart. "Slow yourself down. These reports aren't right. This is just some money-making entertainment thing that people aren't supposed to take seriously. They called you Native American." He cocks his head in doubt, emphasizing the absurdity of it. "You think your Nonna's Nonna was spending time with the local Navajos back in Sicily? This"—he points toward the papers—"is just consumerism gone wrong. Fake science getting into the wrong hands. We have no reason to consider this information real data. At worst, it's nothing more than a scam. At best, they mixed up the results. Who knows? But don't you go doubting the family we worked so hard to create."

"It could be real." I back away and lower myself into a chair, too weak to bear the weight of the thoughts assaulting me. "Remember when the Mayers did this and found out Judah was Irish? They redid the test with two other companies and all three reports showed identical results. I think he found, like, twenty-two Irish cousins he never knew he had."

"First of all, promise me you are not going back online to look for cousins." Chip's voice is rough, commanding.

I shake my head. "It already says there are no matches for any relatives closer than four generations removed." I point to the bottom of Kai's report.

He looks down toward my finger but doesn't read the words. "Well look, the Mayers' experience doesn't mean that there wasn't a screw up this time around, okay?" We're quiet for a second as we stare at each other. "Just slow your roll for me. That's all I'm asking. Let's take a step back and digest this information for a few hours. Maybe it was just a shock to see the reports not matching up. Nothing is going to change, so let's sit with it for a minute, let it simmer. If we give it a little time, perhaps clearer thoughts could prevail?" He raises an eyebrow at me.

I want so badly for him to be right, to prove that my anxiety has gotten the best of me once again. "Yeah, okay," I say, nodding, as I make my way back over to the fridge, where I pull out a package of whole wheat wraps and a head of lettuce so I can get lunch started. "I guess that makes the most sense." I don't expect that a few hours of ruminating will do anything to quash the dread I'm feeling in the pit of my stomach, the vine full of worry burrowing inside me. My mind is already running on overdrive, wondering what the next step should be, how we should try to figure out what happened. In spite of myself, I feel like something has already been taken from me—ripped out of my grasp, stolen. I'm not sure how I'm supposed to just ignore this new sense of uncertainty, of not knowing where our boy came from, of not having any information to cleave to for even a dusting of foundational or emotional security.

As I pull a few more items from the fridge, I try to talk myself down. I tell myself that it's crazy to think, even for a split second, that Kai might not be my child. Of course he's mine, and there is a reasonable explanation for the results we were sent. I try to convince myself that eventually, I will be laughing about my ridiculous overreaction.

And yet.

As I move the butter knife in concentric circles, spreading hummus across four whole wheat wraps, I can't stop worrying. Is it possible that I have another ten-year-old son somewhere out there, living in someone else's home? Or is my genetic child still a frozen embryo, waiting in a lab in Connecticut? What if there was another unfortunate family at UCLA the day that Kai and Teddy were born who are also caught up in this, and now, somewhere out in the wide world, I have another child who has no idea he has been living the wrong life?

By nighttime, I'm still fixating, despite Chip's pleas to the contrary. Each of his brisk, clipped movements feels like an admonishment as he climbs into our king-size bed and pulls the white duvet up around his waist. He plucks his iPad from the nightstand, his gaze shifting pointedly away from me, down to the news article on the screen.

I sigh dramatically from where I'm still standing in the middle of the bedroom with my toothbrush in my hand, and Chip looks back up at me.

"I can't argue about this anymore," he says. "You're Scottish, you're Spanish, you're part penguin. These companies are just pandering to consumers."

"I don't know how you can be so cavalier." I run my bare toes against the scratchy Berber rug beneath the bed as I stare down at him. "They have millions of people in their database. Millions. It's real data, Chip!" I point the green toothbrush at him, laying into him like this is his fault. A dollop of fizzy toothpaste plummets to the Berber.

"You know what?" Chip sits up a little straighter against his pillow, a hint of irritation creeping into his voice. "Do you want to just get DNA tests? Like, real, legit paternity tests? Otherwise you're going to be a basket case forever."

"Yeah." I turn back toward the bathroom. "I think it's a good idea."

I don't mention that I already reached the same conclusion hours earlier, while we were shepherding the boys around South Street Seaport, talking about everything except what was actually on my mind. Chip's cell phone rings from its perch on the wireless charger beside him, and I head back to the bathroom to take care of my teeth.

His mother, no doubt. Don't get me wrong, I love Lynn Rigsdale dearly, but Chip has asked her repeatedly not to call us after 10 p.m., and still she does. Some days Chip seems incredibly miffed by the liberties to which his mother feels herself entitled, and other times, like tonight, he is clearly delighted by the sound of her voice, regardless of the hour.

I take my time with my teeth as I listen to Chip's end of the conversation. Gone is the exasperation that I heard moments ago; and instead, he's regaling his mother with tales of his latest work-related drama. Who knew there could be drama at an investment bank, but that's Chip—he could find a human-interest story inside a can of green beans.

It turns out that the investor on the other side of his latest deal is the brother of some peripheral high school friend of his. As I listen to him hypothesize with his mother about what ever happened to this guy and that guy from his stodgy private school back in Connecticut, I feel an unwelcome sense of jealousy at his ability to compartmentalize, or to simply not worry at all. He's always so sure of everything, of how things will work out, of himself.

He's hardly rushing her off the phone, so I reorganize the top drawer in the bathroom vanity while I wait. Beneath the tubes of toothpaste and shaving oils, I spy a package of Coco-floss, a high-end dental floss that Chip brought home from a cosmetics store last month. I used to get really fired up about artisanal floss—one of my many offbeat indulgences from before we had kids—so when Chip saw this new floss at a Sephora, he thought of me and picked it up. Sadly, this brand leaves an aftertaste akin to Crisco mixed with shoe polish. After trying it once, I thanked Chip profusely and shoved the packet deep into a drawer when he wasn't looking. I reach now for the fluorescent box, pull out a long piece of the distinctive turquoise-and-orange-braided thread, rip it off, and toss it directly into the trash. Chip will see it there and think that I've used it.

He's wrapping up the call, finally, so I make my way back toward the bed, stopping to rub at the spot of toothpaste on the rug and then to pull our blackout shades more precisely into place on the way.

He hangs up the phone and looks back at the tablet in front of him as I lower myself onto the bed next to him.

"Huh." He chuckles as he turns his screen in my direction. "Did you know they sell paternity tests at Walgreens?" He tilts the device closer to me so I can see. I'm surprised that he was searching DNA tests while so casually chatting it up with Lynn. "How many people do we think are doing paternity tests on the regular?" he says on a laugh.

"I'm glad you think this is funny," I say. "I am not using some random drugstore test. We're using a lab. Quest, Labcorp, I'm sure they all do it."

"How are you going to take Kai to a lab? You're just going to tell him that you're worried we got the wrong embryo or that the hospital might have sent us home with one of the wrong babies?" His smile vanishes. "I don't think so. That's a hard no for me."

"Of course not," I say. "Do you think I've suddenly turned brainless?"

He raises his eyebrows at me as if to say, *If the shoe fits.*

"Oh no," I deadpan, "there goes my brain, slipping right out of my ear. Look, it made a mess on the bed."

I cross my arms against my chest, waiting for him to speak. He only rolls his eyes at me.

"I'm pretty sure we can get a sample at home," I say. "I'll just tell Kai it's follow-up for the ancestry testing. That they needed more information or something. He won't care."

"Fine, whatever." Chip waves a hand in the air. "I think you're blowing this whole thing out of proportion, but whatever you need to do."

"I hope you're right," I shrug as I pick up the novel that has been sitting on my bedside table for a month, some crime drama that I cannot get into. I pull out the bookmark and attempt to focus on the words in front of me, but my thoughts are still careening in a million directions. I can't stand that it's currently only Saturday night, which means I will have to wait out the remainder of the weekend before I can start making any useful phone calls about this situation.

My thoughts keep churning, tumbling all the way back to the day the boys were born. We were there in the hospital room the moment they arrived. I saw both babies before they were whisked off to the nursery. I held their wiggly bodies, inhaled their scents as I kissed them. Wouldn't I have noticed if one of them was different—like, an entirely different little human—when we saw him again only a couple of hours later? I remember how I instantly felt bonded with each boy. Chip and I had endless discussions before the babies were born about whether the love for a child truly materializes the minute he or she is born, or whether that was all cliché. Those questions became moot as I held Teddy and then Kai, for the first time each. I was overcome with such astounding emotion, a fierce and violent love that took over my whole being.

But now I feel my stomach clench as I worry that maybe it wasn't Kai I was holding in that moment, that it could have been another baby boy. Is it really possible that Kai wasn't meant to come home with us? I can't fathom such a possibility, not even a little. And yet I can't let it go. I need to know why his results don't match up with the rest of ours.

Chapter 3

MAGGIE
JANUARY 2007

As I pull into the parking lot of the Food City Shopping Plaza, exhausted from eight hours at the store, I'm still ruminating about my afternoon. This older guy came in wanting a refund for an air mattress, but he'd already opened and destroyed the packaging, which meant I was only allowed to an offer an exchange. Well, he wasn't having it. He threw a full tantrum, shouting at me about how he didn't like my attitude and demanding to see the manager. Cynthia appeared on the scene and eventually placated the man with a lot of earnest head nodding and a discount card, but after he left, she started waxing poetic about customer service. I let the situation get too heated without seeking intervention, she said. "You've got to know who has your back," she kept telling me, as though she'd have gone to bat for me if she'd been standing there when the guy started insulting my intelligence.

He doesn't know who I am or where I come from. He doesn't know everything I've given up. Who is he to judge me? And I said as much. And what reason has Cynthia ever given me to indicate that she truly has my back anyway?

I wonder fleetingly whether I will ever truly trust anyone other than my sister. My parents stopped speaking to me six years ago, when I dropped out of UC Irvine mid–freshman year. I was so sure then that I was making the right choice—rejecting everything they stood for, pursuing a future that would hold something better for me.

As I approach the door of Food City and cast about in my bag for my grocery list, I decide I'd rather rest my feet for a few minutes before heading inside the crowded store. Mondays are my longest day at BB&B, and I'm not quite ready to compete against all the other after-work shoppers for produce. I give up on the list and pull out my phone instead, looking for a place to sit when I hear someone call my name.

It takes a moment before my eyes settle on Brianna Westlake, who is striding toward me from the parking lot looking as fetching as always in a pair of pale denim overalls with a tight white T-shirt beneath. Her blond hair is contained in a loose bun on top of her head. Instead of making her appear juvenile, the overalls and casual hairstyle somehow lend an air of sophistication to her bone-thin frame.

Brianna is a couple of years older than I am, and she waitresses at Cantina Rosalita, the restaurant where Nick is a line cook. She's in grad school, getting a PhD in psychology or sociology or something. For her, the waitressing is just a side gig, a way to supplement the stipend she receives from her graduate program while she progresses toward her own bright future.

"Hey." I offer a small smile as she reaches me, self-conscious in my drab leggings and tunic. My hand flies to my chest, double-checking that I'm no longer wearing my BB&B nametag. I'm not.

"This is funny, bumping into you now," she says. "I was just going to call Nick."

The sun is setting in the distance, and I have to shield my eyes with my hand to look her in the face. "Oh?" I tilt my head. I wasn't aware that Nick and Brianna had become "phone friends."

"Tripp and I are having a dinner party tomorrow night. Thought you guys might like to join us." We've never spent time with Brianna outside of the restaurant.

"That's so sweet," I answer, "but we don't have anyone to watch Wyatt, our baby." We could probably ask my old roommate, Kiara, but I'm not really interested in spending a night with Brianna and her boyfriend, watching them be perfect with all their perfect friends.

"Okay." She shrugs, like it's irrelevant either way. "Another time, then. I've gotta run, though. Class soon." She leans toward me and surprises me with a quick kiss to my cheek before she offers a little wave and heads into the market.

"Bye," I call after her, but she's already too far away to hear me.

I watch her for a moment as she walks away, wondering if I made the wrong call, and then I lower myself down on the bench beside me. The wood is still warm from the Arizona sun, even in January, and it heats my legs through my flimsy cotton pants.

I dial Tess's number and then listen to the phone ring on the other end.

"Sorry," she huffs into the phone as she picks up. "I'm just walking out of New York Sports. Hang on."

I picture my sister slinging some stylish gym bag over her shoulder and pulling her long blond hair out from under the strap. Her fancy-brand tank top is likely soaked with sweat from an hour on the treadmill or elliptical.

"Okay, hey." She's back. "What's the latest? Is he in?"

The last time Tess and I spoke, I was about to tell Nick about the surrogacy ad. To my own surprise, the notion of carrying someone else's baby for a fee had niggled at me, poking at me for nearly a week by then. I kept trying to talk myself out of the idea, but with the kind of money offered, I was smitten by the possibilities. I could go back to school, get a college degree, start thinking about an actual career.

When I mentioned the ad to Tess a couple of days ago, her reaction was calmer than I expected. Once she realized I wasn't joking, she just asked a lot of questions.

"He's in," I tell her. I replay last night's conversation in my head, remembering the way Nick's face darkened like a brick when I first broached the idea. "He made a couple of comments about me carrying 'another man's kid,'" I admit, "but he didn't erupt, never said he didn't want me to do it."

"Another man's kid," she repeats. "Nice."

A pock-marked teenager wearing a Food City vest pushes a long train of shopping carts across the lot, and I watch him maneuver them into place beside the entry of the store as I consider how to respond.

"So now what happens?" Tess asks, interrupting my thought. The sound of a car horn follows her question through the phone.

The incessant background noise of our calls is a stark reminder of one of the reasons I prefer Arizona. Even in this busy shopping center, the relative bustle doesn't rise anywhere near to the chaos that was the soundtrack to my childhood in Manhattan.

"I have to get matched with intended parents," I explain. I've been hunting down information about surrogate pregnancies over the past few days, and I finally understand how it works. Mostly.

That magazine with the ad disappeared before I went back to work the next day, but a few internet searches during Nick's hours at the restaurant provided a wealth of information. Even though I couldn't remember the name of the place I'd seen advertised, the search engine I used was chock full of choices. Through a series of clicks and a few phone calls, I ended up speaking to someone at a place called Seven Sisters Surrogacy. A brief conversation allowed me to re-confirm that I meet all the minimum requirements: I'm within the correct age range, I've successfully carried at least one child to term,

I'm a non-smoker with a healthy weight, and I don't have a criminal record. The fact that I live with a domestic partner also cuts in my favor, because intended parents like to know that their surrogates have a support system at home. After the call, I filled out online applications from four difference agencies.

The woman from Seven Sisters also explained that although my personal stats make me an excellent candidate for gestational carrying, my geographical location is less than ideal. Apparently, Arizona is not, in her words, a "slam dunk" state for surrogacy contracts. The laws here are somewhat murky when it comes to the enforceability of these agreements. Living in Phoenix is not as desirable as a place like San Francisco, since California is widely considered the safest choice for surrogacy contracts. Even so, she said, a number of Arizona courts have recently interpreted the laws favorably enough that lawyers are finding ways to make surrogacy work in the Grand Canyon State. Moreover, it's not that simple to find healthy, stable women who fit all the medical parameters and are willing to go through the indignities of pregnancy without the reward of a child left to raise after the fact.

"It's apparently kind of like eharmony," I say, fully aware that she hates that dating site. "I have to get chosen. All my information goes into some database out there, and then parental hopefuls comb through files until they find someone who sparks their interest, someone who checks their boxes."

"So, what?" she prods. "You have to list your hobbies, your hopes and dreams? Like, 'Maggie enjoys traveling and long walks on the beach'?"

I laugh loudly as an older couple walks past me, the husband pushing a cartload of overstuffed grocery bags toward a curb cut, as he glances in my direction. "Not exactly," I say. "The questions are a little more targeted. They want to know things like, would I be willing to terminate a pregnancy for a serious genetic abnormality? Would I agree to reduce from three fetuses to two?

Easier stuff also, like would I be willing eat all organic food if it's paid for by the intended parents, would I be able to pump and ship breast milk after the birth of the child . . . that kind of stuff."

"Huh."

"What?" Maybe she's going to judge me about my plans after all.

"Hey Stevie," she calls out as her voice begins to echo a bit. "The doorman," she whispers into the phone, making clear that she just entered her West Village apartment building. I picture her in her lobby, living the shiny life our parents wanted for her—for both of us. I'm certain it doesn't matter to our mom that Tess is not remotely enthused about being a lawyer. "Go to law school," our mother had told her again and again, "you'll be qualified to do anything." But when Tess came out on the other side of that JD, it turned out she was qualified to do precisely one thing: work in a large corporate firm. She's tepid about her job but gratified to be giving our parents just what they need from her. At least one of the Fisher girls ended up with an impressive degree and a six-figure salary.

"What were you going to say?" I nudge.

"No, it's just complicated, that's all. Breast milk after the fact. Aborting perfectly healthy fetuses. There's a lot I wouldn't have thought about. You sure you're game?" The ding of an elevator sounds in the background.

"Thousands and thousands of dollars," I say into the phone.

We're both silent for a second, and I wonder if she's lost reception in the elevator, but then I hear her sigh. I start talking again before she can interrupt.

"I'd be helping people create a family. There's something pretty awe-inspiring about that, don't you think? Even though Wyatt came as a surprise, I can't imagine my life without him. What if I could never have a kid of my own without someone else's help? It's too awful to even imagine. I don't have many marketable skills, but this . . . this I can do and do well."

"If Wyatt is the proof of your baby-carrying skills, I guess I can't argue. Listen, I've got to hit the shower before I start growing mold. Talk later?"

I'm relieved she isn't pushing me today. I've grown weary of repeating all the reasons why it's important to me to pay my own way when I go back to school, why I don't want to be anyone else's problem to fix. "Sure," I say. "I'll call you if there's any news."

We say our good-byes and I stand up from the bench, stretching out my stiff limbs. I'm still feeling reluctant to begin the unpleasant process of food shopping on an inadequate budget. Long lines are visible through the market's foggy window, heaping carts and fidgety people waiting under the yellow lights at the two open checkout lanes. The store is clearly understaffed for the number of shoppers inside.

I release a defeated breath as I feel around in my tote again, searching for the shopping list. I wonder whether Food City pays their cashiers more than what I earn at Bed Bath & Beyond. There are no "Help Wanted" signs here as far as I can see, so it's probably a moot point anyway. My hand finally lands on the notepaper, but as I pull it out, my bracelet catches on the zipper and beads start spilling onto the sidewalk, miniature pieces of pink and green hail bouncing to the ground and disappearing.

The bracelet was a gift from Nick on Wyatt's first birthday. I scoff now, thinking that an engagement ring wouldn't have fallen prey to a zipper, that metal wouldn't have splintered into unbound pieces of disappearing confetti.

I don't know if Nick even remembers the plan he and I made to get married after three years of being together. There are still several months remaining until we hit that benchmark, but I've begun to doubt whether he has any intention of ever making good on the agreement.

If I get selected by some couple out there to be a surrogate, will that wreck us? Are we as fragile as that cheapy bracelet?

While Nick's out there building his career, I'm stuck in a never-ending cycle of mind-numbing, low-paying work. The quiet nights while he's out at the restaurant haven't been so fulfilling, either. Surrogacy could be the thing to finally uncork my other options, my potential for more than just punching buttons at a register and handing out coupons.

As I enter the supermarket, a hot burn creeps from my heels up through my calves, reminding me of the hours I've already spent on my feet today. Even if gestational surrogacy will be more strain than our relationship can bear, I think it's a risk I'm willing to take.

Chapter 4

DONOVAN
JUNE 2018

*A*t 11:00 a.m. on Monday morning, I am standing in the small courtyard behind my office building with my cell phone pressed to my ear. One of the perks of working at the real estate and design firm of Hopper Bredworth in New York City is the office's prime location near Union Square and the charming postage stamp of outdoor space tucked away behind the building. I've been out here lingering in the late-morning sunshine because of the sensitive nature of the many phone calls I've had to make so far today.

My first call this morning was to the pediatrician, who took two hours to get back to me. I shuffled papers around at my desk, waiting, and then scurried back down the internal stairwell when I saw a blocked number flash on my caller ID. When I was finally able to unload to her about those DNA reports, her response came nowhere near alleviating my concern. Dr. Pine did not have an extensive opinion on the veracity of commercial genealogy testing services, except to say that from what she understands, she believes the tests to be generally reliable. She also informed me that no, her office does not perform paternity tests. She was, however, perfectly willing to write me a prescription for a paternity test that we can complete at any Quest or LabCorp location.

I have always been very happy with Dr. Pine, who has been looking after the boys since a few weeks after their birth, but something about the precision of her word choices today as she reflected on the Relativity results had me thoroughly coming apart.

Before going inside to log into the LabCorp website and figure out the logistics for the paternity test, I looked up the number for the hospital at UCLA where Kai and Teddy were born. I asked to speak to a nurse in Labor and Delivery. A woman who introduced herself as Nurse Shontz finally came on the line. I told her that my ten-year-old son was going to be working on a project over the summer, researching questions of nature versus nurture, and he wanted to add some information from his own life. Would it be possible, I asked, for Nurse Shontz to tell me how many other white, male babies were born in their hospital on the same day as my child?

The nurse seemed excited about the fake project I concocted and cheerfully explained that I would have to call the birth registrar for the information I was requesting. She gave me the phone number and then told me to ask for Felicia, who she thought would be the most helpful.

So now I'm on with Felicia. Actually, Felicia has me on hold. As the delivery nurse predicted, Felicia did seem happy to help, but Felicia also explained, before putting me on hold, that the records going ten years back are kept in a different area and are somewhat haphazard since the BirthPlace at Westwood, the division of UCLA where the boys were delivered, hadn't been operating for long back in 2008.

I've been pacing across the empty cobblestone patio for close to ten minutes, listening to tinny hold music as sweat builds around my hairline, and I'm beginning to wonder if she's ever coming back.

"Hello, sir?" I finally hear a human pick up on the other end of the phone, but it's a man, and I hope I'm not going to have to explain myself all over again.

"Yes?" I confirm that I am, indeed, still waiting on this end of the line.

"Yes, um, those records are in a different location, though, you see. If you want, we can write up a request, but we're going to have to get back to you in a few days, maybe next week."

"Oh." I stop pacing, as I realize this is a dead end for now. "Okay, yeah, let's do that, write the request please."

He takes my information, and we hang up. I have a sinking suspicion that I might not ever hear back from them. Red tape, hospital bureaucracy, overworked employees.

When I sit back down at my desk, huffing from the four flights of stairs, I see that Erica, one of the junior associates, has left a new draft of plans on my desk. My team has scored the relocation of Wenzo, a large pan-Asian restaurant that is looking to overhaul its image—or, rather, we've scored the opportunity to pitch to them. The project, if we get the client to officially sign on, will be one of the firm's largest, and I'm thrilled by the opportunity to lead this effort. Was thrilled. Up until this weekend, I was extremely wrapped up in each step of the process—searching for the perfect space for the client, brainstorming layout concepts— but the truth is, ever since I saw those DNA reports on Saturday, I've thought of almost nothing else. I sink into my leather swivel chair and gaze at the large, glossy pages on my desk detailing the way various proposed spaces could be transformed to meet Wenzo's needs. The pictures blur in front of me, becoming nothing more than random shapes of grey and beige.

I push the stack of oversize drawings to the side before jiggling my mouse to wake up my screen. The sunshine streaming from the window behind me creates a glare at this time of day, but today I'm too thirsty for answers to waste time dealing with the shades. I pull up the webpage for LabCorp, click on the dropdown menu, and select *Schedule a paternity test*. I see that the company doesn't even require prescriptions. I guess this is not something that Dr. Pine deals with on a regular basis. Maybe everyone is bypassing their doctors altogether now that paternity tests are available in Walgreens, like Chip said.

I click through the options and see that there are "legal" tests and "at-home" tests. I want the most accurate test there is, but the descriptions make clear that the tests are equally reliable. The legal test is for court cases, where the medical procedure has to meet certain standards with respect to the chain of custody. It includes safeguards to ensure that results aren't tampered with (as in, to influence the outcome of a court case for child support or custody), but the actual medical accuracy is the same. If you simply want information for personal use, LabCorp recommends the at-home test.

In light of the fact that the at-home test is significantly less expensive than the legal test, I am happy to follow LabCorp's advice. Not that I wouldn't dig deep into my life savings to confirm my biological connection to Kai if I had to.

There is a special link for New York residents, so I click on it, and I learn that if you live anywhere in New York state, you actually do need a prescription, or a court order, to purchase a paternity test, even just the at-home test.

Sorry for doubting you, Doctor Pine.

After I've filled out the mailing address and billing information, I have the jarring realization that Kai is supposed to leave for overnight camp with Teddy in just a few days. What if the test doesn't arrive in time for us to collect a sample before he goes? I'd prefer to do the test at home in order to prevent Kai from discovering the true nature of this testing, but maybe time constraints mean that going to a lab is our only option.

Below the main contact number on the website, there is a special number to call just for questions about DNA testing. I dial, trying to quell my embarrassment about making this call at all. An automated message begins speaking to me—a woman's voice thanking me for putting my trust in LabCorp—and then a real person picks up.

I swallow my discomfort and ask the woman how long it takes for the paternity test to arrive in the mail. It's FedExed overnight, she tells me. And how long will it take to receive results, I ask, after we mail back the samples? It will be three to five business days, and I can have the results emailed. What sort of package does the testing kit arrive in? Will other people be able to tell what it is from outside the box? No, she assures me. It's an unmarked box branded by FedEx. It may contain the return address of LabCorp, but there will be no indication of what is inside. I thank her for her help, and her tone is so gentle in response that I feel like she can see inside my thoughts, inside my soul. In my fragile state, it feels for a moment that this anonymous woman on the other end of the line is the only one who understands me at all.

I pinch the skin on the inside of my wrist, forcing myself back to reality, back to my job and the tasks that I'm certain have been piling up all morning. I finish my order on the LabCorp website, wishing I could achieve some modicum of detachment. Then I reach for my desk phone and buzz Erica at her desk.

"Could you come talk these through with me?" It's not really a question—more of a summons to my office. I close out of the LabCorp screen and click a few times to pull up a digital spreadsheet on Wenzo.

When Erica knocks, I'm plugging my cell phone into the charger on my desk, checking to ensure the ringer is on in case anyone calls about anything having to do with this DNA clusterfuck. Maybe Felicia from the birth registrar will surprise me by calling back sooner than expected. Or ever.

"Come in." I try to sound focused and together, attempting to readjust my equilibrium so I can be a professional broker for the moment rather than just a hand-wringing dad.

Erica pokes her head around the door, her wispy blond bangs as tentative as the rest of her.

"Come," I say again, knowing she needs coaxing before she'll feel comfortable stepping forward, inserting herself into someone else's space. I still can't figure out how she expects to thrive in the world of commercial real estate when apprehension is her defining characteristic.

Even though she was hired as a junior broker, we utilize Erica as though she's part of the design department. Her spatial planning skills are beyond, beyond. The brokering she does . . . well, not so well. When it comes to brokerage, you have to be willing to push and shove until you get your way. Without a certain level of personal volume—aggression, even—there's nothing to prevent competitors from stealing clients out from under you. And let's be honest, real estate deals are all about the commissions, so unless she finds a way to rid herself of that stench of deference, I just don't see her earning out enough to remain on this career path for the long haul. She's lucky to have ended up here at Hopper, at least, which is quite possibly the only real estate firm in New York with such an extensive design division.

She walks in slowly, her pale blue eyes scanning my office like she's checking for booby traps. In her khaki chinos and striped sweater set, she reminds me of a Gap ad, except that she lacks any sort of swagger.

"Okay, walk me through this." I pull the plans back to the center of my desk as she comes and stands beside my chair. I can smell her fruity body-grooming products—strawberry or cherry, like those scented erasers Teddy used to collect when he was in first grade.

As I look again at the plans, I see that she hasn't used the vacant warehouse in TriBeCa that we talked about, but has instead based the design on a different location that we never even considered. No wonder she's worried. As I flip through the pages and contemplate the drawings, however, I see that her idea is rather stellar. The space she apparently wants to present is the defunct church that used to serve as the famous dance club SpackleNine, the one that was so popular in the '80s. A host of restaurants have gone in and out of that space over the years, so many that a number of brokers have declared it to be cursed. I personally tend to shy away from the vampiric old church because I think it has proven itself as a consistently poor choice for eateries. But Erica's vision for the restaurant is sufficiently sublime to make me second-guess my usual position.

Using the 10,000-square-foot space, she has created a garden area, a bar lounge, a main dining room, a salon, and two additional private dining rooms. The dining areas range from 150 to 3,000 square feet, and each has its own theme.

"I was thinking . . ." She looks up from the pages with her wide baby-lamb eyes, waiting.

I nod to nudge her along. She reaches toward the packet and flips back to the front page.

"I was trying to create a concept that's immense but also intimate."

"Yes." I'm bobbing my head along in agreement as I begin arranging each of the pages side by side on the desk so I can view them all at once. My eyes travel from clip sheet to clip sheet, noting the way she has incorporated the building's arched windows, its vaulted roofline, and the vertical stacking of the existing layout to create something surprising and enticing. The Wenzo execs would be foolish to do anything other than swoon over these concepts. Her description of the aura these spaces will create is spot-on—private, yet boundless—and I want to get my head in the game here, to make the most of this explosion of creativity she's sharing with me.

"Maybe we add a street mural here"—she points to a series of arches in one clip sheet, and then lifts another sheet off the desk—"disco balls in this one."

She's done a great job, and she deserves serious praise for it. Any one of the ideas she proffered today would generally have me throwing compliments at her, but this comprehensive, mouthwatering combination? I mean, disco balls alone . . .

"It's a complete turn-around from the image Wenzo wants to leave behind." I force myself to sound as excited as I know I should be. "No more mass-produced Asian fast food. It's a sexy, high-end vibe, exactly what they asked for. Really excellent, Er." I collect the pages and hand the stack back to her.

"They're coming in at three to see the designs," she tells me, looking toward the open door of the office rather than meeting my eyes, "and then they might want to go downtown to see the physical space."

"Today?" It's not really her place to schedule a client meeting on her own, but I suppose I should be proud that she's finally showing some initiative. Any recrimination might squash that gumption down, so instead I tell her, "Excellent, that's just what I was going to ask you to arrange."

"Thanks," she says, but her shoulders tense again.

"Why don't you check in with the street team? And have a list of backup spaces just in case, though I don't think we'll need it."

"Okay." She looks at me with an indecipherable expression. "Okay," she says again, then turns quickly and scurries out as though she's only just made a narrow escape.

She's always timid, but her nervousness today was so exaggerated. There must be something else she is not telling me—one more question to which I do not know the answer.

Chapter 5

MAGGIE
SEPTEMBER 2004

I 'm standing at the South Rim, looking down into the abyss that is supposed to be the Grand Canyon, but all I see is emptiness. I borrowed my friend Albert's car and took the long drive from Los Angeles—seven, maybe eight hours of driving alongside dirt and cactus plants. I thought when I got here, I'd be able to stare down into the earth's depths and find *something*, some meaning, a way to move forward from here. I realize now that I've put too much importance on this trip, as if it was a momentous pilgrimage toward a better life rather than a drive to a canyon.

My eyes rove over the formations of dust below me, hopeful ambers and russets, quiet traces of lavender, and I am reminded of a family vacation to London we suffered through during one winter break when I was a kid. My mother kept insisting that we had to visit the Prime Meridian, the imaginary line where the Eastern and Western hemispheres meet. It was like the equator, Tess explained to me, except vertical instead of horizontal. She said there was a marking on the ground outside the Royal Observatory in Greenwich, England, where tourists liked to congregate and have their pictures taken, one foot on each side of the line.

It happened to be Tess's thirteenth birthday that day, and she was sure that something amazingly mystical was going to happen if she stood in two different hemispheres at the exact hour of her birth. She was reading *MacBeth* in her "gifted" English class, and I remember that she had also taken up a brief fascination with witchcraft around then. It shocks me now, as I gaze blindly into the canyon, that our parents found her nascent interest in magic and sorcery endearing, when each of my own attempts to step outside the box created such strife between us. Perhaps it was the very fact of their tolerance that led Tess to move so quickly on to other interests.

As usual, my parents were happy to indulge Tess that day, so we made sure we would be at the Observatory well before 10:56 a.m., the precise time at which Tess was born. We took a ferry up the Thames from London—a grand adventure in itself that gave us the chance to pass beneath London Bridge and sing all about it falling down. Our teenage self-consciousness was dulled by the miles between our voices and home, and we sang with abandon, both of us glad to make our mother smile.

What we had not budgeted for when we planned our day was the crowd at the latitudinal marker, lines of tourists waiting to snap photos with their legs splayed across the line. My dad pleaded with a group of Italian travelers, explaining the importance of the timing, until they generously allowed us to cut in front of them for our moment on the marker. We stood in size order while an older Italian man wrangled my dad's oversize Nikon and captured the shot, each of us with one foot on either side of the divide, just in time.

My parents were thrilled that we had completed the mission successfully, but not Tess. She was oddly quiet and deflated the remainder of the day. She didn't even perk up during the show in the planetarium with the vibrating seats. She never offered up the cause of her sudden dejection, but I imagined then that she had been hoping for something more while she stood on both sides of the world at once—some sort of cosmic message or adjustment—and that moment had never come.

This is how I feel now, standing on the edge of this enormous gorge, this actual wonder of the natural world, on my own birthday. I had hoped to find some sort of understanding or direction here. It's been exactly six months since I last got high, and I know in my heart that this is the year I will get my act together.

I lean over the black railing slightly, cautiously, wondering what it's like down at the very bottom of the canyon. I came here hungry for awe, hoping to feel a jolt of energy or some sort of spiritual surge, something to acknowledge the work I've put into rebuilding my life over these last six months, but all I feel is disappointment. It's as though my insides are mimicking the scenery. It's all just one big hole.

I close my eyes and take a cleansing breath. There are so many tourists standing on either side of me that it's difficult to get into any sort of serious meditation zone, but I attempt to at least drown out the noise in my own head.

"You know, you should be more careful than that."

I open my eyes in irritation, ready to rebuke whoever just saw fit to interrupt my attempted calm, but I'm unprepared for the openness I feel toward the face of the man standing beside me. He is a pretty average-looking guy somewhere near my own age. He has brown hair cut close to his head, brown eyes above a slightly crooked nose and a chin full of stubble. Beneath the scruff I can make out a whisper of lingering scarring, probably from acne in years gone by. He's wearing a navy-blue T-shirt and a pair of jeans so worn that they must be his favorites. I cock my head at him, unsure if I am willing to engage, but he just keeps going.

"Two to three people die every year from falling into the Grand Canyon." He juts his chin toward the abyss beyond the barrier. "You might want to be more careful than leaning over the rail with your eyes closed."

"How does someone with a Queens accent become an authority on the Grand Canyon?" I ask, friendly in spite of myself.

He holds up the little pamphlet in his hand, showing me the title, *Canyon Trivia*. He shrugs. "I picked it up at the last rest stop."

I reach for the water bottle in my bag and nod politely, ready for him to be on his way, but he keeps talking.

"Here's my favorite one, though." He opens the booklet and takes a step closer to show me.

I look down at the thick orange writing and bark out a laugh before I read aloud, "Americans eat enough peanut butter each year to fully coat the floor of the Grand Canyon."

He smiles at me—a move that transforms his face and jolts me out of complacency. His shining, mischievous eyes and straight white teeth are apparently the sight I've been waiting for all day; suddenly, I'm a little less ready for him to move on.

"Peanut butter," I say again as I sip my water. "Who knew? I've always been more of a jelly girl myself."

"Nick," he says, and extends his hand to shake.

"Maggie," I answer. My hand fits neatly into his own.

He holds on for an extra beat as he smiles down at me and adds, "And it's Scotch Plains."

"What?" I retract my hand, feeling suddenly awkward in the heat of the afternoon sun, sticky and blundering.

"The accent," he clarifies. "It's from Scotch Plains. New Jersey. But I just moved to Phoenix."

"Huh," is all I say, an acknowledgment that he has spoken. I don't mention that I'm planning to move to Phoenix as well. I don't tell him how I've finally gotten my act together after three years of living on other people's sofas. "Nice tat," I say instead, nodding my head toward the image of a crisscrossed fork and knife that occupies half of his forearm.

"Thanks. I cook," he explains. "And despite reports to the contrary, it seems I can still get myself buried in a Jewish cemetery, after all."

I'm surprised to hear that he's Jewish, but then I'm not surprised, because I was already feeling that the Universe had sent him my way for a reason, and perhaps he's one more way I am supposed to be getting my life on track, something I can report home to the parents that might actually bring them pleasure: the nice Jewish boy I met at the Canyon. It's so cliché, it's almost vintage. My mother would love it—at least, I think she would.

"You cook?" I ask. "I cook too—mostly eggs, yet shockingly, it hasn't led me to tattoo an omelet on my arm." I hold up my own wrist to show him the rainbow-colored hamsa tattoo that does adorn my skin. It's a Middle Eastern symbol meant to represent the hand of God, one of three tattoos I committed to during the first year I was living on my own.

He opens his mouth to comment but we are interrupted by the arrival of another guy. This one also looks to be in his twenties, and he's holding an old-fashioned metal canteen by its thick strap. He has long blond hair held back in a ponytail and a plaid flannel shirt tied around his waist.

"Hey," he says as he gives Nick a friendly slap on the back. "I found the meeting site." His eyes travel to me and he smiles noncommittally. He's exactly the kind of guy I would have gone bonkers for in high school, a Kurt Cobain lookalike. But three years later, out here in the desert, he does nothing for me. "We have to get down there," he prods Nick.

"We booked a helicopter tour," Nick explains to me. "It was nice to meet you." He smiles, and I can see regret in his dark eyes, like he thinks this was a lost opportunity, like it might have been something. "I hope you find what you were looking for," he adds before hurrying away with his friend.

I don't tell him that until he turned to walk away, I thought I had found exactly what I'd been seeking.

Chapter 6

DONOVAN
JANUARY 2007

C hip thumbs through the pages of an out-of-date *Men's Health* magazine in the waiting room of the surrogate services office as I take in our surroundings. I'm not sure what I was expecting, exactly, but that doesn't negate the fact that I am comforted by the large ficus tree resting in a bronze oblong pot in the corner and the two matching prints of sailboats framed on the wall. The décor, as horrific as any found in a dentist's or nutritionist's office, is oddly calming.

The young receptionist calls our names and stands with a file folder, waiting for us to follow her into Melanie Collier's office.

"Come in, come in!" The illustrious Melanie Collier, surrogate matchmaker, steps into the hallway to greet us. She has blond, wavy hair and thick-rimmed Buddy Holly glasses. I am reminded of the television character Murphy Brown as I absorb her persona. She's younger, maybe forty, but she has the same no-nonsense, can-do body language, not to mention the distinctive feathery hairstyle. She extends a hand to shake, and her grip is as firm as I would have expected. Chip and I trail her into her office, where we heed her instruction to sit in the two burgundy armchairs facing her desk.

We did our research before coming to this office in Connecticut. We spoke to our doctors; we spoke to our friends and our friends' doctors. We solicited advice from a female friend with a heart defect who used a surrogate several years ago and another friend who donated eggs to her sister. We joined internet chat rooms and read news stories. Ever since we got married in San Francisco last year, Chip has been talking about kids. I'm quieter about it, but I think I want to be a father even more than he does. When he talks about our theoretical children, it seems almost like whimsy, a pipe dream. For me, my desire to father a child, multiple children, is fierce, always has been. Maybe it's a result of my upbringing in a large Italian family, but I want children so badly that I am generally averse to talking about it, to feeling the pain of knowing it's likely an impossibility.

Chip insists that my doubt is too old-fashioned for today's enlightened world. Thankfully, he can't see inside my brain to the relentless vortexes of apprehension, the questions that swirl in my mind in spite of myself. Who's going to help two gay men bring a child into the world? Is it even fair of us to attempt to raise a kid in this kind of family? Will our child be ridiculed every single day for having two daddies? I want to believe that attitudes and society at large have evolved, that Chip and I aren't just living in some progressive bubble where we've surrounded ourselves with likeminded individuals and have been able to remain blissfully ignorant of lingering prejudices in the world at large, but I can't wrestle down the uncertainty.

"You look nervous," Melanie says after she's taken her seat behind the desk. Her eyes are on my face, not Chip's, as she singles me out. "You're right to be nervous." Lovely. "This is a long, arduous process we're about to delve into, but if you want it badly enough, I am the person to make it happen."

Melanie is an attorney. She is also a "surrogacy agent,"

meaning she finds surrogate mothers to carry babies for couples who are unable to have a child on their own for one reason or another. A modern-day matchmaker, she can draw up surrogacy contracts, oversee the surrogacy process from start to finish, and bring joy to those who expected to be perpetually childless. She is also the mother of twins who were born through surrogacy. She has long sections on her website about LGBTQ family building and about the warm and open environment her office provides for same-sex couples. I believe that we are in a safe space here. And yet. Is anything about trying to conceive a child with the help of a stranger "safe"? I can't help thinking about all the potential disasters, all the ways this process could end up shattering my heart into a zillion pieces.

Chip takes my hand and squeezes.

"We have questions," he tells her, his tone polite, upbeat.

"Good parents always do." She half smiles as she waits for him to continue.

"We're very excited to start this process," he begins, "but we would both like to contribute genetic material. Can we try to find a surrogate who might be willing to work with us twice, and an egg donor whose eggs we could use for both the first and second pregnancy, so that our kids could be genetic half-siblings on their mother's side?"

"Wow." Melanie shakes her head a little and I know there's a judgment about to be shared. "You guys are real go-getters, huh? Over-achievers like everyone else who lives on the Upper East Side, am I right?" We actually live in the Village, but we are planning to move uptown once we become fathers.

"What do you mean?" I ask, already defensive and likely failing to hide my irk. But in a breath, I remind myself that I am not angry at this woman who has already classified us as a "type" in her mind; I am petrified by the possibility that I might never be a dad. Certainly, copping an oppositional attitude with Melanie Collier is not going to help.

"You haven't even started the process for the first child"—
she rises suddenly to adjust the window treatment on the opposite
wall, starts fiddling with the blinds' tangled cords—"and you're
already talking about the second. I love it. There's nothing
better than enthusiasm. It'll help keep us going during the more
exhausting parts of this process." She finishes with the blinds
and sits back in her chair. "Now how about this." She folds her
hands into each other and leans back in her swivel chair, her silk
blouse straining slightly across her chest.

"A more practical solution might be to find a surrogate
who's willing to carry multiples and an egg donor with a high
egg-retrieval yield. Should the stars so align, we can then have
the harvested eggs separated into two groups, where 50 percent
of them are fertilized with your sperm, Chip, and the other 50
percent with Donovan's. We then implant the viable embryos,
maybe two from each of you. This is all subject to best practices
at the fertility clinic, but if we're lucky, the plan works, the
embryos take properly. You get multiples who are genetically
related to each of you, and they are also genetic half-siblings,
like you said." She pauses for us to digest what she's described
and then adds, "Some people call these kids 'twiblings.' Cute,
right?" She seems utterly thrilled.

"We'd get four kids?" Chip asks, incredulous but not altogether horrified.

Four babies at once might be worse than none at all, I think.

"No," Melanie clarifies, sitting forward again to explain.
"The embryos probably wouldn't all attach, and if they did,
well, my recommendation would be to find a surrogate who is
willing to reduce in that scenario. You do run the risk of ending
up with two children fathered by one of you and none by the
other, but you can do what some of my other clients have done,
and just agree not to find out who is the father of each child.
Then you simply proceed as though you are each the father
of both of the children, which is as it should be anyway, no?"

Chip and I look at each other. His light eyes are wide, questioning, wondering what I think of this suggestion. He shrugs almost imperceptibly, like it's up to me.

I have to admit, I kind of like the sound of this plan.

"What if there's a medical emergency?" I ask. "Wouldn't you need to know who the father is, like for a kidney transplant or something?"

"Well, yes," she allows, "that's the fly in the ointment. But for most people, something like that never comes to pass. Or by the time it does, so many years have passed that when you find out which one of you fathered him or her, it no longer matters at all."

We spend another hour and a half with Melanie after this, going over all the details of the work that needs to be done before we can find ourselves holding a new infant, or two, in our arms. We need to choose our fertility clinic, find an appropriate egg donor, meet with a social worker, review profiles of potential gestational carriers, have a phone call with the potential carrier, meet her and hopefully love her, sign contracts, fund an escrow account, send legal clearance to the clinic, pay for the carrier to travel to our clinic for testing, do the embryo transfer, file for a pre-birth order so our names can be on the birth certificate immediately following the birth, travel to the state where the surrogate lives to be there for the birth, travel home with our new family. Sounds totally simple. I think I'm going to vomit.

Melanie explains that she will begin the search for our gestational carrier, or GC, as she keeps saying, by running ads throughout the country, ads that will appear on paper placemats in waffle houses, in the back of *PennySavers* in supermarkets, in college newspapers and women's magazines. It seems implausible to me that this is the way carriers are found, but she promises she has had a great success rate in the past.

"Yes, you do have to weed out many of the people who call in," she responds to my question. "There are always people looking to get something for nothing, but we know what we're doing. By the time we present you with a file of applicants, they will be only serious candidates who have been well vetted. There will obviously be medical testing, which will rule out drug and alcohol addiction, and even diseases that could affect her ability to carry safely. You'll see. But first, we have to figure out what is important to you." She takes a sheet of paper from inside the file folder on her desk—some sort of checklist. "Do you care about the race of the carrier?"

Chip and I look at each other and both shake our heads no.

"Religion?" She asks next.

Again, we shake our heads no.

"Would you want the carrier to terminate the pregnancy in the event of serious genetic defect?"

"Potentially," I answer cautiously.

"We'd have to see what it was first," Chip says, pragmatic as ever.

After several other questions like this, she starts asking about finances. We are obviously going to be responsible for all medical costs related to the pregnancy, as well as any travel expenses, but then she starts asking about things I hadn't thought about at all.

"Many intended parents pay for extras like maternity clothes, or someone to clean the GC's house so she doesn't have to overextend herself during the pregnancy. Maybe she'll be put on bedrest at some point and will need additional help in the house or with any children she already has."

The list goes on and on. My head is spinning, but I'm also beginning to feel something akin to an electrical current running through my body, like this is a real, legit possibility. Despite all my prior expectations to the contrary, I might truly end up becoming the father of my very own child.

Chapter 7

MAGGIE
FEBRUARY 2005

A droplet of my own pee falls onto my hand and I don't even bother wiping it away as I stare at the two lines on the pregnancy test, stunned. This is the third test I've taken since getting home from my long day at the animal hospital, and I keep getting the same result. I don't know why I'm so surprised. I didn't even realize I was late until I overheard a woman in the waiting room at work ask one of the vet techs if she should expect her new dog to menstruate and get blood on the floor of her house. By the way, I've learned that the answer is yes, dogs that haven't been spayed do indeed bleed, and it can get quite messy.

It's only been four months since Nick walked into the veterinary office holding someone's lost Cavapoo, a designer puppy that he hoped had been microchipped with the owner's information. I checked them in at reception, and he didn't blink when he saw me behind the desk. I figured he didn't remember me from the Grand Canyon six months earlier. While he and the puppy were in the exam room with Doctor Turk, I ran my fingers through my hair and dug for the lip gloss at the bottom of my purse anyway. After the exam, Nick lingered in the front room until the dog's owner arrived, even though I told him it was unnecessary for him to wait.

He leaned an elbow on the reception desk as he looked down at me. "How could I leave now?" he asked, eyes narrowed. "We still haven't had a chance to talk through the benefits of tattooing an omelet on your arm."

I sat up at full attention and tried my best to formulate a witty response, running the gamut of jokes in my head about the fork tattooed on his arm, but I came up with nothing, and he continued talking.

"Well this is some kind of kismet, don't you think?" he asked.

Kismet happens to be one of my favorite words, one of my favorite phenomena. Did that make it extra kismetic? I didn't mention that I'd thought about him several times since that day at the Canyon, that I continued to feel as if it had been a missed opportunity, a chance for something important. I didn't say anything about the fact that he was better-looking than I remembered or that I had, just this morning, repeated that statistic about peanut butter and the Canyon floor to my roommate, Kiara. Instead, I just let my eyes shift back to his tattoo, the one I'd thought about too many times over the past few months.

Well, fork me.

It feels like it was only a hot second from that moment at the vet's office until this one, where I'm standing on the cold, hard tile of the tiny bathroom, staring down at this undeniably positive test. I'd be lying if I said that up until this shocking development, I hadn't been patting myself on the back lately. After moving from LA to Phoenix, I had found myself not only a steady job at the animal hospital and a peppy, responsible roommate but also a successful boyfriend. I had begun saving a little money, still hoping to make it to back to school for a teaching degree. I thought that I was finally lining up all those ducks, getting my life on track. Over the past few weeks, I've even been considering reconnecting with my parents, now that I believed I was nearing a place where they might be genuinely proud of the life I'm building.

This whole child-out-of-wedlock situation is clearly going to throw a wrench in that plan.

I try to imagine what Nick will say. I have to tell him, but our relationship so far has been mostly hot sex, tasty meals, and mediocre movies. We aren't really ready for ultrasounds and dirty diapers. Amazingly, I feel a surprising excitement about the baby anyway. Maybe after so many years being on my own, I'm ready to have someone dependent on me, someone I'm responsible for, unconditionally. Would it be crazy to say that I feel the tiniest inkling of love for the little pipsqueak already? Maybe it's just the *idea* of the baby that I'm loving— but either way, and despite all the drama that is inevitably on its way, there is no possibility that I am doing anything other than keeping this baby.

There is a knock from the outer hallway, and I don't even drop the pregnancy test before scampering out of the bathroom to open the apartment door. Nick is standing on the other side, right on time, in a crisp, black button-down and dark jeans. I take in his polished, freshly shaven appearance and wonder again how I could ever have considered him average looking.

He notices my outfit—scrubs from work, still covered in cat hair—and his dark brow furrows. "What's wrong?" he asks, clearly wondering why I am not ready to go to the "Un-Valentine's Day" party at his friend Darren's, whatever that is supposed to be.

"Oh, come on," I joke, "if this outfit doesn't scream 'over it,' I don't know what does." I laugh self-consciously, wondering how to phrase the little bit of news I need to share.

"What's that?" His eyes are on the pregnancy test. He knows what it is.

I hold it up and we both look to the results window.

"So, um, it's positive," I say, unnecessarily.

His eyes widen and I can see his mind working through this information. He kicks the door closed behind himself and cocks his head to the side as he considers me.

As the silence stretches, I brace myself for whatever's coming next.

"Let's get married!" He nearly jumps as he says it, startled, as though the idea has popped out of his mouth of its own accord.

"What? No!" I can't marry someone I've only known four months. This isn't reality television.

"No, seriously," he says, stepping toward me and taking my free hand into both of his. "You know we're a great fit, and we were probably going to end up getting married anyway. We'll just do it sooner so we can raise this kid together, be a family. And we'll never tell anyone that I proposed on Valentine's Day, because I am not that cheesy." His lopsided smile is so hopeful, so enticing, that I have to talk myself down. Marrying someone I've known less than half a year is something the old Maggie would do—but not this me, not anymore.

He starts getting down on his knee, I guess thinking to propose properly.

"No, no, no, no." I yank him back to a standing position. "Don't. Don't do that. Let's not. This isn't . . . we can't get married. It's too much. Too crazy, too much all-at-once insanity. Let's think this through." I pull him over to the denim-covered sofa, one of the many items of furniture Kiara already owned before I moved in to take her old roommate's place.

"Sit," I instruct. "Let's just take a minute. A breath." I lean out from the couch to place the pregnancy test on the glass coffee table. It makes a startling clatter as it lands, as if I threw it, like I couldn't wait to get it away from me.

We both stare dumbly at the test stick for another moment.

"What if," I say as I look back at Nick, "we don't get married, but we try living together? We could wait until after the baby is born."

"What if," he counters, his eyes darting away from the coffee table and back to me, "we try living together, but we don't wait until the baby is born?"

"Move in together—like, now?"

Nick nods.

I suppose it's less extreme than marriage. And it would allow us to adjust to living in shared quarters before the baby comes. I don't know if I'm ready for this, but maybe that's the whole point. "One transition at a time does make more sense to me than doing everything at once. Except . . . I can't just leave Kiara. I committed to living here for a year, and I still have six months left." I don't add that Kiara has become my closest friend in Phoenix, and I feel a little blue at the thought of dissolving our arrangement early.

I do some on-the-spot calculations in my head and then offer another idea. "So, let's say I move in—but not until September, when my lease term is up. There should still be a month left before the baby is born."

"We wait until September to move in," he parries, "but we get married when the baby turns one."

"Three. Three years old." I'm worried that if we make an agreement to marry each other when the baby turns one, it will be all we think about. "The first year is supposed to be the hardest with a kid, right? So why would we want to judge our compatibility entirely on that year?"

"Really?" Nick's brows scrunch together as he studies me.

"You should see these people who come into the office with their new puppies. They're totally shell-shocked. They're overwhelmed by the responsibility, sleep deprived, and just generally freaking out. One lady was wearing two different shoes. And that's puppies."

At first he looks at me like I've lost my mind, but then he starts nodding slowly.

"Okay," he says, taking my hand. "Maybe what you're saying makes a little sense, in a totally roundabout, Maggie kind of a way." He takes my hand and continues. "I like you. Really, really like you. So maybe it makes sense that we take the pressure off. Since I don't want to blow my chances with you entirely, I'm willing to wait you out. Unless this is just a secret ploy to let me down easy, and 'not yet' is easier for you to say than 'no way, never you'?"

A laugh escapes me at the ridiculousness of his suggestion. Of course it's Nick. So I wonder what the real reason is, why I want to wait so long. Maybe I'm just not sure he knows who I am yet. Other than being the mother of his child, I could still be anyone at all.

Chapter 8

DONOVAN
FEBRUARY 2007

*W*e're back in the office of Melanie Collier, the surrogate matchmaker, with multiple files open in front of us, and we have narrowed the candidates down to three. My favorite is the Jewish twenty-four-year-old from Arizona. The woman has one child and lives with the child's father, which means that she has a support system at home. He's a moderately successful chef in Phoenix. She herself works as a cashier and has said that her reason for answering our ad was because she is saving to go back to school and become a teacher. I love the idea that our needs could align with another person achieving her own dream, too.

Chip likes a thirty-seven-year-old woman from Florida who has three children of her own and has already acted as a surrogate for two other families. I'm concerned that the Florida woman is too old. Chip is worried that Arizona has dicey laws about surrogacy; he's more comfortable going with someone from Florida because the regulations there seem more favorable to surrogacy arrangements than they do in Arizona. He is also giving a lot of weight to the fact that this woman seems to be a career surrogate—less potential for drama, he thinks.

Melanie also showed us the paperwork for an applicant from Colorado, a thirty-year-old woman with twin daughters whose husband recently passed away, leaving her strapped for cash. Colorado has no specific laws pertaining to surrogacy, but the courts there generally rule favorably to intended parents in these situations. However, all three of us are concerned that this woman might be in a precarious emotional state after losing her husband. Not to mention, she lacks the emotional and physical support of a partner at home to help her through the pregnancy. I've watched my sister Gina muddle through three pregnancies. I remember the way she relied on her husband, Pete, during the first two, and also how taxing it was on her when Flora was born so shortly after Pete's death. I don't want to be a part of another birth where a woman might still be grieving.

"Let's get rid of Colorado," I say, closing the manila folder and pushing it to the side of the conference table. Truth be told, none of these applicants seems perfect. It would have been great to find someone from a place like California, a safe-haven state as far as surrogacy laws go, but I suppose not everyone is amenable to carrying a baby for nine months and then giving it up, no matter how much money you might be offering them to do so.

"We can run the ad for another month," Melanie offers as she begins collecting the folders in front of us, "see what else comes in."

"No," Chip says. "Let's work with what we've got." He looks at me, and I nod.

"Can we do the phone calls with both of them, then decide?" I ask Melanie.

"Absolutely," she says, making a note in the journal beside her.

"Let's start with Amber, the one from Florida," I say—trying to be a team player, giving Chip's vote the first opportunity.

"I've got a good feeling about Amber." Chip winks at me. He unbuttons his cuff and starts rolling up one sleeve, then the other, like he's getting ready for battle.

"You have a good feeling about everything." I swat at him, hoping that this time, his eternal optimism is well placed.

━ ━ ━ ━ ━ ━ ━

Nine days later, I find myself nearly shrieking at Chip in our apartment, "I can't give you more specifics, I just got a bad vibe!"

We are attempting to enjoy Vietnamese takeout together, a Wednesday night ritual we've created for no discernible reason, but we cannot stop arguing about which surrogate to choose. Amber, the woman from Florida, Chip's first choice, said all the right things on the phone. She talked about how she loves helping to build families, how special it is for her to know that a parent has a child to love because of her help. She said her husband's job as an electrician is sufficient to support their family, but that her ability to serve as a surrogate periodically supplements their income, allows them to add to their savings. They even used a portion of the payment from her last surrogate pregnancy to fund a family trip to Orlando. But when we asked her about her attitude toward same-sex parents, she stumbled. Putting aside the fact that she hesitated, her response—"It's just not my business what you do in your home"—rubbed me really, massively, upside-the-head wrong.

"Not everywhere is SoHo," Chip argues as he takes the container of lemongrass-spiced vermicelli from the coffee table and begins ladling more noodles onto his plate. "They live in rural Florida. Flo . . . ri . . . da." He draws it out slowly that second time like perhaps I didn't understand the first time he said it.

"Yeah, I get it," I snap back. "Our country is full of bigotry. It doesn't mean I want one of those people carrying our children. Even if she thinks she's openminded, clearly, she is not. It's not like we don't have another choice." I walk over to the white granite countertop that separates the living room from the kitchen, lift the other file, and wave it in his face, causing one of the papers inside to fall out and float to the floor. "How could you not love this one?" I reach down to retrieve the paper, which turns out to be the handwritten letter the woman in Arizona sent us. Her flowery note explains that she squandered her opportunity to attend college, dropping out of UC Irvine after less than a single semester. She's gotten her act together, she says, and is now trying to find a way to finance her education.

"I know." Chip puts his plate back on the coffee table, leaving his glistening noodles to linger, untouched. "She sounds perfect. Except for where she lives, and that's kind of a big deal. We can't just ignore it."

"It's not like there haven't been successful surrogacy arrangements out of Arizona before," I push. "She's not going to back out. You could just tell. Couldn't you just tell?" He doesn't answer, so I keep going. "Every last detail about her is right. A former East Coaster with liberal political views, open-mindedness. She's even a Yankees fan, for God sakes."

This is the third day in a row that we are having the exact same fight. We might as well have just recorded last night's argument and watched it back tonight.

I can't keep going back and forth like this.

"Look," I say, "let's get Melanie to find us more applicants. I just can't with Florida. If Arizona makes you too nervous, let's see who else is out there. These can't be the only two women in all of America who are willing to do this for us." I haven't offered this concession before.

Chip rises and walks to where I'm standing. He reaches out to take the Arizona file from me and then puts his free hand to my cheek with a sigh.

"Let's not wait," he says. "I love that you are trying to work with me, that you always try to meet my needs. What I need most, I think, is to be a father with you." He kisses my lips lightly and pulls back. I can see that he has arrived at some sort of conclusion in his mind. I brace myself for whatever he is going to say next.

"Let go with Arizona."

Chapter 9

MAGGIE
APRIL 2007

*I*t's nearly 7:00 p.m., and Wyatt and I have just finished baking muffins for tomorrow's breakfast. I'm wiping down the kitchen counter while he plays with his action figures in the living room. My goal is to have him tucked into bed in short order so I can shower and brighten up my appearance a bit before Nick comes home. Our rhythm has been off recently. If I'm honest, it's been shaky ever since I decided to do the surrogacy.

My old roommate Kiara thinks he's right. She and I come from very different backgrounds, and as much as I love her, when she gets all "God this" and "God that," I kind of just tune out. She thinks God didn't intend for families to be created in many of the modern ways, like IVF and surrogacy. But I see no reason to spit in the face of science. If God didn't intend for these possibilities, why create people smart enough to dream them up? Wouldn't God have thought about that too?

Now that I've been matched with intended parents, Nick has become especially reticent. When I try to tell him about Donovan and Chip, he clams up, tightens his lips into a line, and starts staring off into space.

"Wyatt, buddy," I call into the other room. "Time for bed!" I toss the batter-stained dishtowel back onto the countertop and head to the living room, where Wyatt is maneuvering a figure of Captain America into the Batmobile. He's muttering something in his version of Captain America's voice, but his speech is still fairly primitive, and I can only make out the word "protect," which he says a couple of times in a row.

"C'mon kiddo." I lift him up and toss him over my shoulder.

"Sack of potatoes!" he demands, and I oblige him by maneuvering his body in such a way that he slides down behind me and hangs against my back, his head dangling comically low, just above my rear end, as I keep a secure hold on his feet. He erupts into fits of laughter, as he always does when I get him into this position. I start turning in circles, escalating his hysteria, and I realize I feel more relaxed in this moment than I have in weeks. As we spin, I'm hit by a fresh wave of love for this kid. When I think of all the awful things I did when I was using, I can't believe I've been given the gift of this fresh, perfect little person.

He has been a pleasure from the day he was born. Which is a good thing, because I was not ready to be a mother. Sometimes, when I least expect it, I hear my mother's no-nonsense voice inside my head—"Who said anything about 'ready'?" She'd probably say in response to my thoughts, "You just get in there and do it." If my defunct relationship with my own mother is any indication, I clearly still have lots to learn, but with Wyatt helping to guide me down this path, parenthood has started to feel just right, like it's exactly what I was meant for.

___

A couple of hours later, I finally hear Nick's key in the door. I'm nestled into the corner of the sofa, a latch-hook rug open in my lap and a near-empty bottle of Amstel on the table beside me. When he steps inside and sees me there, multiple emotions flash across his face, the final effect being one of guardedness.

"Hey," he offers half-heartedly before heading to the kitchen. I can hear how tired he is from his voice, the one word filled with more air than timbre. There's a muted hiss from the other room as he opens the refrigerator door, and then the sound of plastic crinkling as he shoves leftovers onto a shelf. As usual, he's brought something home from Lexington Grill, the steakhouse where he's just been promoted to sous chef. I smile when I hear him open a beer; I know that it means he's coming to sit with me so I can help attempt to take the weight of the day off his shoulders.

"There was a bachelor party that came in tonight." He rubs a hand across his forehead as he comes back into the room and lowers himself onto the recliner chair across from me. "Only six guys, but they ordered every dish on the menu. Literally everything." He sniffs the palm that had been rubbing his face. "Garlic."

"On a Wednesday?" Usually it's mostly businessmen at the restaurant on weeknights, maybe a few families. The more boisterous crowds don't typically show up until the weekends.

He shrugs. "Wyatt's good?"

"Miss Sue says he made a new friend at daycare. A little girl named Poppy." We just started sending Wyatt to a full-day program so I can begin hunting for a higher-paying job.

My first interview was for an administrative assistant position at a law office. The listing said a bachelor's degree was "preferred." The frizzy-haired interviewer should have just admitted that she wouldn't hire anyone without a college degree rather than interrogating me about my life choices for the forty-seven minutes I spent sweating in her office.

I had another interview this morning, this one at a large medical practice. The posting was for an office manager, which was described as "an individual who can staff the front desk and help with filing and office organization." Based on my days at SunMeadow veterinary, I felt pretty confident heading into that interview. I explained to the interviewer, a middle-aged woman named Brenda, that I left my job at the animal hospital when I got pregnant with Wyatt because I wasn't supposed to be around cat feces all the time during pregnancy. Brenda got very emotional, telling me about how she had to give away four cats of her own when she was carrying her first child because she developed a sudden allergy to their dander.

I fold up the latch hook I've been working on and start tossing the round clusters of yarn back into the cardboard box. This hook-rug kit is a project I began when I was pregnant with Wyatt. It's a two-foot-by-three-foot mat with a picture of a mama bear and her cub beside a blueberry bush on it. I only progressed as far as the mama bear's eyes before Wyatt was born, and then this project, along with so many other parts of my life, fell by the wayside. Maybe having babies on the brain again reminded me about it—or maybe I'm just ready to be a person who finishes what she starts.

"It went well at that gastroenterologist's office today," I say, and Nick nods encouragingly as he takes another sip of his beer. "I think I bonded with the office manager." I laugh. "It was all about cats and pregnancy."

As soon as I say the word pregnancy, I regret it. It's been several weeks since Nick purported to accept my decision to serve as a gestational carrier, but his body language is still saying otherwise. He argued that with his new salary, I can return to school, but the fact is, between raising Wyatt and keeping food on the table, we have enough expenses as it is. And I want to be responsible for my own success. I have a perfectly good uterus that has no other occupants at the moment. I see no reason why I shouldn't rent it out for a little extra cash.

Now that I've killed the mood, I figure I might as well go for broke and tell him the other news of the day.

"I booked my flight," I tell him tentatively. "They're paying for it, obviously. But I'm flying out to meet them next Thursday.

I'm going to bring Wyatt. Tess said she can look after him while I have my meetings, and it'll be nice for him to see his auntie."

Nick nods, his Adam's apple bobbing, as he takes another long sip of beer. But then he rolls his eyes. "You're really doing this?" He sounds equal parts annoyed and surprised.

"Nick." I don't want to have the same argument for a third, or seventh, or nineteenth time.

"Look, I get it." He holds up his free hand in a gesture that might be surrender, or at least an indication that he doesn't feel like having another fight. "I said I'm okay with it. All the parts you haven't thought about, even, I'm okay with those too. Like when other guys congratulate me after seeing your stomach, and I have to be like, 'Nah, man, it's not my kid, but thanks.' I've been preparing myself for that. But seriously, two guys? I thought maybe you'd move on and find a hetero couple. You really want to help bring a kid into the world so that it can be raised by two dads?"

Hold up. This is the first time Nick has said anything like this. "Wow." I swallow and blink a couple of times before I'm able to continue. "I completely did not realize I was living with a homophobe."

"I'm not a homophobe," he says loudly, but then he stops, probably remembering Wyatt sleeping nearby, and he starts again more quietly. "I just think it's really fucking selfish. Of you. Of these two dudes. Everyone wants what they want so badly, and no one is thinking about what it's going to be like for that kid. You want your money, these guys want a baby. So fuck it, who cares if a child has to spend his whole life getting ridiculed not only because he's a test tube baby but also because he's being raised by two gay guys in a world that just isn't as accepting as you think it is."

I'm stunned. I've been so delighted by the idea that I am going to be part of creating a family, bringing a child into a world of love, and helping two people build the life they've dreamed of. If I'm honest, I've been a little proud of how progressive the whole thing is, too. The world is changing, and there's an increasing number of families with same-sex parents out there now.

"Science and society are evolving together, Nick!" I shout back, unable to keep my volume on low. "It's people like you who are going to be left in the dust. Shame on you." I stand up, frowning. "Like it or not, a homophobe is exactly what you are, and you need to adjust your attitude, starting now."

A bulb flickers in the ceiling above Nick's chair, which feels appropriate, as my entire view of him is suddenly precarious. "I have no problem with gay people," he argues. "What I have a problem with is giving them a baby, or two babies, who didn't get the luxury of choosing that life."

"Nobody gets the luxury of choosing their life! Did you choose your parents? I sure as hell wouldn't have chosen to end up with parents who valued my accomplishments over my well-being, parents who were so controlling that I can't even speak to them anymore. These guys in New York sound like amazing people, full of so much love to give a child. If they are who they seem to be, any child would be lucky to be raised by them." Spit flies out of my mouth as I finish this tirade. I'm so incensed that I can't even figure out where to put my hands right now.

Nick looks up at me from where he is still attached to the velvet armchair, and something in him seems to deflate. "Yeah," he says, more subdued now. "I guess we just have to agree to disagree." He stands to take his empty bottle back to the kitchen, and all I can do is watch as he drifts farther away from me.

Chapter 10

DONOVAN
JUNE 2018

*H*ave you ever found yourself standing at the edge of a skyscraper, somewhere like the rooftop of the Standard Hotel, everyone around you partying it up, and for the briefest moment, you wonder what it would be like if you just fell over the railing? What would you feel, falling like that? Would you hear people screaming in your wake? Or would the city suddenly fall silent, like everything had halted in the world around you, and there would be only a quiet stillness, nobody moving but you, no one to catch you at the bottom?

This feeling of vertigo is exactly what hits me as I read the results of the paternity tests. I don't even waste time closing the door to my office before I click on the email attachment to download the report. Chip convinced me that we should both get tested as possible fathers to Kai; as long as we were bothering to submit the test for one of us, he argued, why not get full information?

I read the words at the bottom of the report again. *The alleged father is excluded as the biological father of the tested child.* This is what it says on the report for Chip's test as well. *Non-matching alleles observed at the loci listed.* I feel paralyzed as I read the information on the screen over and over again. *Alleged father lacks genetic markers that are contributed to a child by a biological father.* I haven't even called Chip. I just keep reading it, again and again. *The alleged father is excluded.*

"Hey, Don?" A voice at the door pulls me out of my trance and I look up to see Erica standing in the doorway holding multiple unwieldy rolls of plans. I quickly close the window on my computer.

"Yeah, sorry. What's up?" My voice sounds off, muted and viscous, but maybe I'm the only one who notices.

"Hey, I just wanted to give you a heads up about an issue we're having with the client," she starts—hesitant, as usual.

I suddenly feel as though I'm suffocating, as though someone has literally stuffed a pillow over my face and I simply, utterly, cannot breathe. "You know what, I'm sorry." I erupt from my chair and grab for my bag on the floor. "I'm having a bit of a family emergency. There's something I've got to take care of. You handle it. I trust your judgment."

She watches me, her eyes and mouth agape, as I haul ass out of the room. I imagine she continues watching me as I book it toward the elevator, but I am focused mostly on trying to get air into my lungs. I need to get outside, need air. I hurry to the stairwell, past the heavy metal door, and down the concrete steps, as the feeling of a vise pinching my chest continues to intensify. My peripheral vision dulls, the cream-colored walls around me fading nearly to oblivion, and I worry that I might faint, but I keep hurrying down toward the street exit.

When I finally emerge into the humid summer sunshine, there are so many people milling about on the sidewalk that there is no relief. I haven't had a full-on panic attack like this since I was a teenager. I can feel the sweat pooling in my armpits, on my chest. I hurry to the crosswalk and make my way to toward the little park in the middle of Union Square. At the closest bench, I drop my bag to the grass and pull my phone from my pocket to dial, barely able to form a coherent thought.

On the third ring, she finally picks up.

"Hey," she says happily into the phone.

"Mom," I choke out. "Oh, thank God."

"Honey, what is it?"

As soon as I hear her voice, the reaction is almost instantaneous. My overactive amygdala shifts gears, bringing me out of the panic state. My lungs begin to open, and it feels as though I can swallow again. I sink down and lean back against the warm bench, grateful for the tree branch providing shade above me.

"I was having an attack. Like high school. But I'm okay now. It's going away." I huff into the phone as I undo the top two buttons of my dress shirt and rub a hand against my damp chest. A group of young women are gathered on a patchwork raft of picnic blankets several feet away from me, chatting happily into their takeout containers.

"Are you sure? Where are you?" I can detect the concern in her voice. I'm not the only one who remembers how awful those panic attacks were for me.

"No, I'm okay. It's just . . ." To my horror, I start to cry.

"You got the report."

I don't answer, but simply let out another weepy yelp.

"Listen to me, baby, breathe," she tells me, and I do as she says, crying softly and focusing on my breath. I watch people coming and going throughout the park—men in suits, nannies with strollers, everyone seemingly so relaxed. Two birds pick at a pizza crust protruding from the overstuffed trash can beside my bench.

My mom does the best she can, saying all the right things about how we'll figure this out and how family isn't just about blood. Her effort is not in vain. After a few minutes of listening to her calming words, I'm more collected, more focused. It's not the substance of what she's said, though—more of a trained response from the years she coached me through my teenaged panic. The strategies she pieced together from the self-help books, the therapists, even a couple of episodes of the *Donahue* show, they've left her with a bit of expertise when it comes to me and my panic.

"You know what, Ma," I finally interrupt, sitting up a little straighter and rubbing the heel of my hand against my face, scrubbing against the wetness beneath my eyes. "I'm good now. I have to go."

She sighs heavily into the phone. "Good" is so far from where I am, and we both know it.

"I'll keep the phone with me," she says.

I dial Chip next, but of course, he doesn't pick up. It's always so hard to get a hold of him during the day. I send him a text to call me when he can, and then I look up the number for the Yale Fertility Clinic on my phone. I notice two text messages from Erica and a sudden pile-up of emails in my inbox, but I cannot focus on anything right now other than the fact that Kai is not my biological son.

I leave a message for Dr. Pillar and ask that they have her call me as soon as possible.

⸻

So it is that Chip and I find ourselves sitting across from doctors Pillar and Brookstone in a small conference room at the Yale Fertility Center in New Haven a week and a half later. Dr. Pillar's curly hair has grown longer than I remember it being before, and a few deep lines across the olive skin of her forehead are evidence of the time that has passed since we last saw each other.

Back when we began the surrogacy process, it was Dr. Pillar who ordered the extensive battery of tests on Chip and me, as well as the significantly more exhaustive examination of our surrogate. Only after receiving acceptable results across the board did she authorize fertilization of the eggs her team had harvested from our donor.

Other than a couple of follow-up phone calls, we've had almost no interaction with her since the successful births of our babies back in 2008. Though now when I say "*our* babies," it feels like I ought to use that term loosely.

Dr. Brookstone is the director of the Fertility Center and the Center's Fertility Preservation Program. He wasn't here when we availed ourselves of the Center's services all those years ago, but even if he had been, we probably wouldn't have met him. Every procedure we did at the Center was considered routine, even ten or eleven years ago, and Dr. Pillar was more than capable of overseeing our case on her own. Or so we thought.

Based on their expressions as they study us from across the glossy conference table, I would hazard a guess that nothing about our situation qualifies as "routine" any longer. Dr. Pillar was unwilling to even engage in discussion with us until she re-ordered the paternity tests and supervised the testing herself. So now, for the third time, we have received test results that prove Kai is not genetically related to Chip, to Teddy, or to me.

Dr. Pillar was able to access the records from the BirthPlace at UCLA, and it turns out there were six other babies birthed in the hospital on the day Teddy and Kai were born. Five of them were girls, and the one other boy was Asian. There were four babies born the day before our boys arrived—two girls, a black boy, and a white boy who was seven weeks premature, meaning that he weighed less than four pounds. We were in the delivery room when our boys were born. We held them each before the nurses whisked their tiny bodies off to the nursery. We certainly would have noticed if one of them had returned from the nursery weighing literally 50 percent less than he had an hour before. None of these baby profiles seem to allow for the possibility of the switched-at-birth scenario.

The next logical explanation is that the fertility clinic screwed up with the embryos—implanted our surrogate with the wrong fertilized egg, meaning that they took an embryo belonging to another patient, with genetic material from other parental hopefuls, some other egg, someone else's sperm, and implanted it into our surrogate's uterus. How could they make an error of this magnitude? And does this mean that one of our fertilized eggs ended up being carried by another woman? Is our baby somewhere out there in the world, thinking he belongs to a different set of parents?

"It's simply not possible," Doctor Brookstone is explaining, the salt-and-pepper whiskers on his chin lending authority to his words. "The Center has had strict protocols in place since well before my tenure whereby the chain of custody for a fertilized embryo could never be interrupted. There is no possible way that your surrogate could have been implanted with the wrong embryo. That kind of error does not get made in this institution—not now, and not eleven years ago, when you first arrived here." He removes his eyeglasses and starts wiping one of the lenses with the corner of his lab coat as he glances over to Dr. Pillar, as if he expects her to say something. She nods at him, and he sighs.

"Look," Dr. Brookstone continues on an exhale, "as far as we can conjecture, there is only one other possibility. It's a long shot, but at this point, it's the only idea that is a logical possibility. With your permission, we would like to contact your gestational carrier and collect a DNA sample from her as well."

"Our surrogate? Why?" Chip is sitting forward in his seat, his long torso pitched at an angle suggesting that he is getting ready to rise, to leave. Are they saying that the boys have belonged to the surrogate all along, that we thought they were the result of the implantation but in fact they were her babies to begin with?

"But we've already confirmed that Teddy is biologically related to Chip," I interrupt, answering my own question.

"Strange things can happen in our field," Dr. Pillar responds gently. "Let's just rule her out as a mother before we start any wild goose chases."

"And when that DNA test comes back negative for any connection," Chip pushes, "then what?"

"Well, then . . ." Doctor Pillar looks blankly at Dr. Brookstone and then back at us. "Then, I don't think we know."

It's only a few hours later when I see Maggie's name flashing across the screen of my cell phone. Chip has been at the gym since shortly after we got back into Manhattan, training for another marathon. I've been in our home office, reorganizing the drawers of my desk for the past twenty minutes, trying to distract myself by purging my files of old insurance bills and MasterCard statements.

"Donny," she says, and I can hear the worry in her voice. "I just finished work and had this message waiting about going to a Quest lab. What's going on?"

It's probably been a good three or four years since we've spoken, and I feel badly now that I haven't done a better job of keeping up with her. After everything that went down for her in California, it just got harder and harder to know what to say. Even so, once somebody houses your children inside her body for nearly a year, a certain lifelong bond is created.

I lower myself onto the wood floor of our study and lean my back against the wall as I fill her in on the Relativity DNA tests, the negative paternity tests, and the meeting at the Fertility Center.

"Well, clearly they screwed up with the embryos," she says when I'm done. "Whatever they claim their protocol is, they obviously didn't follow it. What are you going to do?"

"Chip and I have been asking ourselves that question all afternoon. Are we even supposed to try to figure out where the embryo came from?" I put Maggie on speakerphone and start shoveling the stack of old papers into a black garbage bag.

"Does it matter?" she asks gently. "You and Chip are his parents, his family."

Maggie's kindness brings me back to that moment in the delivery room in California. Teddy was the first baby to arrive, and as Maggie had asked, the young doctor handed him straight over to me. I held him, all slimy and warm in my arms, as Chip cut the umbilical cord with that bent-looking medical scissor. I looked down at Maggie, who was smiling back at us with a sheen of sweat coating her forehead. Her eyes were a little shiny as she told me, "That boy is finally where he belongs." Then she got back to work pushing out the second baby.

Maggie's sister, Tess, ended up coming to California to look after Maggie's son during the delivery. She brought Wyatt to the hospital the next day to meet the babies. He was only two years old, and the social worker suggested he should have the closure of seeing the babies outside his mother's body before we carried them away to the other side of the country. Some nurse on duty that day who didn't know any better put a big sticker on Wyatt's T-shirt that said, "I'm a big brother!"

Chip and I looked at the little boy in panic, unsure what to say to make the moment one of clarity but also kindness.

"No," Maggie had explained to everyone from where she was still recovering in bed, "the babies belong to our friends, Donovan and Chip. They are the daddies. Wyatt and I are just their very good friends."

Tess reached out to take the sticker off Wyatt's shirt, and the poor child started to cry that he wanted to keep the babies.

"No, sweetie," Maggie said again as she reached out toward him and pulled him onto the bed. "Remember that time when we watched Mittens because Miss Lydia went on vacation? And then we had to give him back when she got home?"

Wyatt nodded as he wiped his hand under his nose.

"Well, this is like that. Chip and Donovan are back from their vacation, and now it's time for us to send the babies home with them." Wyatt nodded, making a visible effort to stop his carrying on.

A bubble forms in my throat as I remember Wyatt like that—too young to understand what was happening, but so eager to cooperate with his mother. At that moment, I thought we'd be very lucky if our sons grew into little gentlemen like Wyatt. I also remember wondering whether Maggie planned to have more children who would grow to be as sweet as that little guy.

I swallow hard so the emotions my memories are evoking won't creep into my voice. Maggie doesn't need that.

"You guys should sue that clinic six ways to Sunday," Maggie is saying on the other end of the line, drawing me back to the present. I'm touched again by how protective she is of Chip and me. She's been that way from the beginning.

There's a sudden wail in the background, like a child crying.

"Caleb," Maggie says, her voice slightly muffled, "if you don't give him back his giraffe right now, there will be no cookies at all. Sorry," she says, her voice louder again. "These kids are at it again," she apologizes.

"Wait, what?" I'm stunned. "What kids? I thought you couldn't . . . Who . . . ?" I have so many questions that I don't even know where to start.

She gasps a little into the phone. "Oh, gosh, no! Not *my* kids. Sorry. I drive my neighbor's kids home after school every day since we're coming from the same place anyway." Her tone changes a little as she adds, clearly more for their benefit than mine, "Usually they're very good company, but I think they've forgotten their manners today."

"You're teaching now?" I find myself smiling for the first time all day. I close the trash bag and depress the speakerphone button, moving the phone back to my ear. "I'm so thrilled to hear it."

"Ethics-based art classes for K through 5," she says with pride. "Listen"—the shrieking in the background is intensifying—"I've got to run and get these kids settled down. Do me a favor and keep me posted about all this, okay? And no matter what answers you find about where the embryo originated, don't you forget who that boy's fathers really are."

Chapter 11

MAGGIE
FEBRUARY 2008

The sound of a door closing wakes me from where I've been napping on the couch. As I sit up, the extra weight of my engorged breasts is instant torment, reminding me why I felt the need to lie down in the first place.

"How was it?" I ask, twisting to face Tess and Wyatt as they unload themselves behind me in the small vestibule of my apartment.

Wyatt is already crouched down, struggling to open the Velcro of his red and blue Spiderman sneakers. He mumbles back at me, "Good, good, good." Dark curls fall toward his face as he focuses on his shoes, and I sigh internally thinking about how much he hates it when I cut his hair.

"What should we do with this one?" Tess asks. She's holding a pile of mail in one hand and an obnoxiously large bouquet of pink ranunculus flowers in the other. Her eyes travel toward the kitchen.

It's been four days since I've been home from the hospital, and I'm wondering if I should email Nick and tell him to stop with the incessant flower arrangements. I'm just afraid that if I acknowledge the deliveries at all, he will use that as an opening, an opportunity to get back under my skin. His eleventh-hour regret over his actions doesn't mean that I can necessarily forgive his nasty comments, his jealousy, his surprising bigotry. What I know for sure is that I need more time to decide how I feel, and the overpowering scent of calla lilies and roses permeating the one-bedroom walk-up Wyatt and I have been renting in LA is not helping to clear my head.

"Maybe you should leave it outside with a note that says, 'Up for grabs'?" I suggest.

Tess rolls her eyes at me and walks toward the kitchen with the flowers. As she opens cabinets, searching for another make-shift vase, I wipe my sleeve across the back of my neck, drying away more sweat. My hormones are all over the place, and I've been perspiring like it's my job since the day after giving birth to the twins. Tess, on the other hand, looks like a Barbie doll in her tight white tank top and capri jeans. As she stretches to reach something from a top shelf, her torso elongates, accentuating an elegant curve in her back. I wonder if I will ever get back the body that I had before I embarked on this journey. Even though I was never as slender as Tess, her taut physique reminds me how much my own form has changed over the past nine months. Would Nick even want me if he saw me now, with my cartoon-ishly large breasts, my mushy belly, and all the post-delivery blood still flowing out of my body in crime-scene quantities?

I thought this delivery would be easier because birthing a child was something I had already done once before—thought my body would know what to do. But delivering little five-and-a-half-pound Wyatt wasn't quite the same as popping out two surprisingly large babies in one sitting. Teddy arrived weighing more than eight pounds, a real achievement for a baby who's a twin. When Kai finally saw fit, thirty-five minutes later, to make his first appearance, at least he had the good grace to be smaller than his big-ass brother.

I feel renewed anger at Nick, thinking about how his behavior left me without the support system I expected to have in place after giving birth. Months ago, I declined Chip and Donovan's offer to pay for two weeks of post-partum household help because I thought Nick and I would manage on our own.

As if she can hear my thoughts, Tess turns to me with a can of ground coffee in her hand. "Are you sure you don't want me to stay a few more days?" She pulls a plastic container out from a drawer and starts pouring the coffee from the can into the Tupperware.

I hesitate. I could definitely use a few more quiet days languishing in sitz baths and calendula ointment and experimenting with other home remedies meant to speed the healing of my nether regions. But it's time for me to start forging my own path forward with Wyatt. Tess shouldn't have to give up even more of her vacation days just because I've landed in yet another tight spot.

"I can," she says. "I can push the flight." She pulls a scissor from a drawer and starts cutting the stems of the flowers.

"It's fine." I lean back against the sofa and look up at the popcorn ceiling. "I'll miss you, but I'm okay. There's no reason for you to pay a change fee for the flight. Go home and use the rest of your vacation days for an actual vacation."

Her pale lips turn up at that, like the idea of her taking a real vacation from her job is a joke. She picks up the completed flower arrangement and opens the freezer to grab a bag of peas before carrying everything over to where I'm sitting.

"Here." She tosses the frozen veggies at me.

I waste no time placing them between my T-shirt and sports bra. The frosty bag helps immediately with the burning sensation emanating from my chest, but the dull ache from the engorgement persists. Tess puts the flowers on the small brown coffee table in front of me before lowering herself onto the sofa.

"Front and center, huh?" I shift my gaze away from the flowers and whatever it is they're supposed to represent.

"Could you stop pushing everyone away? Just for once, let someone stick around in your life?" I never gave Tess an exact play-by-play on why Nick and I fell apart, so I should probably cut her some slack for stepping into his corner now. "You could at least speak to him, hear what he has to say. Maybe there are more reasons to be *with* him than reasons to be apart from him. Being alone isn't synonymous with being brave or being strong. Maybe it's just evidence of bad judgment."

I open my mouth before I even know what I'm going to say. She doesn't give me the chance to come up with anything clever before she stands and walks over to the play area I've set up for Wyatt. He's sitting next to a large plastic clock, pushing at all the buttons, but the toy remains silent.

"Here, buddy." Tess takes the clock and slides the power button into the "on" position. She shakes it a couple of times and looks at me. "Batteries must be dead. Where are extras?" She's already scanning the room like I would ever be the type of person to keep a well-stocked supply of batteries at the ready.

"Hmm, let me think. Oh, right—they're at the bodega on the corner."

Her lips twist in annoyance at me, but then she turns to Wyatt and smiles. "Let's go to the store and get batteries?"

"No shoes," he responds earnestly. Wyatt hates wearing any footwear—prefers to be barefoot at all times.

"No shoes, no batteries," she responds in the same earnest tone, like she's really sorry to say it.

"No shoes," he repeats, his little lips slick with his saliva.

"Then no batteries." She shrugs.

Wyatt looks from Tess back to the oversize clock, his eyes roaming over the colorful buttons, but he holds his ground. "No shoes," he says again.

"Okay," she says, casually, but with finality, and she walks back toward the couch to sit down.

If it were me, I'd probably have just carried him to the store barefoot—saving myself the hassle of negotiating, but definitely not helping the kid learn anything useful. Except maybe that his mom's a sucker.

"Tell me more about BoomStander," Tess says, as though we weren't just in the middle of an argument.

BoomStander is the internet-based celebrity gossip publication where I've been working as an administrative assistant. It'll only be another two weeks until my truncated maternity leave ends and I return to my desk. Wyatt will finally start at their in-house daycare at the same time.

I'm still so grateful to have found a position anywhere at all, considering that I was already five months pregnant when I began my California job hunt. I was so large that I probably looked like I was well past my due date. As it happens, I've been enjoying the position more than I expected. When I explained to Sandra, my now-boss, that I wouldn't need a full maternity leave because I wasn't keeping the babies I was delivering, she got super excited about the fact that I was carrying babies for a gay couple and practically insisted that I take the job. She lost all interest in my educational background, or lack thereof, and only wanted to know about the intended parents and the details of their parenting plan. Would they both be called "Dad"? Did they have a network of similarly structured families so the babies would grow up with a community? Did I know which of the guys was planning to be the primary caretaker? At some point, she confessed her regret over the fact that she herself hadn't turned out to be gay, declaring the LGBQT lifestyle seemed kinder and gentler than the hetero existence in which she had landed. You've got to love Los Angeles. If only I could send Nick out here for a few months, plug him into a more enlightened way of thinking.

I fill Tess in on my job, describing the laid-back office culture, the Ping-Pong tables in three of the conference rooms, and the extra-large medicine balls many of the employees use at their desks instead of swivel chairs.

"Probably sounds pretty crazy to a white-shoe attorney from New York," I say with a small shrug.

"Speaking of shoes . . ." she says quietly as she uses her chin to point in Wyatt's direction. He's sitting on the floor by the front door, attempting to put on his socks and sneakers. Like everything else in life, it appears that Tess is also a better parent than I am. That's my big sis, though, always right about everything. Maybe she's right about Nick, too.

But when I think about calling Nick, I cringe. I can't stop remembering the last fight we had before I left. It was a Tuesday night, and I had been on the phone with Chip, trying to explain what it felt like when the babies were kicking inside me. I told him that it was sort of like being on an inflatable raft in a river and floating over a log. There was pressure, lots of it, but only in a muted way, like if someone was poking you in the arm, but from the other side of a pillow. I kept coming up with stranger examples, and at some point our conversation devolved into nothing but stupid jokes and hysterical laughter. I heard movement on the other side of the room and looked up from the couch to see Nick leaning against the wall, his lip curled up in apparent disgust as he glowered at me.

I ended the call with Chip to see what bug had crawled up Nick's ass this time. Ever since my pregnancy had begun to show, he'd been impossible.

"I don't understand why you fawn over those guys so much. You know they're not into you that way, right? Where is your dignity?"

"Excuse me? What the actual fuck is your problem?" I demanded as I stood from the sofa. I almost never cursed anymore, not since having Wyatt, but I couldn't stand the way he was judging me, especially when I wasn't even certain exactly what he was judging.

"All you do is call those two guys in New York. It's like you don't even have a life of your own anymore," he said, spittle flying out of his mouth. "You're just this vessel. A uterus for hire."

"Don't you ever think of what it's like for them?" I walked toward him, lugging all my anger with me. "I have their children with me, day in and day out, and they have absolutely no control over what I do to their babies. Can't you try to imagine how scary that is for them? I could be doing shots of tequila all day long and giving their babies fetal alcohol syndrome, and there's nothing they can do to stop me. They have no power over whether I eat raw eggs, unpasteurized cheese, sushi. I could decide to drive down to Mexico for vacation and just never come back. I'm trying to be kind, to help give them peace of mind. Not everyone has it so easy where they can just stick their dick in their girlfriend and magically end up with a kid nine months later." I noticed I was pointing at him, and I lowered my hand.

"It's embarrassing," he shouted back, "the way you're playing up to them all the time. If you're so worried about them, maybe you should just move to New York, where you can be with them all the time. They can feed you organic produce and folic acid tablets all day long. You can watch them make sweet love to each other and ask yourself over and over again when it's going to be your turn to get in there."

I gasped at his cruelty.

"Maybe I *will* move to New York!" I shouted back, suddenly certain that I wanted to get myself and my child as far away from this man as possible. I stormed off to the bedroom, yanked a duffel bag off the top shelf of the closet, and started stuffing my clothing into it.

In the end, I decided I wasn't ready to go back to the East Coast. But I had to get away from Nick, who seemed in that moment to be filled with nothing but anger and the ugliest kinds of negativity. So instead of New York, Wyatt and I went west. Part of me hoped Nick would stop us, that he'd make some grand gesture and convince us to stay. Instead, he offered to carry our luggage to the car, warning me, in an oddly timed moment of gallantry, that I shouldn't be lifting anything heavy. He didn't even argue about Wyatt coming with me, which only made me angrier. As we drove out of the building's lot, I spotted him in the rearview mirror, still standing next to the empty parking spot, arms crossed in front of his chest, watching us leave him behind.

I've been out here in LA for four months now, and I've started to build a new life. I have a solid job, and I've made a few friends in the building. Wyatt and I use the weekends to go on adventures around town, down the road to the pet store or a few blocks over to visit the tar pits. But I'd be lying if I said I didn't miss Nick.

"It looks like I'm going to be popping into the bodega," Tess says as she stands again. "Want me to pick up anything else?"

"Maybe more peas?" I say as I move the bag from my left breast to my right.

"You sure you don't want to try pumping just to relieve some of the pressure?" she asks, eyeing my bulging breasts.

Chip and Donovan decided they would formula-feed the babies in order to spare me the hassle of overnighting breast milk across the country on a regular basis. In order to let the milk dry up as quickly as possible, I've resolved to suffer through whatever pain is necessary.

"Nah, I don't want to give these boobs reason to produce any more milk than they already are." The thought of leaking onto my dress shirts after I return to work doesn't really appeal to me.

After Tess leaves again with Wyatt, I decide to straighten up a little. I sweep up the clutter on the coffee table: two half-full juice glasses, Wyatt's dinosaur coloring book and crayons, and the stack of mail Tess brought in yesterday, which I still haven't bothered to sort. I drop the dishes in the sink and then lean against the counter while I flip through the pile of envelopes and catalogues. Tucked between a phone bill and a Toys "R" Us catalog, I find a postcard. There is a picture collage on the front, and the word "Colorado" is scrawled across the middle. I flip the card over and see that Donovan has sent a note.

He and Chip rented this obscenely large retrofitted RV in order to road trip the entire way home to New York. They had too many concerns about bringing newborns on a commercial airliner to fly back.

Donovan's handwriting is neat but small, and without my contacts in, I have to squint in order to read.

> *Dear Maggie,*
> *Who knew they even sold postcards anymore?*
> *We were passing through Denver and we decided*
> *to spend a few extra hours here as tourists—I've*
> *always had a hankering to see this city. We just*
> *wanted you to know that you are on our minds*
> *as we bring our babies home. We are still simply*
> *baffled, bewildered, and beguiled by the kindness*
> *you've done us (and don't start up again about*
> *how you only did it for the money—Chip and I*
> *know better). The babies are doing fantastically*
> *well, and you will forever be our biggest hero.*
> *Much love,*
> *Donovan*

I'm heartened to have heard from them, even if it's an arm's length postcard. I flip the card back to the other side and study the pictures. I've never been to Denver, but one of the pictures on the front looks just like the red rocks in Sedona. It makes me unexpectedly homesick for Phoenix, and for Nick.

Chapter 12

DONOVAN
JULY 2018

*I*t's a sweltering Sunday afternoon, and we're loitering outside a suburban shopping mall, along with several other sweaty parents, awaiting the return of the camp bus. Britt Lindeman, an uber-fancy mom we know from the boys' school, is standing on my other side, talking Chip's ear off about the letters she received from her son, Hudson, and how much he loved his brief stay at overnight camp. Next summer she plans to send him for the full seven weeks rather than the fourteen-day mini-program we did this year, and she wants to know if we expect to do the same for Kai and Teddy. She's clapping her hands in excitement at Chip as she imagines the possibility of our kids being together again.

Britt Lindeman falls into the category of women who love us simply because we are gay. After spending so many of my teenage years struggling with the idea of coming out and then putting up with incessant jibes from alpha males in my Italian neighborhood, I definitely prefer an attitude of people like Britt, who can't get enough of us. I've come a long way in coping with reactions from the straight community anyway, because once you have children with another man, it's like you're coming out over and over again, every time you and your partner take the kids out in public. That was one thing I didn't fully realize before we had the boys. Whenever people see you co-dadding, it's like announcing from a bullhorn that you're gay. When you arrive for back-to-school night or take your kids out for burgers, it's as if you're wearing a sign that says, "Yup, two dads over here, because we're gay, yes, totally gay. Gay as glitter, and unicorns, and Europop. Gay, gay, gay." We're lucky that in New York, our gayness only seems to add to our cache (Britt and her Chanel handbag are proving my point at this very moment, as they collectively sidle closer to Chip).

When it comes to straight people judging us and our family, there are basically four different groups, and Britt, as fan-girl, fits into the category that is my second favorite. My top choice is those people for whom our sexual orientation carries no extra implications, but merely registers with them as a part of who we are. Unfortunately, those people tend to be few and far between. In third place are the folks who you know aren't comfortable with your orientation, but they're also sorry they feel that way. Those people pretend, aggressively, that which way you lean is of no consequence at all to them, when in fact it's all they can think about in your presence. And then, of course, there are your anti-gay Neanderthals—the ones who can't resist telling you how you're wronging society, wronging God, wronging your parents, causing climate change or weapons of mass destruction, or who knows what else, simply by existing as you are. When those people see you with children . . . that's when things can get ugly. Chip and I have learned to avoid rest stops in rural areas at all costs—not because we can't take the heat but because now that Teddy and Kai are older, they understand what's going on, and why should they have to deal with bigotry?

A big white charter bus with a green leprechaun on its side finally pulls up at the stoplight across from the shopping center, and several of the parents start cheering in excitement. Britt's high-pitched words fade to muted clouds of dust as I steel myself to see the boys. I've not looked into Kai's face in person since receiving final confirmation that he and I are not genetically related. I remind myself, again, that I've known for years about the absence of a genetic connection between Teddy and me, and it hasn't impacted our relationship in the slightest. I have to approach Kai in the same way.

After the bus pulls to a stop, the doors open and campers begin tumbling out. The kids all look disheveled and satisfied, with rolled sleeping bags tucked precariously under their arms, grubby sneakers on their feet, trophies peeking out from back-packs. As though it's been choreographed, each boy pauses on the top step and scans the crowd for a parent before hopping happily off the bus.

Finally, I catch a glimpse of Teddy, his blond hair still somehow perfectly coifed. *Just like his father.* In spite of myself, I am stung by the thought. I maneuver through the crowd of excited parents and lift Teddy into a bear hug before his feet hit the parking lot. I feel tears spring to my eyes as we connect, and I am overcome by my love for this child, and for his brother.

"Ooof," Teddy says when I squeeze too tightly. I lower his feet to the ground and release him as Chip emerges beside me. I look back to the bus to see Kai waiting at the top step, just like all the boys before him. When our gazes connect, a wide grin takes over his face.

I will not cry. Not here. Not now. I should have thought to grab my aviators out of the glove box in our Land Rover. He bounds down the steps and I open my arms. He jumps straight into my chest and clutches me so tightly that this time *I* am the one getting smothered.

"Yuck, you're so sweaty." He pulls back and wrinkles his nose.

And just like that, I am at ease again. This is my kid, through and through. No matter his biological origin, this child is one and the same with the infant I bathed in the kitchen sink of our old apartment, the baby I wrapped in swaddling blankets in the middle of the night, the toddler I taught to swim at the old Reebok Sports Club, the boy who asked me to sit in his room during late-night thunderstorms until he was well past nine years old. Now he's whispering something to me about how Teddy brought home a trophy.

"Can we get sushi?" Teddy appears beside us, bursting with energy despite the long bus ride and their departure from Vermont so early this morning. "Dad said."

I glance over at Chip, who laughs and shakes his head. "No, I didn't." He wraps an arm around Kai and corrals us toward the other end of the parking lot.

"You did." Kai looks from Chip to me. "The night before we left. Pa?" Kai looks over to me for validation, his big eyes wide with excitement and hunger.

"Fine, whatever." I smile at them. "We'll stop somewhere after we get back to the City, but I promised Nonna we'd bring you guys over for Sunday dinner tonight."

Kai and Teddy catch sight of our SUV and hurry toward it; they're already lifting the door of the trunk and throwing in their bulging bags before Chip and I have reached the front of the car.

Chip grabs my hand before heading to the driver's side. "We've got this," he says quietly.

His words slide over me like a balm, and I allow myself to hope for the first time since learning the horrible news about Kai that maybe he's right. Maybe there is nothing to do here except enjoy our kids. What does it matter where our son came from? As far as we know, there's no one out in the world searching for him or crying over his absence, so why not just put this whole thing to bed and let us keep enjoying our family?

My mother keeps glancing at me across the table, where I'm wedged between Chip and my sister, Gina. The worry lines in her forehead seem to be deepening by the minute.

"Donny, you didn't have any of the garlic bread," she says, shoving an oblong basket toward me.

"Ma, I'm fine, stop." I push the bread away, toward Chip, who's just finished refilling his plate with second helpings from several of the ceramic dishes on the table. I look mournfully at the lasagna on his fork and remind myself that not everyone has a turbo-charged metabolism. Kai rises from his seat and rounds the table, passing by his two older cousins, Flora and Ethan, until he reaches my father's chair. "Nonno, can I?" He motions to my dad's lap. My dad is leaning back in his chair, hands resting on his rotund middle. The creases around his eyes deepen as he smiles at his grandson.

"You're not getting too old for this?" He hauls Kai onto his lap without waiting for an answer.

Kai picks up my dad's fork and claims the last bites of pasta on the dish in front of them, as if the plate is his own, as if everything about this life is his for the taking.

"Can we be excused?" fourteen-year-old Ethan asks, and I hear Gina sigh beside me.

"Not yet," she answers on a huff. "Nonna worked hard pre-paring this meal so we could all take time to enjoy it together." She widens her eyes at him in a way that says, "Don't you ask me again."

He nods, but his lips tighten in protest.

"Check this out," Teddy says to Ethan, then crosses his blue eyes, shifting both pupils down toward his nose. Ethan laughs and then shows everyone how he can curl his tongue into a shamrock, his foul mood already forgotten. Gina often bemoans her kids' mercurial mood swings and the trials of single parenting, especially during puberty, but right now she's smiling at Ethan's theatrics like she can't help herself.

Flora leans across Teddy's seat and drops a half-eaten piece of garlic bread onto Ethan's plate.

"Gross! I don't want it if it already has your spit all over it." He picks it up and makes as if to toss it back onto his sister's plate.

"Guys." Gina's word is a bite, decisive. Any trace of a smile has disappeared. Even so, with her dark hair pulled into a low braid, she looks more like another teenager sitting at the table than the middle-aged mother that she is.

"It's fine, let them get up," my mom says, so much softer than she was when we were that age. The sudden scraping of chairs and clattering of porcelain dishes fill the air as the kids clear their places before scrambling to the basement.

Once it's quiet again, my mother asks, "So, they liked the camp?" What she wants to ask is whether I've had more panic attacks, whether I'm about to have a complete emotional breakdown, whether we've figured anything out about Kai, his history, his future. But she starts with camp.

"They loved it," Chip says. "They're already planning what they want to bring next summer, how they want to set up their bunk bed if they get to share again."

"Next summer." Gina says it like a declaration, like we've made some sort of collective decision, and I realize instantly that yes, we have made a decision. Or rather, *I* have made a decision.

"Yeah, next summer," I say, and then I turn toward Chip. "We're going to drop this search for answers about Kai."

Chip cocks his head and raises an eyebrow, his whole body poised in question as he waits for me to say more.

I shrug, as though it's suddenly obvious, and then look back at my parents. "Even if the clinic did use the wrong embryo, what does it really matter, right? What good will it do us to find answers like that at this point?"

"What about the doctors?" my dad asks, leaning back in his chair again, showing off that paunch of his. "Don't they have a duty to their other patients, a legal obligation, to report what they've done with a patient's genetic material?"

His question makes me think of that book about Henrietta Lacks we read in our book club a few years back, a true story about a woman in the 1950s whose cancer cells were harvested without her explicit consent. The doctors kept this woman's tissue without her knowledge, and then they performed studies on her cells without ever informing her. By experimenting on her cells, doctors learned how to grow cancer outside the body, in a lab, and that knowledge became the basis of all sorts of groundbreaking inventions, from a polio vaccine to—coincidentally enough—IVF.

I remember the book because of the heated debates we had in our twelve-person book group about the medical ethics. Several of our friends felt that the doctors' decisions were within acceptable boundaries of medicine at the time, and that the benefits to society far outweighed whatever wrongs might have been perpetrated against the Lacks family.

I wonder if our situation is like that. Two people out there in the world have provided biological material, this time in the form of an egg and sperm, and although those people are not aware of how that material has been used, the benefits of allowing events to proceed on their current trajectory far outweigh any arguments in favor of alerting the providers of said material.

"Whatever duty they might have, they're pretty much grasping at straws at this point." I glance over at Chip, who nods in agreement. "Maybe they check the records for every single fertilized egg that was in the clinic when we got pregnant and then follow up with all of those patients. And then what happens when they find the person whose egg Kai came from? We have to give him back? Yeah, no."

Before I can add anything about the preposterousness of such an idea, Chip chimes in, "The people at the clinic insist that the embryos simply couldn't have gotten switched. Their protocols." He waves a hand in the air, like it's shorthand for all the explanations they gave us.

"Don't you think we should just let it go?" I ask, looking at my mother.

Her dark eyes shift immediately toward my father, looking to him for an opinion, so I keep hammering at the point.

"There are plenty of people out there who don't know who their genetic parents are. Certainly, there are plenty of kids who don't know who their fathers are." I think again of the paternity tests available at every corner Walgreens. "But beyond that, there are the babies who get left on church steps, at firehouses—it happens, and they survive."

Everyone is just letting me talk now, allowing me to convince myself. And it's working, the convincing. I'm talking myself into this.

"Of course I would prefer to know more about Kai's genetic history, but not if the price of information is possibly losing the right to keep him."

I am beginning to get more comfortable with the fact that Kai is not genetically mine. It's okay because, as I am finally realizing, nothing has to change. Shame on me for taking so long to get here, but I finally understand that so long as we get to keep our family together, everything will be all right.

Chapter 13

MAGGIE
JULY 2018

The ringing from my backpack surprises me, as I don't usually get cell reception out here in the sticks. I'm just finishing my lunch break at the summer camp where I'm in charge of the crafts curriculum for academically talented children ranging in age from four to thirteen years old. I stop wiping the sandwich crumbs from my denim cutoffs and quickly fish around in my pack for my phone, sighing as I do. The heat of the Arizona summer sun has me in a constant sweat, making every movement feel objectionable.

When I see the 203 area code, I imagine first that it's spam, but then I remember the clinic in New Haven. "Hello?" I answer, unsure whether I will be able to hear anyone on the other end. I drive out to Prescott every day because I haven't found any similarly creative summer teaching opportunities near Sedona. My cell reception is even worse out here in the desert than it is when I'm surrounded by the red rocks near the house. Amazingly, though, this call has come through.

"Ms. Wingate, this is Dr. Pillar from the Yale University Fertility Center calling. Is this an okay time to talk?" Her tone is pushy, as though she is not really giving me a choice.

I glance at my Swatch and see that I still have about eight minutes before the next period starts. "Yeah, sure," I say, and walk the few steps back to the shaded picnic table where I finished my sandwich moments ago. I lower myself onto the splintery bench, waiting for her to continue.

"We've received the results of the maternity test from QuestLab, and you are a match for Kai Rigsdale," she says.

"Well, right." I run my finger over a pair of initials carved into the wood of the table. "I carried him," I remind her. "I was the GC."

"Right," she says, "but you are also his biological mother. The test confirms it."

"Wait, what?" I look up from the picnic table, as though the doctor is sitting on the bench across from me. Maybe the reception isn't as good as I thought. "Did you just say the report shows that I am his biological mother?" I repeat it back to her, sure that I've gotten it wrong.

"Yes, exactly."

A counselor is heading in my direction, a group of eleven-year-old girls trailing behind her. I rise from the bench and head toward the mess hall, away from the approaching campers.

"But that's impossible," I argue as I walk. "Those embryos were transferred into my uterus fertilized. I didn't make either of those babies."

"Well yes, but it seems that only one of the embryos that we transferred managed to implant in your uterus effectively— the one that became Teddy Rigsdale. The other one must have failed, and then you conceived a baby on your own, the natural way."

"But if I was pregnant with the one embryo, I couldn't have gotten pregnant on my own. That's impossible."

There is silence on the other end as I climb the steps to the mess hall porch, and I am hopeful that the doctor finally realizes how ridiculous she is being.

"Doctor?" I finally prompt, but then I hear a beeping on my phone, indicating that the call was dropped. "Wait! Hello?"

I quickly press the call-back button, but now I have zero bars showing up and can't get any sort of signal. I start high-tailing it to the main office so I can use the landline. "Tom," I bark at the CIT who's staffing the front desk, "I need to use the phone in Calla's office. Family emergency. Can you send someone down to the barn to cover for a few minutes?"

After pushing all the right buttons to get through the automated menu and then sitting on hold for another six minutes, I finally get a real, live human being on the phone. I explain that I was on a call with Dr. Pillar and we got cut off. The operator apologizes but says that Dr. Pillar has just gone into an exam room for a procedure and cannot be interrupted. She's going to have to call me back. I give the woman the phone number for the landline, as I'm certain that she won't reach me a second time if she tries my cell. Then I add a list of frenetic instructions about how if she returns my call between 5:00 p.m. and 6:30 p.m., I will be driving back to Sedona, and she can try my cell but I will have my son in the car with me and likely won't be able to speak freely, so it might be best that if she can't return my call before 5:00 p.m., to please try me tonight at my home number, which I rattle off for the woman.

Having done all I can at the moment, I have to return to the craft barn, where I will calmly teach children how to do a Chinese staircase pattern with their lanyards as I try not to imagine what on earth Dr. Pillar could have meant. What I understood her to be saying is so far and away beyond the realm of human possibility that I know it's best not to dwell on it until I can have a real conversation with the doctor. For now, I will simply pray that I misunderstood. The alternative—that the second Rigsdale baby, Kai, is actually my own biological child—is simply unthinkable. I look down at the blank screen of my cell phone and try not to see the gaping hole, the abyss that I could fall into, if it turns out I was carrying my own baby all those years ago and then accidentally gave him away.

Chapter 14

DONOVAN
JULY 2018

*E*rica isn't calling me back. We're scheduled to meet with the Wenzo execs in three days, and I regret that I've been too distracted by of all the confusion about Kai to focus on this project properly. But now that Chip and I have opted for blissful ignorance, I'm trying to get back in the game on this pitch.

Unfortunately, while I was busy fixating on embryos and alleles, everything seems to have fallen to shit at the office. This morning, as I arrived with my non-fat half-caf mocha latte, I noticed that many of the younger associate brokers were giving me not-so-subtle sidelong glances. As I tried to determine whether I was imagining the surreptitious rubbernecking, the way they all stopped talking as I walked by, I began to realize that, in retrospect, this worrisome behavior from the firm's junior associates has been going on for weeks. I was just too muddled up in the brain to register it. I called over to Wen King Partners this morning and got the runaround from their end as well. Now, as I sit at my desk waiting for multiple return calls that are not materializing, I also grasp that Erica has been acting somewhat shifty and unavailable recently, and a narrative finally begins to crystallize in my mind. I've been at this job for long enough to know when something is dirty, when someone has been double-crossed. And apparently this time, the stooge being screwed over is me.

I scroll through my emails, trying to focus on other clients and potential leads, but the fact is, Wen King is the biggest fish I've landed in quite some time, and it's hard to get excited about anything else when this deal is looking increasingly like my best missed opportunity.

As I read through an email from the manager of a Turkish bath and body products company who is looking to open a pop-up shop in midtown, my phone finally rings. I realize with a thud that it's my cell, not my office phone, that's ringing from beside my keyboard.

"Hello?" I answer without looking at the caller ID.

"Mr. Gallo-Rigsdale, it's Dr. Pillar from the Yale Fertility Clinic."

"Hi, Dr. Pillar." I glance at my open office door but decide privacy is not necessary for what we need to discuss. "I was actually going to call you today." I lean back in my swivel chair. "Chip and I talked, and we don't want to waste your resources on a wild goose chase with respect to the embryo's origin. I think it's time to shut down this inquiry and chalk it up to medical mystery."

"Mr. Gallo-Rigsdale." Her tone is firm, suffused with some sort of warning that has me instantly on edge. "We received the DNA results from Maggie Wingate's test. She is a perfect match to your son's profile."

"I don't understand what you're getting at." I sit up straighter in my seat to focus, thinking, yes, Maggie was a good match for us, a great match.

"She is the biological mother. The test confirms it."

"That's not possible," I explain calmly, relieved that she is simply mistaken. "Maggie was our carrier, yes, but we transferred fertilized embryos. She didn't conceive those babies on her own." I pick up the skyscraper fidget toy I have on my desk and absently start disassembling the thing.

"I understand," Dr. Pillar says, "but only one of the embryos you transferred seems to have implanted successfully. It appears the other one, which we thought was a success, never matured. There are any number of possibilities as to why it didn't take—belated rejection by the endometrium, a blighted ovum, undetermined blastocyst arrest—but that's not really the point. Your carrier must have ovulated shortly after the implantation, and then conceived an additional child all on her own."

Well, the doctor definitely has my full attention now.

"It was so close in time to the first conception that nobody realized the discrepancy," she continues. "But I've been looking over the records from the pregnancy, and it all makes sense now—why the second sac was smaller than the first, why one baby was so much smaller for the duration of the pregnancy. It's because he was conceived at a different time. Their gestational ages were different."

"But that's impossible," I argue. "It's like Biology 101. A woman can't get pregnant if she's already pregnant." I may not be an expert in female anatomy, but even I know that much.

"It *is* extremely rare," Dr. Pillar explains, "but there are documented cases of this happening. It's a process known as superfetation. Hormonal irregularities can lead a woman to ovulate when she is already pregnant. If that egg is fertilized during the appropriate window, there is no reason it can't also implant into the uterus of an already-pregnant woman. It's incredibly rare, but unfortunately, *not* impossible."

I'm stunned. This can't be right.

"But . . ." I'm silent, thinking, trying to process. I notice that I am now standing, half a skyscraper still in my hand, though I don't recall rising from my seat.

"When patients come in for fertility treatments, every now and then, there are surprises," Dr. Pillar says. "And the fact that you opted for your GC to do a natural-cycle transfer made that all the more likely. She was never given the progesterone that would have shut down her ovaries. It makes sense that she could have ovulated again after the embryo transfer."

"But she wasn't allowed to have sex," I remember suddenly. "Right? Wasn't that one of the rules?" We could sue her for breach of contract. Except that the courts in Arizona probably wouldn't pay much attention to us, and even if they would, it wouldn't change the fact of Kai's parentage.

"We did a blood test nine days after the transfer to confirm the pregnancy," she tells me, and I am reminded of the call we received with the thrilling news that the transfer had been a success. They told us then that the blood test wouldn't indicate how many of the embryos had implanted, but at least one had attached. "After that, the carrier would have been cleared for intercourse. Based on the gestational measurements of the babies that we recorded throughout the pregnancy, I would guess that they were conceived approximately two and a half weeks apart."

My desk phone starts ringing, and I see that it's Erica, finally calling me back. Well, now Erica is going to have to wait.

"Wow." I drop back into my leather chair with a thud, trying to digest what Dr. Pillar is telling me. "So, okay, I guess that's good then, that we know what actually happened here, what Kai's genetic history is. We loved our carrier. It's kind of nice to know that she's the person who Kai came from, and now we have access to genetic information if he ever needs it." I realize that means Nick is the biological father, which means we can have medical history for Kai on both sides of the family.

"Mr. Gallo-Rigsdale . . ." Dr. Pillar's tone is demanding, halting. "The carrier never agreed to hand over her own biological child. We may have a situation on our hands. She might want custody of the child."

Not for a moment can I believe that Maggie might want to take our son away from us, that she might claim he is *her* child. It was only the other day that she was telling me that Kai was *my* child, no matter who contributed the genetic material.

"No," I say quickly, "I don't think so. She wanted us to have our family. She knows Kai is where he belongs, that there is no question in that regard."

"I am legally obligated to reveal the test result to her, to inform her of this development," Dr. Pillar says, and I hear contrition in her voice. "I'm sorry Mr. Gallo-Rigsdale, but I think you should find yourself an attorney."

Chapter 15

MAGGIE
MARCH 2008

*A*s one of the hottest new companies in LA, BoomStander has already rebranded itself in the weeks that I've been absent. No longer is it simply a pop-culture blog; the company is now expanding into a commerce platform as well. As part of their push to be at the forefront of life and style, they also run an excellent daycare facility onsite.

When we reach the wide glass doors of BoomBabes, Wyatt becomes instantly transfixed by the brightly colored climbing equipment and oversize toys that are visible just inside. He barely gives me a second look when I kiss his forehead and hand him over to a redheaded young caregiver, a woman who looks like she just stepped out of a shampoo commercial. He runs off, beelining straight to the play-kitchen. *Just like his daddy*, I think wistfully before remembering my festering anger at Nick.

I head off to my post in reception, two flights down.

As I approach my desk, I notice that it's covered with congratulatory flower arrangements and greeting cards. My co-worker Bara spots me first and rockets out of her chair to welcome me with a too-tight hug. This embrace is followed by a similar squashing from Jean-Marie, and even a low-key squeal of delight from Amanda. The display of affection feels more appropriate to long-lost friends than recent acquaintances, and yet I find myself leaning in, enjoying the sensation that I belong somewhere.

"Oh my God," Bara says as her eyes roam over my frame from my ears to my ankles. "You look like you were never pregnant." Bara is a recent college graduate with the body of a twelve-year-old boy. I could probably fit four of her into the pants I'm currently wearing.

"That's definitely a lie," I say with a smile, "because I'm still sporting at least half of the weight I gained—but I appreciate you for trying."

"Okay, bust out the pictures, let's see those babies!" Amanda gives me a light shove on my arm as she peers pointedly into the gaping tote bag that's still hanging over my shoulder. Amanda is only a few years older than I am, and she has mentioned several times that she can't wait to get pregnant after she and her fiancé get married a few months from now. Bara's ponytail bounces as she stands beside Amanda, nodding in agreement.

"No. Guys." I'm silent for a beat as they gaze back at me expectantly. "It's not like that. Once I handed the babies off to their dads, that was the end of my involvement." I rub my hands together like I'm wiping off dust. "Kaput."

"Yeah, but . . ." Bara's round blue eyes grow wide as she puzzles through my response. "You have to have taken at least one picture, right? Not even right after the delivery?"

Without warning, I'm hit by an intense rush of panic that I've given away too much, that I've lost some part of myself. The feeling of emptiness is harsh and frightening—but then, as quickly as it arrived, it's gone.

I move closer to my desk and drop my tote down to the floor beside it as Amanda and Bara watch me. "There are pictures," I explain, "but they belong to the dads. I didn't take any. Not my kids." I shrug, punctuating my detachment, then flop into my desk chair, relieved to be off my feet. My body doesn't feel like my own yet, and I wonder if I've rushed back to work too quickly. "It was like watching a good friend's children—my responsibility, but not my babies." I jiggle my mouse to wake up the computer. "Ooh! I do have a really cute shot of my sister with Wyatt when she was in town, though. Want to see?"

I pull my digital camera from my tote and click around until I find the right picture. When I land on it, the image makes me grin all over again. Wyatt's sitting on Tess's lap in front of a fountain at the Grove shopping complex. Tess is smiling brightly at the camera, oblivious to the fact that sweet little Wyatt is holding an open bottle of water and pointing it down into Tess's lap. The picture was taken at the exact moment that the water began spilling from the bottle, but before anything actually landed on Tess. I laugh every time I look at it, especially when I remember Tess returning to my apartment with soaking wet cargo pants and a very giggly Wyatt.

I hand the camera to Bara, who laughs out loud and then passes it to Amanda's waiting hand.

"Hilarious," Amanda declares. "You should post that."

"I'm not on Facebook," I confess.

"Seriously?" Bara glances at Amanda in disbelief and then looks back at me.

I don't want to admit to them that I'm concealing my single-mom, entry-level job status from all my pretentious old prep-school friends.

"But you work at a media and pop culture company," Amanda starts to argue.

"I'm only an admin," I say. "Answering phones and keeping order in the office doesn't require me to have an active internet presence. It does, however, require me to catch up on whatever I missed since I've been gone." I smile apologetically and turn my eyes back to the computer.

As they each return to their own seats, I log into my email

and find a to-do list from my supervisor, Sandra. It's mostly busywork that I can handle with relative ease, but the list is three pages deep, so I figure I'd better get started. I also have an email from the daycare center telling me that Wyatt is already busy playing trains with two other little boys and that I can come visit at lunch time if I'd like.

As I marvel again at how lucky I am to have found this job, another email appears on the screen, this one from Chip Rigsdale. Curious, I click on it right away.

> *Hi Maggs!*
>
> *The boys are doing great, and Donny and I are loving being home on paternity leave with them. It's going to be rough leaving them every morning once this period of time expires. I just wanted to tell you that I think your boy Nick is trying to make a statement, and that maybe you want to sit up and listen. Donny says I'm being a busybody (again), but so be it. We just opened a baby gift from Nick, and I would say it's a definite declaration.*
>
> *He sent us a personalized baby book—you know, like one of those scrapbooks where we can record all of their firsts, save a lock of hair, and so on. The book is incredibly cute, lots of teddy bears and firetrucks, etc., etc., and the front cover reads, "Happiest with our Dads." He also included a card, and I won't rehash the entire treatise he wrote, but suffice it to say, he thanked us for opening his eyes about different kinds of families, and then he went on, and on, and on, and ON, about how much he misses you. I'm sure he's hoping that one of us will reach out to you on his behalf. Well here I am, babe.*

Throw the poor guy a bone! Look, I wouldn't presume to tell you how to live your life, but I do feel strongly that you are punishing yourself needlessly. The man is SORRY. How many more bouquets does he have to send you before you relent, Woman? Donny and I only want to see you happy. You've done so much for us, and I'm just trying to return the favor here.

Talk soon,

Chip

I can't. I can't do this right now. I've been back at work for a hot second, and I need to focus on my job. Not Nick. I've been trying so hard not to miss him, but the constant barrage of flowers and emails has made it very difficult for me to remember why I was so angry at him. Bigotry, I remind myself again, intolerance. Chip's email suggests that Nick has evolved, but I'm still not sure I'm willing to open myself up to him again.

Instead of figuring out how to respond to Chip, I turn back to Sandra's list and start with task number one.

———

Later that evening, Wyatt and I are meandering home from where the bus has dropped us. As I navigate the uneven sidewalk, pushing the stroller over bumps and cracks, our moving forms cast long shadows against the sidewalk.

The lingering sunshine is a reminder that springtime is coming. The seasons aren't all that variable in LA, but the longer hours of daylight do mark a certain passage of time, a reminder of how long we've been here.

After a busy first day back at work reconciling expense reports, organizing travel arrangements, and calendaring a staggering number of internal and external meetings for senior management, I am wiped out. Wyatt, on the other hand, seems to be completely energized from all his creative play with the other children at BoomBabes. His sudden enthusiasm for every tree root and sidewalk divot fills me with contrition that I haven't done a better job of stimulating his mind or socializing him since Tess went back to New York. At least now he will have BoomBabes to look forward to each weekday.

An uninvited voice pipes up inside my head to say that LA was never supposed to be my final destination—just a safe place to wait out the pregnancy and plan for the future. Now that I have the final payment from Chip and Donovan, it's time for me to start figuring out my next steps.

As Wyatt and I continue toward home, I mentally sift through my options. I enjoy the office culture at BoomStander, and it's possible that I could find a degree program in LA that would allow me to continue working for the company part time. I've also been toying with the idea of moving closer to New York—near Tess, and even my parents, if we ever get back on speaking terms. But I think I would feel too guilty moving Wyatt to a place that's a full plane ride away from his father. At least in LA, it's only five hours in the car if Nick ever wants to see his son—

"Daddy!!!!!!!!!" Wyatt suddenly shouts, as if he has heard my thoughts.

And then I see him.

Half a block ahead of us, leaning against the railing that leads to my apartment building, stands Nick. His arms are folded across his broad chest and there's a cautious smile on his tanned face. I barely have time to register the wash of joy that runs through me at the sight of his face before Wyatt wriggles out of the stroller and begins running toward him.

I take another second to look over at Nick before I realize that Wyatt's headed straight into the busy street between us without any awareness of the cars barreling in each direction.

"Wyatt! No!" I break into a run, chasing after him. He's already several feet ahead of me, and he's darting off the sidewalk with improbable speed. Cars are careening in both directions, and an old blue Chevy is headed directly toward him.

Suddenly, everything is moving in slow motion. I see Wyatt's little feet moving farther away, Nick racing toward us from the opposite side of the street, the face of the man driving the Chevy, his eyes turned down toward the dash. With every ounce of energy I have, I run. It feels like I'm running for both an eternity and a split second. Finally, finally, my hands connect with Wyatt's back and I rejoice at the contact. I shove him, hard. We both fall to the ground, and I feel the sting of the concrete scraping my knees as Wyatt emits a wail. I hope I haven't hurt him, but I thank God that he is clear of the car's front bumper. Then I hear the blast of a horn, so close it's nearly inside my head, and I turn toward the Chevy, knowing that it's too late.

When I wake up, I'm in a dark room, and I feel an impossible weight on my abdomen. There is beeping from a machine somewhere. I turn my head and see Nick sitting in the chair beside my bed, his eyes closed.

"Nick." My throat is scratchy, and the word comes out as barely a whisper.

His eyes open slowly, but when they finally focus on me, he jolts upright. "You're awake!" His chin is covered with more stubble than I'm used to.

There is an IV in my arm and a breathtaking throbbing in my head. My mind plays a quick reel of Wyatt in the street, the blue Chevy. I force out the only word I can. "Wyatt?"

"He's fine. He's with Lydia from your building." He glances over his shoulder toward the brightly lit hallway. "Let me, I'm just—I'd better grab the doctor." He hurries out of the room and leaves me to absorb the relief of Wyatt's safety on my own. I begin to drift off again, my lids too heavy to keep open.

The next time I wake up, sunshine fills the room. My throat feels like it's lined with needles. Nick is standing by the door with his back to me as he talks with someone in the hallway.

"Water," I croak, but I'm quieter than I mean to be.

"Mommy!" I hear Wyatt's voice before I see him. He's seated in a large armchair beneath the window, a coloring book open on his knees. "Daddy, water," he calls over to Nick.

Nick begins lifting a finger to his lips, as though he's going to shush Wyatt, but then he and the doctor notice that I'm awake.

"Well, good morning," the older woman says as she and Nick both move toward the bed. She fills a small cup with water from the plastic pitcher beside me and hands me the cup; I take small, wonderfully redemptive sips as she fills me in.

"You took quite a hit," she says, "but it looks like you'll heal up fine. A jagged piece of the car perforated your abdomen, but the ambulance made good time, and we've stitched all your parts back together."

"Humpty Dumpty," Wyatt mumbles from where he's resumed coloring.

The doctor's lips turn up and she shakes her head good-naturedly. "Not even that bad."

I try to nod, but I just want to go back to sleep.

———————

I open my eyes to what feels like early morning. The ferocious pounding in my head has decreased to a more manageable headache. I turn in the bed and start to move, but Nick comes rushing from the other side of the room.

"No, no, no, don't strain."

"How long have I been here?" I ask as he props a pillow behind me so I can sit up slightly. I notice that he's still wearing the same shirt he had on when I first spotted him outside my apartment.

"Three days." He starts pouring me a fresh cup of water.

"And he hasn't left your side since they brought you in," a heavyset nurse says as she comes into the room and starts pushing buttons on the machine next to the bed.

"I guess I'm a stay-put kind of person," Nick says into the room without meeting my eyes.

The nurse moves to my bedside and pushes away the coverlet. "I'm just going to check the wound," she says as she begins removing bandages from my stomach. I keep my eyes focused on her face as she peels away the dressing so I don't yet have to confront the visual of whatever damage lies below.

Even with the painkillers flowing through my veins, I wince against her ministrations, but she seems pleased with what she finds.

"Well, you won't have to stay put all that much longer." She looks at Nick over her shoulder before turning back to tell me. "Seems you're healing up good."

"Careful," Nick says, "if you give her too much confidence, she might attempt a jailbreak. A bit of a runner, this one." Even though he says it like he's making a joke, his shoulders are rigid.

I blink at his words. Is that what I've been doing? Running away? Again?

Even here, battered and bruised in a hospital bed, I can feel my anger at Nick still simmering inside me. His presence is allowing me to relive all the horrible things he said, the way he let me just take Wyatt and leave. But a different voice, maybe a more reasonable one, is telling me that I am the one who put us into a complicated situation with the surrogacy arrangement—that I was too quick to react, too slow to empathize. Now that Nick is actually standing in front of me in his favorite black T-shirt and distressed jeans, the biggest part of me just wants him to stay. I want him to watch bad TV at my bedside until I'm recovered and to bring me home afterwards.

After the nurse leaves, he returns to the chair he's been occupying nearly constantly for the past few days.

"Did you come to apologize?" I ask, willing him to plead for forgiveness, to give me a reason to relent.

"Really?" He lets out a breath that might be a laugh before meeting my eyes. "Twenty-seven separate flower arrangements, and you still have to ask?"

I wait for more. I will not do the work in this conversation.

"I was a moron. I was so insanely jealous at the idea of you carrying someone else's baby that I did everything wrong. The fact is, I think that what you did for Donovan and Chip . . . well, I think it's pretty extraordinary. It's quintessential Maggie, bucking the establishment in your endless quest for goodness." He pauses, takes a steadying breath. "I sit outside on our deck every night, nursing a warm beer and wondering how I allowed jealousy and ignorance to turn me stupid. I should have fought harder before you left. I never should have put you in the position to want to leave in the first place. Leaving is your MO, I know that. But it doesn't have to be that way with me."

He stands and walks toward a duffel bag that's sitting beneath the window. I watch as he pulls out a small paper shopping bag that's been folded over itself. He reaches inside to reveal a pile of pamphlets.

"If you're feeling well enough, maybe you could flip through these."

I push myself up a bit, trying to sit, but I'm arrested by another twinge in my abdomen.

"Here, stop." He lifts a remote from the side of the bed and uses it to raise the top portion of the mattress so I'm more upright. He hands me the small stack, and I see that the brochures are for colleges—Arizona State, Grand Canyon University, Brown Mackie College, and a number of others.

As I appraise the possibilities that he has just placed into my hands, something inside me begins to melt, and I hope it's not just the effects of all the meds coursing through my system. It feels like something has shifted inside me, and I'm feeling ready to forgive him. I guess near-death experiences have a way of changing perspectives.

"Have you actually apologized, though?" I say it as I think it.

"What?"

"Are you sorry? I need to hear it."

"Oh my God, yes!" His voice is filled with relief as he takes one more step toward me, then falls to his knees beside the bed and grips the edge. "I'm sorry! I am sorry, sorry, sorry."

I glance down at the University of Phoenix brochure that's on top of the pile, allowing myself a moment to absorb his words. When I look back at him, the cautious hope I see in his expression makes me catch my breath, allows me to fill my lungs with air that I hadn't realized was missing for all these months.

"I've heard good things about Arizona State," I say, looking down at the pile again.

"Here." He stands and reaches for the catalog, thumbing through the pages until he finds what he's looking for. "The education major."

I eyeball the shiny pages and see that Arizona State offers a degree in elementary ed and another one in art education, the two areas in which I am most interested.

"It wasn't just the pregnancy," I say gently, worried that I'm sabotaging a newfound alliance before it's even solidified.

"I know," he responds in the same subdued tone, acknowledging that we had already been falling apart well before I decided to carry those babies. "You called it, years ago. When I asked you to marry me and you said life was going to drag us down, that we should wait. I think it's happened now, that we've seen it. Wyatt, the restaurant, the rent—it's been hard, no doubt. But I'd still rather do shitty and hard with you than easy, breezy with someone else. This isn't a proposal, but I'm just throwing it out there so, you know . . ."

I wait.

After a beat, he continues, "If I have to pass another day without your babbling mouth and your crazy ideas and your wild hair, honestly, my brain might actually explode. I mean"—he flinches a little, like he's bracing for something—"unless you'd say yes now?"

His full lips are open, as if he has more to say but is waiting, holding himself back. I think he is literally holding his breath as he waits for me to respond.

"Well, no," I say lightly, trying to be the reasonable one in this situation, even though reason has never been my forte. "Not *now* now. But now-*ish* is a definite possibility."

The corner of his lip tilts up and he starts to say something.

"But"—I interrupt before he can get the words out—"maybe next time some candlelight, or rose petals . . . A little something more in the pomp and circumstance department wouldn't kill you."

He takes my face in his hands and plants a warm, wet kiss on my lips, sealing the deal.

I guess Wyatt and I are going back to Phoenix.

Chapter 16

MAGGIE
FEBRUARY 2009

*T*he study group I joined for my Intro to Child and Adolescent Development class is made up entirely of other late-to-the-game students like me. I'm not even the oldest. Joy Kliber worked twenty years as a waitress before returning to school for a teaching degree, and Mark Shafer spent twelve years working as a personal trainer. Now he wants to teach PE to elementary school students. Crystal, our fourth member, is a hairstylist. We old-timers found each other right away when classes began, feeling out of place with all the recent high school grads. At twenty-six, I'm hardly elderly, but with a three-year-old son and a husband at home, I relate better to forty-two-year-old Joy than I do to the sorority girls toting wine coolers around campus.

Tonight we're meeting at the Denny's restaurant near Crystal's apartment to prep for midterms. We've just finished reviewing the chapter on attachment theory, and now we're moving on to my favorite topic: paracosm, which is a phenomenon where children invent their own complex worlds. It's sort of like imaginary friends and secret languages, only on a much larger, more involved scale.

"I don't have that many cards for this chapter," Crystal tells us as she pushes her pink-framed reading glasses into place and flips through a pile of flashcards. She taps her long fingernails against the laminated tabletop in consternation as she looks back at us.

Mark reaches across our plates of breakfast-for-dinner foods and takes the stack of index cards from her. He has thick, dark hair and a fleshy, boyish face. I imagine school children would love having this energetic muscleman teach them how to play dodge ball and badminton.

He shuffles the cards he's holding like a dealer at the Bellagio. "I think this is more of a theoretical topic than a memory-based exercise."

"Right," I say. "I just found an article about Emily and Anne Bronte and how they created a world called Gondol when they were kids. The article says that imaginary world play can be an early indicator of giftedness."

"Don't you mean Charlotte?" Crystal asks. "Emily and *Charlotte* Bronte, not Anne?" She's squinting at me, like she is questioning her memories.

"Nope, Anne was the younger sister," I say.

"No, I don't think so," she shakes her head. "No, that's definitely not right." She's becoming agitated, as though I've declared something outlandish, like gravity is just a figment of her imagination.

"Are you seriously questioning *the* Maggie Fisher?" Mark scoffs. He gets so competitive and bent out of shape about the high marks I earn in class that I've begun to hide my graded papers before he has a chance to spot the ninety-eights and one hundreds or any of the glowing comments written underneath.

"Let's stay focused," Joy pipes in, clearly sensing my discomfort. She leans back in her chair and rests an open binder on her large stomach, reminding me of how I used to place bowls of ice cream on my pregnant belly when I was carrying the twins. At the thought of pregnancy, my mind flashes back to the appointment I had at my obstetrician's yesterday, but I immediately push the images away; I'm still trying to come to grips with everything Dr. Lustrin had to say.

"The point," Joys says, "is about world building and why children might do that. I think that by creating their own worlds, kids are somehow better able to ground themselves in actual reality. Maybe by comparison?" She sounds confused as she begins rifling through a packet of articles that our professor handed out early in the semester.

"It's sort of like Facebook, if you think about it," Crystal pontificates. "Users curating photos, posting proof of their happy moments, leaving out all the crap that happens the rest of the time. The feed turns into a fake world, what they wish their worlds looked like, instead of representing what's truly real."

"It's an interesting theory . . ." Joy looks at me for verification.

"I wouldn't know. I'm not on social media." I shrug.

Joy starts to say something, probably to let me know how much I'm missing by opting out, but I interrupt with, "It's just not for me." I don't want to get into the fact that I'm embarrassed by the way my life unfolded after high school, by my early start to childbearing and my late start to educating myself.

"It's worth checking out," Mark says, stabbing a fork into one of the pancakes that remains on Crystal's plate. "Great way to keep up with people. And news. That's where I've been getting all the breaking headlines." He shoves the entire pancake into his mouth.

I shrug again and sip the bitter cup of decaf I ordered with my dinner. Crystal starts suggesting other fake worlds we can investigate—children's stories, amusement parks.

As the three of them debate, my mind wanders back to Facebook. I wonder if it's time to adjust my perspective. My life has actually taken a number of positive turns since I graduated high school. Sure, I was a screwed-up nomad for a few years, but I've gotten my act together since then. I'm working my way toward a teaching degree at a respectable school, I have an adorable son and a successful husband who's creating a name for himself in the culinary industry. Even if Dr. Lustrin's theories are right and I can never have more children, I'm hardly the near-homeless single mom that I was a few years back. Not to mention, I'm sure many of my former classmates would envy my decision to settle in Arizona, with its slower pace and better climate. It feels good, I realize, to take a step back—take stock like this—and recognize that I'm finally in quite a good place, literally and metaphorically. Sometimes the best part of these psychology classes is the introspection that results from studying psychological phenomena.

We buzz through the remaining chapters and an additional order of French fries. I manage to restrict myself to just a few of the fries, knowing that Nick will most likely bring something decadent home from the restaurant later and I've already shoveled a week's worth of carbs into my mouth tonight.

We say our good-byes, and Joy and I walk through the parking lot to our cars together. The sky is completely dark, but the lot is almost as well-lit as the restaurant's interior.

"Don't let Mark rankle you," she tells me as we cross the concrete, the pavement warm beneath my flip-flops even now, so long after sunset. "He's just jealous because it doesn't come easy to him like it does for you."

"I just work hard," I say, dodging the compliment, as I pull her into a quick half-hug.

"Sure, sure," she says with a laugh and waves me off. "Drive home safe."

As I navigate my way through the Phoenix streets toward home, I realize that Joy might be right. The coursework for this program *has* been a breeze for me. I've even taken extra credits each semester with the hope of earning my degree sooner. After all those angry, wayward years during my teens and early twenties, is it possible that I'm finally landing where I actually do belong?

When I get home, Nick's pickup isn't in the driveway, and I feel a stab of disappointment. The house is quiet when I step inside, so I ditch my backpack in the mudroom and go looking for Trish, the teenage sitter from down the block.

I find her on the floor outside Wyatt's room, reading a book. She puts a finger to her lips and stands to follow me back to the kitchen.

When we're far enough from Wyatt's room, she tells me, "He's been asleep since seven, but this book just pulled me in." She smiles up at me, revealing the dimple in her left cheek.

As I count off dollar bills to pay Trish for the night, I think to myself that there must be at least a dozen sophomore boys in town who are in love with this shiny girl. I hand her the money, and she tells me again how much she adores Wyatt, which in turn makes me adore *her.*

After she leaves, I pour myself a glass of wine and sit down at the kitchen island to wait for Nick. I can detect the lingering scent of fish nuggets—the dinner Trish made for Wyatt—in the air, and I think again about how lucky we are to have such a perfect sitter right down the street. She's so perky and kind, and an excellent resource for our busy family. In contrast to my sullen, introspective, overly emotional high school self, she's all rainbows and dew drops, probably every parent's dream child. She reminds me of Tess.

But I'm not that girl anymore—that miserable, aggrieved teenager. On a whim, I grab my glass and move over to the small desk that's built into the corner of the kitchen. I power up my laptop, and before I know it, I'm logging on to Facebook and creating an account.

As I scroll through names and click on pictures, I'm astonished at the vast magnitude of this database. So many names I haven't thought about in years keep appearing on my screen as I search from one old friend's page to another. There are high school friends, day camp friends, people I knew through Hebrew school, others from my apartment building. Stranger yet, so many of these people seem to be friends with each other, as if everyone has always known everyone else, and I was the only one who wasn't aware.

As I'm poking through more pictures, a dialogue box appears in the corner of my screen—a real-time message from Tess.

> **Tess:** *Finally. Welcome to the future.*
> **Me:** *This website is crazy. Everyone is on here.*
> **Tess:** *Duh. You should search ex-boyfriends. That's the best part of FB.*
> **Me:** *Yuck. Still working on forgetting most of them.*
> **Tess:** *There's probably an alumni page for your high school class. We have one for my grade. That's kinda interesting too.*
> **Me:** *Ok, checking it out now.*
> **Tess:** *Good luck getting out of the vortex. This site will suck you in and never let go!! XO*

She's not wrong, either. I glance at the clock and realize I've already been snooping around on here for forty-five minutes. My eyes shift toward the window, wondering what's keeping Nick, but then I decide to follow Tess's advice and look up the page for my high school class—graduates of 2001—and just like she said, there it is.

One of my old classmates, a guy named Patrick Podell, seems to run the site. There's announcement after announcement wishing various classmates happy birthday. I see a post from Serena Hendricks, who I remember as one of the quietest girls in the grade, announcing that she has an upcoming art show at a gallery in the Hamptons. I glance at the date and realize the post is more than a year old. Even so, I continue scrolling through the other, older posts, reading about births, promotions, new homes, all the wonderful milestones that people imagine for their adulthood when they're children. I wonder if it's all real or if they are mini-paracosms, people's fantasies about the way life would turn out.

As I continue reading, I see a link posted by a girl name Fiona Drescher. She was someone I always liked, even though we weren't really friends. She was a part of the uber-popular crowd, and I didn't have the patience for any of her friends, but I thought she had an interesting edge.

She writes, "*Was I the only one who missed this? I always knew that guy was a creeper.*" Her words ignite an immediate sense of dread in my gut, and I scroll down to the comments section in hopes that this isn't going where I think it is.

Maya Sanders: *Had no idea. So crazy!*
Jon Epstein: *What a loser. So glad I didn't play an instrument.*
Lydia Reid: *Thank God someone spoke up. Here's to brave young women.*

The comments continue in that vein, each one making me more nervous about what the next one might say. I finally click on the hazy photo Fiona posted. It's a picture from a newspaper, I can't see which one, but the article is titled "Music Instructor Fired from Elite Private School for Student Abuse." The words of the article are blurry, and I have to bring my face close to the screen in order to decipher them. I can't believe my eyes as I read that Trent Whitestone was fired before the start of the school year in 2002. The article says that a student's parents came to the school alleging an inappropriate relationship existed between the adult music teacher and their minor daughter. Although they were unable to substantiate their allegations with any proof, Whitestone admitted to initiating a romantic encounter with one of the school's then-seniors. Trent insisted the relationship did not progress beyond one encounter, but the school terminated its relationship with Whitestone. Although the administration encouraged the parents of the student to press charges, the parents declared that their innocent daughter had been through enough, and they were simply relieved to see the situation handled in a swift and efficient manner by the school.

I don't know how long I sit there after finishing the article, just staring at the screen. I'm stunned. All these years, I thought my parents blamed me, that they wanted no part in defending me, that they possibly even questioned whether I'd made the whole thing up. I think back now to the nights I spent living in the front room of Anne-Marie's apartment. She was the first friend I made when I reached Long Beach; she had three other roommates and a significant drug problem, and I lay there night after night on her ratty velour sofa, half-conscious, thinking that I was better off amongst those wayward deadbeats than I was living with adults who didn't believe in me. I was so full of anger, at my mom especially, for not having my back. The way she railed at me . . . it was a big explosion of emotion, even for someone as volatile as she always was. And then they just let me go. That was the most upsetting part of it all. When I finally called home after a few weeks of being on my own, there were no pleas from my mother to return home, no apologies. I can still hear her exact words before she hung up: "Figure it out. Or don't."

Reading this article now, I don't understand. I can't work out why they would let me think we were on opposite teams and then go to bat on my behalf without ever telling me. It doesn't make any sense.

A flash of light illuminates the back wall of the kitchen, and I know it must be Nick pulling into the driveway. I drain the last sip of wine from my glass before going to the front door to greet him.

"You're still up," he says, clearly surprised.

I glance at my watch. It's 1:27 a.m. "Yeah, I was waiting for you and then I got sucked into the internet."

As he kisses me on my cheek, I take a deep breath, searching for floral or musky scents, anything that might provide evidence of another woman in his night. All I catch is garlic and something a little bit earthier, like mushrooms.

"What kept you?" I try to sound like I'm chill, casual, rather than a caricature of a jealous wife, the foil from a sitcom.

"Oh. Nothing. Just a busy night." He doesn't meet my eyes as he walks toward the kitchen carrying a brown bag full of leftovers. "Hungry?" he asks as he sets the bag on the counter. He lifts the round containers out, one by one, and a pleasant aroma of grilled herbs fills the air.

I shake my head and study him, trying to decide whether to push him about the fact that he's been unusually late getting home three times in the past two weeks.

"What?" he asks as he stops arranging the containers and his shoulders straighten. He's bracing for a fight, but not the one I thought. "You want me to tell you again that the damage was definitely from the car accident? Fine, it was from the accident."

"No, nothing." I don't think I want to go there.

We found out yesterday that I have scarring in my uterus. It's possible that we'll be able to have another child anyway. Or not.

"Look," he says after a breath, "it wasn't a conclusive diagnosis, just a theory. We can keep trying."

"We can keep trying," I repeat.

The scarring, the doctor told us, appears to be a result of the trauma I sustained when that car hit me in LA. There's a chance, though, that the tissue damage could be a consequence of carrying twins. The physical stress of gestating multiples can leave a woman's body unable support future pregnancies.

Nick has always wanted a big family. If I didn't serve as a gestational carrier, it's possible that he would have a house packed with kids, like he always dreamed. But the fact is, there's just no way to know. I don't want to talk about it with him anymore. I suppose that means I'm a coward, but I'm not ready to face the fact that I might never have another child, that I'll never again feel myself growing round with life or give Wyatt the sibling he's always wanted. I'm not ready to start with the second and third opinions, the exploration of potential alternatives, the idea that this might possibly be my fault, another consequence of my choices.

"You have to see what I found on the internet," I say instead.

His face changes at my response. "Ha." He's suddenly all light-hearted, glad I've chosen not to rehash everything we discussed last night. "You sound like half the guys I know when you talk like that." His eyes crinkle at the corners, and I'm reminded that I love him and the life we've built together.

"No, you perv." I motion toward the open laptop, matching his tone. "I joined Facebook and found an article about Trent Whitestone. Look."

Nick moves to the desk and bends to read the small print on the screen as I lean against the island, watching him. I can hear the ticking of the analog wall clock behind me as I watch his eyes scanning the words.

Finally, he straightens and looks up at me. "At least they fired the asshole. Those parents should have pressed charges."

He's missed the whole point.

"Nick! Those parents are *my* parents!"

"They are?" His eyes dart from me to the screen and back to me. "How do you know?"

"The timeline and description of events. It's completely obvious."

"Huh." The corners of his mouth turn down as he processes what I've said. "Well, now that you know the school was aware of what happened, maybe you should press charges against the teacher, like they said. The guy shouldn't get away with what he did. Or you could press charges against the school."

"Stop, no. I don't want to press charges. It's probably been too many years anyway. But none of that is the point. The point is—my parents. They went to bat for me. They went after him. All this time, I thought my mom maybe didn't even believe me." I shake my head, as if the movement might clear the confusion I'm feeling.

Nick doesn't answer; he just looks back at the screen, as if he's reading the article a second time. "You should go to bed," I tell him as I move toward the entryway, where I've left my cell phone. "I'm calling my mom."

"Now? It's like four in the morning in New York."

"Yeah, well, I think it's been too long already." I wait, challenging him, but he just shrugs and starts toward our bedroom, kissing my head as he passes me.

"Just be quiet when you come to bed," he says over his shoulder. "I'm beat."

I wait a moment, watching his broad back retreat down the hallway toward our room. It would have been nice if, just once, he could have condescended to engage in a deeper conversation about my family drama, but he still keeps it all at arm's length. My sordid history from before he materialized and saved me. It's like he doesn't want the stains of my past to bleed onto him.

I shift my focus to the phone, dialing my parents' home number and marveling at the things we never forget. I haven't dialed this number since Wyatt was born almost four years ago. Delusional from the post-partum wash of hormones, I let Tess convince me to call them, to tell them they had a grandson. To my mom's credit, she did ask if she could come and visit. I said

I'd call back when I was ready, and now, somehow, years have passed since that conversation.

I put the phone to my ear and wait. After four rings, the answering machine picks up and I hear my dad's voice telling me that the Fishers can't come to the phone right now, but then I hear shuffling and the sound of the receiver being lifted clumsily off its base.

"Hello?" My mother's voice is thick with sleep.

"Mom."

"Maggie." She's suddenly alert. I imagine she's just sat up in bed. "What is it?"

"How come you didn't tell me that you went to the administration about Trent Whitestone?"

She lets out a long sigh on the other end of the phone.

"This is what you're calling about at 4:00 a.m.? It couldn't wait until after sunrise?"

"You said it was all my fault. That I deserved the negative consequences."

"Right. But then I said a lot of other things too. You only heard the parts you wanted to hear."

"But why?" I ask, still stunned. "Why would you let me think you were on his side, the school's side, every side but mine?"

"You had a lot to figure out back then. Maybe you still do if you're waking your parents before the crack of dawn just to restart an eight-year-old argument. I wanted you to grow up, to take responsibility for yourself. I had hoped that was what you were doing."

"But you just let me leave." I repeat the thought that has been tormenting me for years.

"No, Maggie, I let you breathe. I gave you autonomy and agency. You think it was easy for your father and me? Sending you out into the world to figure everything out? We did it because we thought it was best for you, not because it was what we wanted. If you had stopped thinking about yourself for a minute and asked what we wanted, you would have heard a very different story than whatever it was you concocted inside your head. We wanted what was best for you. Plain and simple."

Hearing my mother's decisive assertions takes me straight back to that day in our kitchen so many years ago, the last time I saw her. I remember the pain and humiliation I felt when she laid into me for my choices, my attitude that rules did not apply to me. I remember the sting of it, that instinct that I was just a kid and therefore she had to be the one in the wrong, for not taking better care of me. But now all I feel is that sense of need—that I needed my mother, and she let me down. I'm suddenly filled with a wave of homesickness so strong that it nearly knocks me over.

"But it wasn't best for me. I needed you." My voice is small.

"Are you sure about that?" she asks. It's classic Gail Fisher, going Socratic during every argument, so sure she's always standing on higher moral ground. I feel tears threatening, and I don't want her to hear them, so I am silent.

She huffs, like I'm testing her patience. "Look where you are now. Your husband, the up-and-coming chef; an adorable son—or so I'm told," she needles. "Halfway to a college degree in a field that actually makes sense for you. You would have been happier in fashion?" She pushes, knowing the answer. "I was trying to be a good mother. If you love something, set it free and all that."

"I miss you." I'm surprised I've said it out loud.

"We miss you too." Her voice is kinder now, intensifying the ache I feel.

"I'm sorry I woke you."

"Phsst." She dismisses the comment, and I can see her waving her hand in the air like it doesn't matter to her at all. No bother.

I'm struck now by the absurdity of my behavior. Eight years and less than a handful of phone calls. Keeping them away from their grandson. Wyatt's never even met them. For what? Why? No matter their mistakes, I suddenly can't justify the separation at all.

"Can I come visit?" I ask.

"Of course you can come. This is your home. And you'll bring Wyatt."

I nod, even though she can't see me.

"Tess tells me you're in the middle of your second semester. Don't make things too difficult for yourself. We'll be here after you finish your finals. Maybe you'll call again in the meantime. During daylight hours." She says it with a smile in her voice.

We stay on the phone a few more minutes, catching up a little. It's stilted and I feel awkward, but I'm ready to try to move forward. I don't have to agree with all of her parenting decisions.

When we hang up, I can still feel an echo of anger festering inside me, but the decision to forgive my parents has tamped it down, muted it to a place where I no longer feel that my bitterness should keep us apart. I'm disappointed in myself for failing to consider sooner that my mom's behavior, and my father's choice to follow along, might have been motivated by love and not anger. I'm suddenly running through my entire childhood, as if it's a movie reel on fast-forward. We could have gotten along so much better if my mother had been more open with me, explained where she was coming from. She was propelled by such intense emotions that I often couldn't find the logic in her outbursts, but maybe I didn't try hard enough. Each time she went from zero to sixty without warning, I just blamed her. I listened to her bellow at me, each of her utterances landing like tangible embodiments of her unfair disappointment in me.

In the morning, I'm going to tell Wyatt that we're planning a trip to New York so he can finally meet his grandma and grandpa. Hopefully Nick will be able to join us on the trip as well, so he can meet his in-laws for the first time.

I shut off the light in the kitchen and head for our bedroom, firmer in my new point of view that not every issue between family members needs to reach an actual resolution. Sometimes it's best to just keep the peace.

Chapter 17

MAGGIE
JULY 2018

To his credit, Nick seems more baffled than angry. Ever since we hung up with the clinic, he's been cycling through a host of emotions, from confusion to despair to guilt, but apparently, for once, not blame.

"We literally gave our child up for adoption without even knowing it." It's the third time he has said this since hearing the news, like he simply can't process the thought. After so many years of trying and failing to conceive a second baby, it turns out that our child has been out there all along.

"So what now? Do we just go get him?" He's asked me this several times already as well.

I shake my head again. "I don't know." I'm sitting cross-legged on his side of the bed while he paces the floor. I fiddle with the pile of balled-up tissues beside me on the bedspread. "I think he *has* parents already. I mean, ten years, Nick."

We keep arguing opposite points, both of us playing devil's advocate from alternate positions, then switching sides and battling in reverse.

As we debate, I keep thinking about the things we give away in life that we can never get back, no matter how great the mistake. Virginity. A vote. Love. Every item I can add to this list is something a person would want to take back in order to save it for someone else, to give it away again, but differently. I'm having a hard time coming up with anything that a person might want to take back simply for her own self. I attempt to try on this perspective with regard to my son, Kai. Do I want him back just for me? Or do I want him back to give him to someone else? To Wyatt? To Nick? As consolation for the fertility struggles we've faced over the years? As much as I regret giving our own child away, I regret even more that I'm not sure I do want him back. I have a family already. Nick and Wyatt. Smaller than we had hoped, but our own little unit nonetheless. Bringing a ten-year-old child into this mix, ripping him from his own home and expecting him to blend right into ours—it doesn't seem right. And yet after unknowingly abandoning my child, how can I continue to forsake him now that I'm fully aware of his existence?

"But maybe we have a responsibility?" I ask.

Nick shakes his head. "They've been raising him since birth. It's not exactly like they can exchange him, get a new kid in his place." It feels like he's agreeing with me, and yet we've been talking in circles for nearly two hours, trying to digest this news.

"Just dial, already." The uncertainty of the future is making the mistakes of the past all the more painful. Nick switches on the speakerphone, and we wait as ringing reverberates from somewhere in New York City.

"Maggie." It's Donovan. I wonder if Chip is still working his banker's hours, if my child has been raised by one dad significantly more than the other. I wonder if he's been happy. Has a small part of him always known he was somewhere he didn't belong?

"It's Nick. But you're on speaker, Maggie's here. We heard from the clinic."

Donovan doesn't say anything on the other end—frightened, perhaps, of what Nick will say next.

"Look, none of us expected this," Nick says. "We don't

want to make problems. But we'd like to figure some of this out together, and to come meet him."

A loud breath transmits over the speaker, and I think maybe it's the sound of relief. But then there's silence, a moment too long, before Donovan responds.

"Guys." He says it like a stop sign. "The thing is . . ."

I feel something changing in me at the sound of his hedging. I stand and walk over to where Nick is leaning over the dresser, looking at the phone.

"Our attorney advised us that all communication should go through her," Donovan says.

"I don't think that's necessary," I pipe in, leaning down toward the phone. "We're not looking to uproot everyone's lives here. We just want to meet him. This wasn't the plan, Donny, and you know it."

There's rustling in the background and muffled voices. Maybe Chip is home after all, standing next to Donovan, his eyes as wide as Nick's are next to me.

"Yeah, okay, we can figure this out," Donovan says. "But look, I'm not sure if we're going to tell him, so there's that."

"You're not going to tell him?" I balk, unable to check my emotions. "What's the difference? His mother was an anonymous stranger before. Isn't this better?"

"Except that one of us was his biological father."

We're all quiet as we absorb the statement.

"We might tell him," Donovan backpedals. "It's just. We've had no time to figure anything out. Can we just wait a couple of days before you book your flights?"

"He has a biological brother," Nick says. "Grandparents."

We're all silent again, each of us thinking, all of us struggling.

"Yeah, yeah, no, I know," Donovan says.

"We'd like to bring Wyatt," I add.

"Right," Donovan says. "We just. We have to be careful with Kai."

I feel an unexpected and illogical rage at this man who is telling me how to behave with a child who is my own flesh and blood. I suddenly want to grab the boy out of whatever posh apartment he's been living in and bring him straight to the family where he actually belongs. One glance at the vein pulsing in Nick's neck tells me he feels it too. And yet. We don't know this child.

After a few more rounds of talking in circles, Donovan finally suggests that we reconnect in a couple of days to discuss when and how a plan for a visit might work.

Even though we seem to have persuaded him to grant what we've asked, I'm not feeling particularly victorious at the moment. With little left to say, we make awkward good-byes and end the call. Meanwhile, we have to figure out how to explain to our son, our parents, our siblings—ourselves—that the second child we wanted so desperately has actually been out there all along.

⁎ ⁎ ⁎ ⁎ ⁎ ⁎ ⁎

The next day, I'm sitting on the floor of the master bathroom with my back against the shiny white cabinetry, holding the phone against my ear and listening to Tess on the other end of the line.

"I still don't understand what you mean," she snaps at me, like I'm being purposely abstruse. "How could the baby possibly have been yours? That doesn't make any sense. It's not possible."

I repeat for her, again, the facts that Dr. Pillar explained to me about how it is apparently not impossible for a woman to conceive a second baby when she is already pregnant with a first. It's just so incredibly rare that nobody sees fit to mention it during ninth grade biology. I also rattle off a few of the stories I found online about other women around the world who have conceived multiples this way. There was a couple in Arkansas who conceived a baby boy nearly three full weeks after the woman had become pregnant with a baby girl. An American woman in the 1960s. A woman in Essex, England in 2007. Another in New Zealand in 2015.

"But how do they even know that? Couldn't the babies have just developed at different rates?" Tess asks.

I stare through the glass wall of our empty shower at the brightly colored shampoo bottles lined up along the floor. "There are tests they do on the babies that show proof." I shrug, even though she can't see me. "They use bone age tests and look at the lungs, I don't know. I'll send you the articles. Regardless, the DNA here, in this particular case, proves conclusively that one of the babies was my own. Tess, I literally sold my child."

"Aren't you supposed to wait a certain amount of time after they implant the embryos before you have sex?" she demands. "Can't you ever follow a rule? Like, ever?"

"We waited! I don't even remember how long we were supposed to wait—seven days, twelve?—but we followed the instructions!"

We're yelling at each other, panicked, overwhelmed by the situation.

"Okay, okay, okay," she says, like she has to talk me down from my own unreasonableness. "Let me think for one freaking second." I picture her rubbing her manicured hands over her eyes as her lawyer brain begins to work on overdrive. "I know someone. He does custody cases. That's really what this is at this point. I mean, we could argue it's a contract case, that you agreed to sell one service, and that was to carry someone else's child. You never agreed to hand over your own biological child. But geez, these contracts aren't enforceable where you live, and they aren't enforceable in New York, where the baby lives."

"He's not a baby," I say.

Tess quiets for a moment. My statement carries weight, regret. But then she is back at it, thinking aloud as she rolls full steam ahead. "We could try to sue under the laws of California, since surrogacy contracts are enforceable there and that's where the babies were born. Though I don't know anything about the statute of limitations; I'd have to look that up."

"Tess, stop it. Just stop. Who said anything about a lawyer? Why are you going straight to a legal battle?" I pause before adding the most important point. "I don't think we're going to take him back."

She's silent.

"He has spent ten years living with another family," I continue, "growing up with a different brother. How can we force him out of that if he's happy? And my own family. It's the three of us here. Pulling in a fully-formed, ten-year-old child from New York City to live with us—do we want that?"

"How about it's not about what you want, it's about what's right. He's your son. My nephew. He belongs with his family."

"Look, I'm not saying I'd send him away if he wanted to live with us." I throw the tissue I've been holding toward the trash can in the corner but it falls to the floor, several inches short of its intended destination. "I just want to be fair to him, and I imagine that what he wants is to stay with his adoptive fathers and brother in the life he's always known."

"Really?" Skepticism nearly drips through the phone.

"We're setting up a trip to go meet him. I don't think there's anything else to do yet."

"Fine." She sounds deflated, victim to my opinions. "Let's at least talk through strategy in case you do decide to go to court. Okay?"

"Yeah, okay, fine." I push myself off the floor and catch a glimpse of my disheveled appearance in the mirror above the sink. My eyes are rimmed in red, and the shadows beneath them are darker than usual. I start to run a hand through my messy curls but then give up and just stare at my strange reflection instead. The image staring back is just me, but it's also not. A mother of two, but not.

"As I'm thinking it through," Tess says, "I suppose your best approach is coming at it from a custody angle. Otherwise, you'd end up litigating in California, which wouldn't be good for Kai, or any of his parents, having to travel for the court time. And with custody cases, the question is always, *always*, the best interests of the child. So, just in case you do decide you want your kid back, from this moment forward, you don't so much as take a sip of water without asking yourself if it's in the best interest of your long-lost baby. Got it?"

"Kai isn't a baby anymore," I say again, this time more aggressively. My hand finds its way to my stomach, where I can feel a whisper of a scar through my T-shirt. Beneath that, there is only emptiness. Even though I don't know where Kai belongs, I'm filled with regret over this child who could have been mine.

The front door slams, meaning that Nick is back from his morning hike with Wyatt.

"Listen, the guys just got back," I tell Tess. "I'll let you know when we're coming."

"Shoot me a text after you've told Dad, too." She hangs up without saying good-bye, and I imagine she's already scrolling through her contacts, searching for this attorney's number, being the stalwart sister she always has been. It's no wonder she was always my parents' favorite. At least I will never have to admit this mistake to my mother.

"What did you expect, Maggie?" she would say, "that you could re-invent reproduction and there'd be no risks? Too much re-inventing with you, not enough worrying." After she finished berating me, what advice would she offer? If I had reconciled with her sooner, I would have had more time getting to know her as an adult, more time to collect wisdom from her. Instead, it was only a few intermittent phone calls and two short visits before her brutal diagnosis and then her abrupt decline.

I'll have to call my Dad and confess about all this sooner rather than later, though. A grandson lost.

But first, we have to tell Wyatt. Nick and I decided last night that we shouldn't keep any secrets from him—that there is too much potential for heartache in a situation like this, so we better be honest right from the start. Wyatt was so young when I carried the babies for the Rigsdales that he doesn't remember much about that time, but we've discussed the surrogacy pretty openly with him over the years. Even so, how do we tell him now that the brother he always wanted has actually been living on the other side of the country for ten whole years?

Wyatt and Nick are in the kitchen. Wyatt is holding a bag of frozen blueberries, and Nick is pouring almond milk into the blender. I watch them from the entryway for a moment as they collect ingredients for whatever smoothie combination they've dreamt up this time.

"Hey," I finally say. "You guys look like you got a good workout." Wyatt's hairline is damp with sweat, a couple of wet curls pasted to his forehead, and Nick's grey T-shirt is soggy with patches of perspiration. I've been struck several times over the years by how different Wyatt's rustic lifestyle in Arizona has been from my own sterile upbringing in Manhattan, where I was always surrounded by concrete, glass, and steel. The contrast is all the more glaring at the moment as I consider my other child, nearly 3,000 miles away, living in a place that I couldn't wait to escape.

Nick's holding the top to the blender in midair, as if he can't decide whether to bolt or continue moving forward like this is just an ordinary day. I fix him with a pointed stare and he nods back, ready. He covers the blender, then unplugs it from the wall.

"Your mom and I wanted to talk with you for a minute," he tells Wyatt.

Wyatt glances from Nick to me and back to Nick. There's a flicker of fear—he thinks he is in trouble for something—but the look disappears as quickly as it arrived, probably because

JACQUELINE FRIEDLAND   141

the kid rarely steps out of line. Then his eyes narrow in suspicion. "What? Is this more about my phone?"

We finally caved and let Wyatt get a cell phone, nearly two years after most of his friends got theirs. But as Wyatt makes sure to tell us at every opportunity, we are still much stricter than his friends' parents about when and how he's allowed to use it.

"No, it's not about the phone," I say. "Sit." I gesture toward one of the wooden stools at our kitchen island.

He climbs into the seat, a look of skepticism on his tanned face, as Nick comes to stand beside me.

"We learned some pretty crazy news," I tell him, "and we're trying to figure out how to deal with it."

"Okay?" The word comes out almost impatiently, like he wants me to just get on with it, so I take a deep breath and dive in.

"Those babies I carried when you were a toddler. . ." I start, and he nods.

My eyes stray to Nick, who nods for me to keep going, so I turn back to Wyatt. "It turns out that only one of the babies was the biological son of Chip or Donovan. The other one was actually our own biological child. Your dad's and mine." I take another quick breath and then add, "Kai. He's ours. Our child." It's odd to articulate these facts yet again, when I am still struggling to wrap my mind around the idea myself.

Wyatt's eyes narrow in confusion, just the way Nick's did when he first heard the news last night.

"I don't understand," he says, looking from Nick to me for answers, as if I have the answer to anything at all.

I run through all the science again and explain how it was possible for a second baby to have been conceived during the existing pregnancy. Wyatt listens quietly until I'm finished and then says, "Okay, first of all, yuck." He crinkles his nose as he looks from Nick to me and back to Nick again, making clear his disapproval of any type of sexual congress between his father and me. Then he asks, "But now what?"

I meet Nick's eyes again. I have no idea how to answer Wyatt's question when I still have so many questions of my own. "Your dad and I are trying to figure that out. We'll probably take a trip to New York to meet him."

"Just the two of you?" He shifts in his seat, like he's preparing to argue.

"We'll all go. I wouldn't leave you with no one here. You can have a visit with Grandma and Pops."

"What about seeing him? Kai." His says the boy's name tentatively, like an experiment.

"Maybe on the second visit?" I see no reason to rush into anything, and answering with a question sometimes softens the blow when I tell Wyatt things he doesn't want to hear.

He turns his face away from me and gazes out the glass of the sliding door that leads to the backyard. I look at Nick for guidance, but he only shrugs in response. I open my eyes extra wide at him in a silent plea for him to say something, do something, but he just shrugs a second time and then turns around and walks back over to the blender.

When the harsh sounds of the blender finally stop, Wyatt turns back to me.

"It's weird," he says, telling it like it is. "Right? Isn't it weird to have a whole other brother I've never met?"

I nod, vigorously. "So weird," I agree, trying to validate his feelings, give him the freedom to say more.

"Can you at least take a couple of pictures when you're with him so I can see what he looks like?" Wyatt asks, accepting my decision. "Do you think he looks like me? For his sake, I hope he doesn't have these." He puts a hand to the curls he's always complained about.

"As long as his dads are okay with it, we'll take a bunch of shots. Or . . ." I study Wyatt for a moment. He stands nearly as tall as I am now; a hint of a shadow is just starting to appear on his chin. Maybe he's more grown-up than I give him credit for. "Maybe you *should* come and meet him yourself. I just don't know. None of us knows what's right in this situation. Let me think about it, okay?" I'm regretting that I don't have a more defined position on our next steps, that I can't provide Wyatt with that security, but every question seems to beget more questions. There are so many issues I never could have anticipated when I found that magazine ad back at Bed, Bath & Beyond all those years ago.

My indecision seems to mollify Wyatt rather than destabilize him. His whole posture shifts and he changes the subject. "Will we stay with Grandma and Pops the whole time? Not even one night in a hotel?"

He's suddenly more disappointed that he won't get to order room service than he is by the knowledge that he was robbed of his natural sibling. I don't know whether his attitude stems from the fact that he's a thirteen-year-old boy, meaning he just doesn't look too deeply into much of anything, or from the basic reality that it's 2018 and families today look a million different ways of normal. Either way, I'm relieved that he still seems calm, comfortable.

I walk over to the stool and wrap my arms around his sweaty shoulders. As I kiss his head to signal the end of this big, important talk, I take in his smell—half boy, half man, soap, and sweat—and I am filled with love. Is this the feeling I would get hugging Kai? I find myself hoping not—because if it is, the thought of what I've lost is simply unfathomable.

I need to get myself to New York to see that boy so I can convince myself that he isn't mine, not really, and then I will say good-bye to him one more time.

Chapter 18

DONOVAN
JULY 2018

Gina emerges from the back door of the kitchen again and sets a large bowl of macaroni salad on the tempered glass of the patio table. "What possessed you to go straight to an attorney?" she asks as she rearranges the platters of pickles and tomatoes already on the table.

My gaze travels to the plastic wrap covering the macaroni as I contemplate her question, wondering again whether any of my actions have been the correct ones since the day we decided to try the Relativity test.

"The clinic recommended it," I finally answer. "And I didn't know what she was going to do." I can't seem to stop talking about Maggie, second-guessing the comments she made on the phone about not uprooting everyone's lives. She didn't sound sure about much of anything herself. I wonder again if it was some sort of ploy. Even if her promises were in earnest, what's to stop her from changing her mind and trying to gain custody of Kai?

As if he's been summoned by my thoughts, Kai comes running out the door from the kitchen, along with his cousin, Ethan. Both of them are equipped with multiple Nerf guns, and they make a beeline for the small bit of forest behind the house, leaving the door wide open behind them.

"Door!" Gina and I call out simultaneously. Kai pauses as Ethan runs back to slide the screen closed.

Ethan spares me a quick glance before he bounds back down to the grass and declares with uncharacteristically youthful glee, "Outdoor Fortnite." He and Kai are immediately busy within the trees, setting up forts and outposts that I assume are meant to mimic that video game they both love so much.

I motion for Gina to follow me back inside so the kids won't overhear. As we step into the kitchen, I'm hit by a rush of blissfully cool air and the somewhat less appealing scent of peppery bologna.

"She wants to come and meet him—or re-meet him, I guess," I tell her as I pull a wicker chair out from under the kitchen table and slump down onto the circular cushion. Each time I say it, I feel more defeated.

"And?" Gina asks noncommittally. She unfolds a wax-paper package and begins arranging deli meat on a platter at the counter.

"I just don't know if it's a good idea." I let out a long sigh that's filled with not even a quarter of the apprehension I feel. "Teddy was always the one who used to wonder aloud what it'd be like to have a mom. Kai is different. He bottles things up, lets them fester. I always thought he got that from me." I snort.

Gina doesn't say anything, doesn't even look up, as she continues fanning slices of corned beef into a circle. Her petite shoulders are pinched so tightly toward her ears that I'm feeling a crimp in my own neck.

"What?" I ask.

She shakes her head without meeting my eyes as she returns to the fridge.

"What?" I repeat, this time more forcefully.

She tosses a packet of roast beef onto the counter and looks at me. "Next you're going to tell me you don't even want to tell Kai about any of this, am I right?" Now she has a hand on her hip.

"Well?" I challenge her.

At the sound of footfalls coming up the steps from the garage, we both turn to see Chip walking inside with Teddy close behind him. Gina always leaves the garage open for anyone to walk in, despite my reminders that she should be more careful. She insists that it's safe because so many of her neighbors are cops and they all look out for their own. That may be, but it's not like she has a twenty-four-hour detail outside her house. That surveillance ended two weeks after Pete was killed, when they finally caught the perp who'd shot him point-blank.

"Linzer tarts," Chip says, offering a shopping bag to Gina. She kisses his cheek before peeking into the bag and then shoving it into an empty spot beside her toaster.

"You." She tugs Teddy toward her and wraps his body in a hug. At just about five feet, Teddy is only a couple of inches shorter than my sister.

"Hey, Aunt G," he greets his aunt as he tolerates but does not reciprocate her embrace. His eyes are already focused on the back door.

"Go ahead." She gives him a gentle whack on the arm and turns to say something to Chip, but she's interrupted by the doorbell.

"Oh! That's Graham," she says, as if she momentarily forgot he was coming. She makes big eyes at Chip and me. "Good behavior, boys," she warns as she pulls out her ponytail and hurries to the door.

I rise out of my chair, gearing up to greet Gina's new beau, relieved that she is finally, (finally!) starting to take seriously the idea of dating. Chip moves over to me and raises a hand to my hair line, as if to smooth a wayward lock.

"Stop it." I push his hand away.

The corners of his mouth twist down and he steps back. We regard each other silently for a moment until Chip releases a puff of air and flicks his chin pointedly skyward. Then he marches away from me toward the happy chatter in the entryway.

After a couple of minutes have elapsed with me standing aimlessly at the counter and the three of them still chatting in the foyer, I make my way out of the kitchen. I want neither to be rude to Gina's first prospect in years nor to provoke my sister's ire. I find them all looking at the television in the living room as Chip sits in the middle of the sofa, navigating the cable guide onscreen. Gina and the affable-looking man who must be Graham are standing behind him, watching the cursor move from title to title.

"And here's my little brother, Donny," Gina says as she notices me approaching. Graham is a relatively nice-looking guy with broad shoulders and dark wavy hair, just a little extra padding around his middle. With his white polo shirt tucked neatly into his khaki cargo shorts, he reminds me of the wholesome-looking dad you'd see in a commercial for detergent or bars of soap. His plain-vanilla appearance is so different from Gina's late husband, Pete, who favored leather jackets and snake tattoos. I wonder for a second if Pete would have eventually grown into a clean-cut every-dad like this guy, had he spent the last twelve years raising kids in suburbia instead of lying in the family plot at a cemetery out in Queens.

"Donovan," I say, extending my hand.

Graham's grip is extra firm in a way that is intended to send one of two possible messages. Either his vice-grip is meant to make clear that he is extra, extra straight, in case I was hoping to shove him up against a wall and have my way with him. Or, his firm grasp is meant in a kindly, if misguided, show of solidarity, to prove he has no problem touching a gay man. I squeeze hard in return, giving in for just a moment to my irritation at his "loaded shake," before I release his hand, and my own annoyance along with it.

"Chip said he was listening to the game in the car," Graham says, "and my team was finally in the lead."

"Get a load of the Mariner's fan," Chip jokes as he points a thumb at Graham. Already, I can see this turning into another one of Chip's bromosexual conquests. Straight guys can't get enough of Chip, with his baseball obsession and his impressive memory for sports stats. Everywhere we go, supposedly enlightened men flock to Chip because he allows them to have a friendship with a gay man that feels nonthreatening. The alphas get their token gay friend, and Chip gets the validation of being adored by so many inhabitants of the straight world.

"Are you from Seattle?" I ask. My baseball knowledge takes me far enough to know the states from which various teams hail, but that's about it.

"Born and raised." Graham nods once with satisfaction as he rocks on his heels. "Moved here after law school, but I've still got my hometown pride."

Chip finds the appropriate television channel and emits a satisfied breath as he places the remote on the coffee table. Graham moves toward the couch.

"You guys sit, watch the game, and lunch will be ready in a few," Gina tells them.

"I'll help," I say, following behind Gina to the kitchen, and Graham pauses en route to his seat, looking at Gina, clearly wondering if he should follow her as well.

"It's fine, Graham," she says. "I'm almost finished. Donny will help; he hates baseball. Go." She waves a hand toward the TV.

When Gina and I are alone in the kitchen, she doesn't even pretend to do any food prep before turning to confront me.

"What the hell is going on with you and Chip?" she demands, her dark eyes burning.

"Nothing. What do you mean?" I walk past her to the counter and pick up a platter to bring out to the deck.

"Don't 'nothing' me. Your whole demeanor changed as soon as he stepped into the house."

On the one hand, she is almost too perceptive, and on the other, it feels like she doesn't understand at all.

"You don't get it, okay? You can't know what it's like—thinking a child is yours, finding out he's not. And Chip doesn't get it either. He never thought he was Kai's bio dad. It's a loss you can't possibly understand."

"Oh, I'm sorry." She says it so lightly that for a moment, I think she's truly apologizing, until her next words come: "Don't tell me I don't know loss, that I don't understand it." Her voice is quiet so the guys won't overhear from the other room, but it somehow feels like she's shouting anyway. "You try picking up a call from your husband's commanding officer, finding out that the thing you've been dreading since the day he took a job on the force has finally happened—that your man, who you live and die for, is never coming back. Then you talk to me about loss." A look of disgust forms on her face, like she can't believe she has to explain this to me, that I don't see things from her perspective already. "You still have a living, breathing child. So his biological mother wants to meet him. So he'll find out his genetics aren't exactly what he thought they were. So the fuck what? She could be trying to take him back. She's not. She could be making all sorts of problems for you. She's not. So stop fucking pouting and looking for problems where they don't exist."

"Just because he's not dead, I don't get to be upset?" I demand. "He was my *child*!" I'm yelling now, in spite of myself. Gina grabs my hand; her French-manicured nails dig into my palm as she drags me out to the garage, where we can shout at each other without Chip and Graham—or, worse, the kids—hearing everything.

"He still *is* your child," she says the moment the door closes behind us, her hands going back to her hips. "Is Teddy any less your child?" The anger on her face is so exaggerated that she looks like a caricature of herself.

I pause before answering. I don't love Teddy any less than I love Kai, but I love him differently. I had pinned different hopes and dreams on each boy, I suppose, and now I don't know where those expectations, all that self-reflective parenting, belongs. I would lie down on a bed of nails for Teddy. I've loved him since before we even brought him home. But I'd be lying if I said that over the years, I didn't develop a different feeling for Kai. Seeing what I thought were my eyes in his pudgy baby face, wondering what other traits of mine he would or wouldn't develop and pass on—does that mean I loved him more?

"Don't you say yes." Gina's pointing her finger in my face. "I know you better than that. It's a shame you don't know yourself, too." She turns and climbs the four concrete steps back into the house.

I take a minute to compose myself, and then I follow her inside, prepared to pretend that I'm not in a fight with Chip, not in a fight with Gina, and not in a fight to hold on to my life as I know it.

Chapter 19

MAGGIE
AUGUST 2018

*W*hen we step out of the wide automatic doors at LaGuardia, I'm hit by a wave of humidity so soupy and intense that any nostalgia I might have been feeling for my hometown is instantly extinguished. The scent of car exhaust is strong as we enter a sea of curbside shouts and whistles. Mid-afternoon air sizzles above the concrete, flush with fumes and energy, as travelers attempt to push and stumble toward their final destinations. I already feel a longing for the dry heat and quiet terrain of Sedona.

I hear someone shout Nick's name and turn to see his father, Roy, at the far end of the curb. He's making his way through the clusters of travelers who are congesting the passenger pickup areas. Nick and I both raise our arms high and wave back, corralling Wyatt and our three suitcases, as we attempt to change course and make our way toward him.

"Come here, you!" Grandpa Roy wraps his beefy arms around Wyatt first, and instead of shrugging off the embrace, like he would with me, Wyatt squeezes tightly and looks as if he doesn't want to let go. Roy doesn't seem to notice the way Wyatt clutches at him, hanging on as though this man is his only life preserver in stormy seas. Roy moves on quickly, leaning over to kiss me on the cheek and then giving Nick a strong wallop on the back. Roy's been growing heavier with age, but I think the extra weight looks good on him, softening what were once harsh angles on his face into a rounded countenance so much cheerier that it makes me think of Santa with a clean shave.

"I'm parked this way." He motions with a thumb toward the crosswalk and then lifts the overstuffed tote bag off my arm to heave it over his own shoulder. There's no rancor in his dark eyes, no trace of anger at me for creating this untenable situation with a surprise extra family member, for accidentally depriving him of the other biological grandson he could have had.

When we called to tell them about Kai and his newly discovered genetics, both Roy and my mother-in-law, Nancy, seemed to have more trouble with the science of what we were telling them than with the fact that my get-rich-quick plans from ten years earlier had resulted in the unintentional abandonment of one of their descendants. Nancy finally started typing searches into Google while we talked by phone, only to discover that the biological phenomenon of superfetation is, indeed, an actual thing. I kept waiting for them to berate me in some way, but they—true to their generous, easy-going style—only asked how they could help.

Nick and I have decided to stay in town for a full week, long enough to have time not only with Kai but also with Nick's parents, Tess, and my widowed father. Wyatt didn't meet my parents until he was five years old. He's never seemed to favor one set of grandparents over the other, but I still always feel like I'm playing catch-up when it comes to Wyatt's relationship with my own family. Especially now that my mom is gone.

We slog through the muggy parking garage until we reach Roy's SUV. All the while, Roy is peppering Wyatt with questions about soccer camp. We haven't seen Nick's parents since spring break, but these two seem to be picking up right where they left off. As Wyatt tells Roy about his hopes of getting called up to the junior varsity team in the fall, my eyes meet Nick's, and I wonder if we're both thinking the same thing. We had another son, another child, who could have been here telling his grandpa about his dreams. I don't even know if Kai plays sports.

"Grandma's slaving away at the house, fussing up a storm over Shabbat tonight," Roy says.

When Nick was a kid, his family only celebrated the Jewish sabbath sporadically, more as a novelty than as a religious ritual. But ever since Nancy retired from her position as a nurse at a local pediatrician's office, she and Roy seem to have found religion, Nancy especially. They've been attending synagogue every Saturday, keeping only strictly kosher food in their home, and they've started pulling together holiday-level feasts to celebrate Shabbat on a weekly basis. I sometimes question whether Nancy's recent fixation on religion is a true spiritual awakening, like she says, or is simply a reaction to post-retirement ennui. I suppose that's ungenerous of me; I should just be pleased she's finding fulfillment.

During the hour-long drive down to Scotch Plains, Wyatt continues to type away furiously on his phone. Normally I would admonish him to put the device away and participate in actual human-to-human conversation in the car instead, but he has been so testy with me this week that I don't want to engage. My initial impression—that he was unconcerned by the case of his long-lost little brother—turned out to be dead wrong. As I think about his reaction again now, I berate myself yet again for projecting my own wishful thinking onto my son and misreading the situation entirely.

Wyatt has become extremely defensive on behalf of Kai, arguing that we already made a huge mistake when we gave him away as a baby. We're only making it worse now, he says, by invading the boy's life and going to see him like he's a circus show. Wyatt thinks that if we're not trying to bring Kai home to his real family, we're being selfish by going to see him at all. I've tried to explain to Wyatt that Kai already views Chip and Donovan as his "real family," so he won't be sad not to follow us home at the end of the visit. But Wyatt seems to equate what we're doing with going to visit a puppy in an animal shelter, petting it up, and then leaving it behind in its cage. I don't know who he's texting so aggressively, but I'm glad something other than his anger at Nick and me is occupying his mental energy at the moment.

"Everything okay over there?" I ask.

"Mmmm." Wyatt doesn't look up from the screen, but his cheeks turn pink, and it occurs to me that perhaps all this texting has something to do with a girl. He could certainly use the distraction of a crush at this moment in time, so I don't force the issue. Instead, I turn back toward the window and watch the traffic passing in the lanes beside us as we make our way down the Turnpike. I wonder where everyone else is going, if they are all moving toward life-changing events the way we are.

––––––––

When we finally arrive at the house, it's nearly dinner time, and Nancy comes rushing out in a long white skirt and white fitted blouse to greet us in the driveway. I vaguely remember reading somewhere that it's customary to wear white to usher in the Sabbath on Friday nights, but then I wonder if I'm confusing Shabbat with Rosh Hashanah, the Jewish new year. Either way, she looks lovely, and much younger than her sixty-nine years. She has the same dark hair as Nick, which I imagine she gets from a bottle these days, but her petite frame is nothing like her son's bulkier physique.

"I don't know who to hug first!" she cries, bursting with an energy that seems too big for her diminutive size. She grabs

Wyatt, then Nick, and finally me. When she wraps her arms around my shoulders, the urge to cry is instantaneous. Her warm body, her feminine scent—I suddenly miss my own mother so intensely that I feel I cannot bear it. I know grief can be like that, that it can come at you out of nowhere and knock you right off your feet. Even so, I'm unprepared in this moment, too raw. I step back and wipe at my eyes. Nancy takes one look at me, and it's as if she knows, just like a mother would.

"Oh, sweetie." She reaches out and squeezes my arm. "Let's get you some matzah ball soup."

I laugh out loud at that because nothing says "Jewish mother" like insisting that a bowl of matzah ball soup will cure anything that ails you, whether it's a stuffy nose, a bad breakup, a deceased parent, or the accidental sale of a newborn baby.

We file into the house behind her, then disperse to drop our bags and settle into our rooms for the week. Nick and I are in the guest room, with the queen-size bed and en suite bathroom. Wyatt is delighted to set himself up in the rec room in the basement, where he will have significantly more privacy than he is generally afforded at home.

After I've changed clothes and taken a moment to wash my face and hands, we all gather around the dining room table. Nancy has clearly put great effort into preparing for this evening, covering the table with a silver damask cloth and laying out floral-patterned china. Heirloom sterling silver cutlery and mother-of-pearl napkin rings complete the tableau.

"So beautiful," I remark as we each stand behind our chairs, waiting to pray. I wonder if this opulence, so different from Nancy and Roy's typical come-as-you-are style, is intended to send a message; it feels like a show of solidarity as Nick and I confront the difficult situation our family has landed in.

Nancy lights the candles and utters a Hebrew prayer, chanting out melodic, guttural words that conjure vague memories from my few summers at Jewish overnight camp during middle school. Next, Roy sings the kiddush, a blessing over the wine, the full version of which, it turns out, is much lengthier than the two-line version I learned as child. Nancy joins in to sing the second half of the prayer along with him from across the long table. I glance at Nick, who shrugs and smiles, like he doesn't know where these religious people came from, like he finds their sudden devotion to tradition charmingly adorable, a symptom of old age. I wonder whether age brings some sort of connection to the past—a sense of obligation to commitments, or sacrifices, of your ancestors. Most of what my own parents taught me about Judaism had more to do with the Holocaust than anything else. I never learned the many rituals and prayers that Nancy and Roy seem to rattle off so easily now.

Nancy asks Roy to say the blessing over the challah bread, a simple one familiar to most Jewish children, even Wyatt. *But not Kai*, I realize with a start.

Not only have I deprived that boy of his true family, I've also denied him his religious heritage. From what I remember, Chip comes from a vaguely Protestant family that only bothers with church on big holidays, if at all. I know Donovan's family is Catholic, but I have no idea how serious they are about it. I wonder if my Jewish child has been going to church with Donovan? Whether he's been baptized? Circumcised? I'm supposed to be so progressive, beyond caring who practices what religion, but all those years of my parents making offhand comments about the dwindling number of Jews in the world apparently impacted my subconscious. Their remarks about the importance of passing on traditions to pay homage to Jews who sacrificed for their faith, *our* faith, are now echoing in my head, and I feel as if I've squandered something irreplaceable.

But I still just don't think bringing Kai into our home would be the right move. Ten years is long enough for a person to form a basic identity, long enough for a blood relative to become a stranger.

Nick rips a doughy chunk of bread from the challah and breaks it into smaller pieces, which he arranges on a dish to pass around. We all take our seats as he sprinkles the pieces of bread with salt from his parents' sterling shaker. He catches my eye and squints like he's suspicious. I think he's trying to tell me that he knows my mind has started running wild again, that I should rein it in instead of torturing myself over what kind of parents wouldn't want their own child back. This acknowledgment is enough to stop me from spiraling any farther; instead, I focus on how much I wish I could feel this telepathic connection to Nick more often.

A faint buzzing sound catches my attention, and I know exactly where it's coming from. Wyatt has his gaze in his lap and is surreptitiously attempting to type something on his phone. Without warning him, I reach over Roy on my right and grab the phone out of Wyatt's hand before he can stop me.

"Mom!" He has the gall to sound outraged.

"You know the rules." My shoulders lift, a gesture meant to show him that it's no challenge for me to be firm, to be the enforcer, as though everything is cut and dried.

"Fine, I'm sorry," he backpedals, re-strategizing. "I'll keep it in my pocket, but can I just . . . can I have it back?"

"No." I'm resolute, even though I hate making him upset. Strict adherence to our stated family rules should only benefit him right now, while so many other things feel uncertain. All my training—as a teacher and as a parent—tells me that when parts of a child's life feel out of control, rules and expectations are helpful, stabilizing, even when the child claims otherwise. "You can have it back in the morning. End of discussion."

Wyatt looks over at Nick, but when Nick shakes his head to indicate he won't be any help, Wyatt blows out a loud breath and slumps down in his chair.

"Let me get the soup," Nancy says, and I rise to help her as Wyatt's phone continues to buzz, burning a hole in my pocket.

"I'm just going to stash the phone upstairs," I tell her. "Be right back."

I remove the phone from my jeans as I head up the narrow back staircase, and it vibrates in my hand. Reflexively, I glance down to read the words on the screen.

It's from Summer, the girl who's been Wyatt's closest friend since we moved to Sedona three years ago. While she's not exactly the girl next door, it's close enough. She lives three houses away from us, and I'm pretty sure that Wyatt has been in love with her since the moment she rode her lavender bicycle past our driveway on moving day.

The message, which is clear and bright on the home screen, reads, *But he's only 23, and it's not like he's my teacher.*

We don't allow Wyatt to lock his phone with a passcode, so all I have to do is swipe, and I'll be able to read this chain of texts in their entirety. I push past my doubt, worrying about what kind of trouble thirteen-year-old Summer might be getting herself into, and I swipe to the right. I start reading the texts in reverse order, and a picture begins to present itself, but maybe I am misunderstanding. I swipe up until I get to the first text from today, hoping things will look different if I move in chronological order.

> **Summer:** *I think I should tell him how I feel. There's only a couple weeks till school.*
> **Wyatt:** *You can't. It's gross and you'll get him fired.*
> **Summer:** *From school?*
> **Wyatt:** *From the club.*
> **Wyatt:** ***Actually both.*

As I'm reading, sweat begins to form on my brow, and memories of my own school-day mistakes threaten to waft to the surface. I'm not certain who Summer is talking about, but I'm betting it's Ross Tepper, the middle school tennis coach, who spends his summers teaching adult clinics at Mesa Creek Country Club. That would be the very same club where Summer has been volunteering as a lifeguard in training for the past few weeks. Coach Tepper is astonishingly handsome in a way that has all the sixth- and seventh-grade girls continuously tittering and swooning, and many of the mothers too. I can imagine why he might have taken a special interest in Summer, with her wavy blond hair and long, coltish legs.

Memories of Trent Whitestone assault me. He wasn't a full-time employee of my high school, just someone they brought in to do private instruction with the more talented music students. How I looked forward to last period on Wednesdays for months during my junior year and the beginning of senior year, when I would walk into the music room and find twenty-four-year-old Trent waiting for me in his flannel shirts and ripped jeans, his dark blond hair long and wild like he was Curt Cobain or Eddy Vedder. I used to primp in the bathroom each week before sixth period—fresh gel in my hair, Revlon Colorstay gloss on my lips. I can still see the rust-colored impression my painted lips left on my saxophone reed, bleeding into the wood grain like a scarlet A.

I don't want to get all up in my son's personal life, but I can't sit idly by and do nothing while Summer puts herself into a similar position with the tennis coach—not when I can trace the entire unraveling of my early adulthood back to what happened with Trent. I'm tempted to text back, pretending that I'm Wyatt, telling her all the reasons why pursuing a twenty-three-year-old man could ruin her life. I want to warn her about the ways in which adult men are different from pubescent boys, how they expect more than kisses, more than promises. I can still remember the exhilaration I felt when Trent finally kissed me one afternoon in October of my senior year, the way his stubble rubbed at the sensitive skin on my chin.

He asked me to stay after school that day to work on a solo we had been practicing. After we ran through the bridge a few times, he said he wanted to show me something backstage. He took me into one of the changing rooms and locked the door. I can still smell the moth balls, the pungent odor of the preserved costumes protruding from trunks filling the small space.

"I've been trying to figure out how to get you alone," he said, wearing that flirty grin I had memorized. "You've been torturing me. You know that, right?" He said it as though I had control over anything at all in that situation. His green eyes roved over me as he advanced toward me and added, "No one else is like you."

Of course, I can see the manipulation in his words now, the utter cliché, but back then it was bliss to think that, at last, someone had seen me, the real me. His tongue pushed into my mouth and I accepted it like a gift. But when his hand went to my waistband, I pushed it away, and he got angry. He told me I'd been leading him on since the year before, that I was a tease, and that if I wanted to play in the big leagues, I had to operate by grownup rules. I didn't want to disappoint him, this creative, musical man I had been crushing on since the year before—so, in a move I can still hardly bear to think about, I stepped back toward him, ready to do what he was asking. His lips crashed back down onto mine, and my fear mingled with relief that I had been forgiven, that he was touching me again. But then his grip became rough, too strong, and my fright won out. I pushed away from him and he looked at me in surprise, like he couldn't imagine I didn't want the exact same things he did.

"I can't," I said.

The displeasure returned to his face and his eyes grew cold as he told me, "This was a mistake." That was the last thing he said to me before turning away. He opened the door and strode into the corridor without another word.

The following Monday, I found a note in my locker from the school office telling me that I would no longer be meeting with Trent for lessons, that I was being placed back into regular band. Being removed from the honors music program was a massive blow to the strength of my transcript, but I was afraid to go to the office and complain, so I let it go. I told my parents that I was no longer that interested in music, that I wanted to focus on something else in college, like fashion. I had never expressed more than a passing interest in anything related to fashion, they said. Then maybe graphic design, I said.

They argued with me, which I perceived as their need for me to continue propping up their parental egos through my own musical successes. I had been performing in NYSMMA and other prodigy-appropriate concerts since the minute I was old enough, each achievement another feather in my mother's cap. It was all part of her own quest for excellence, not mine. I just liked filling the air around me with music, and Trent Whitestone had robbed me of that.

To the soundtrack of my parents' snide comments about wasted talents, I shoved my sax into the back of my closet where it couldn't taunt me, couldn't remind me of the pressure of Trent's hands or my own guilty conscience.

It wasn't until June, a couple of days after I graduated, that I saw him again. He was in Central Park with Marisa Cafferty, a girl the year below me in school. They were sitting on a thick Mexican-style blanket in Sheep's Meadow, and they didn't notice me, just a few feet away, as I passed by. Trent had a guitar on his lap, and Marisa was holding some sort of steel drum. They weren't doing anything outwardly untoward, but something about seeing them together made me realize, finally, that Trent had been in the wrong. I went home and told my mother everything, ready to take a stand for myself, for young women everywhere.

Except my mother didn't take my side. She blamed me. If I had been paying more attention when I approached her that day, I might have realized that she was already irritable before I started speaking to her. I should have noticed that she was still in her clothes from the day before, that all the books from our built-in bookshelves were surrounding her on the floor. I should have known better than to interrupt her when she was in the middle of one of her projects, which meant that she would also be more likely to erupt into one of her rages. She told me she had watched me with Trent, and that I had cozied up to him like a puppy dog.

"Someone with a body like yours, that sexy hair that you flaunt," she yelled. "What did you expect would happen?"

As I look down now at Wyatt's phone, I wonder again what exactly I did expect. I shove the phone into the tote I carried on the plane, zipping it into the inside pocket. Summer's mother has become a friend over the years, and I'm now in the tricky position of trying to help Summer without destroying my son's relationship with his friend. The fact that Trent wasn't strong enough to resist a young girl fawning all over him doesn't mean that the tennis coach will act the same way. Even so, I wouldn't feel comfortable without getting an adult involved.

As if we don't have enough drama going on already. I'm fairly certain that Wyatt is going to want to throttle me when I speak to him after dinner, but I can't sit idly by while another girl falls into the same kind of abyss that swallowed me.

Chapter 20

DONOVAN
AUGUST 2018

*C*hip reaches for another piece of jicama from the crudité
I've just finished arranging, and I swat his hand away. "The
point is for the platter to look nice when they get here," I say
as I lift the porcelain dish and move it to the other side of the
counter. Chip rolls not just his eyes but his whole head at
me, like I'm just the most grating individual he's ever had the
misfortune of encountering, and then marches pointedly out
of the kitchen.

"Feeling any better, bud?" I hear him ask.

I glance through the kitchen cut-out. Poor Kai is sitting
on the sofa, a brown paper lunch bag hanging from his hand.
Maggie and Nick are supposed to be here in ten minutes, and
Kai has been growing increasingly nervous. Although he hasn't
articulated it precisely, I believe he's worried that he'll be a disappointment to them in some way. After we decided to tell him
about his birth parents, we gave him the option of not meeting
them at all, but he said that no, he wanted to take this step and
see them in person. Even so, nothing I've said has calmed his
nerves this morning. Sometimes just knowing he has the paper
bag nearby seems to help prevent his anxiety from getting the

better of him. I always thought the propensity to panic was something he had inherited from me. At least I can let go of my guilt about that.

Kai nods back at Chip, a look of certain doom in his round eyes.

Teddy is moping in his room, angry that we're even allowing Maggie and Nick to come. He says they have no right, that they gave Kai away and they shouldn't show up now, making like they're family. I have to admit, I'd like to throw my hat in the ring with Teddy on this one, but Chip has been adamant that letting the Wingates meet Kai is the right thing to do, and that it might provide Kai with some important closure as well.

As I look at Kai now, his fingers running over the edge of that brown paper, the bag at the ready in case he should start hyperventilating, I regret giving in to Chip's self-righteousness. But instead of launching into Chip and adding to the long list of disagreements we've had since finding out that we accidentally took home someone else's child, I walk toward Teddy's bedroom.

At first, it looks like the bedroom is empty. Then I hear sounds of paper rustling. I step in to investigate, and I find him sitting on the cross-stitch rug on the far side of his bed, his back against the bedframe as he studies a photo album in his lap.

"Want some company?" I ask as I walk closer.

"You should show them these," he says, holding up the album. It's a baby book, filled with lists of the boys' various milestones, photos from their first haircuts, their first day at pre-school, their kindergarten graduation. I'm not sure when Teddy took this book down from the living room shelf, but I'm guessing he's had it stashed away since the day we told the boys they aren't genetically related.

"Why?" I ask, trying to let him lead the conversation without imposing any assumptions of my own.

Instead of answering, he looks up at me with those astonishingly blue eyes of his and asks me a question of his own:

"What if Kai likes them better? What if he wants a different brother instead?"

I wish I didn't have the very same fears as Teddy—that Kai might somehow be seduced by his birth parents, that he might prefer them to Chip and me, that he might ask to live with his biological sibling, to experiment with a different kind of life. Teddy needs me to be the parent right now, though, so I push away my own emotional reflexes and force my voice to sound calm.

"Well first of all," I start, lowering myself onto the floor next to him and crossing my legs the same way as his, "there is nobody in the world who Kai loves more than you. You're still peas in a pod, still twiblings."

Teddy looks back to the book in his lap.

"Hey." I try to get him to look at me as I think of something else. "Think of it like movies. You know how you love *Happy Gilmore* so much?"

He nods.

"Then you watched *The Waterboy* and loved that movie too?"

He just looks at me, waiting.

"Does loving *The Waterboy* make you love *Happy Gilmore* any less?"

He shakes his head.

"Our hearts are big," I say, and I realize I'm giving this talk to myself as much as I'm saying the words for Teddy's benefit. "We don't have to make room each time we find something new to love. It's not like letting in the new pushes out something old. I hope that Kai feels really good about his birth parents when he meets them, and you should hope so, too. And by the way, I think he's pretty nervous about meeting them. I bet it'd mean a lot if you came out and sat next to him for a bit."

Teddy thinks for a moment and then closes the scrapbook. When I read the words on the cover, "Happiest with our dads,"

I remember that this was a baby gift from Nick, shortly after the boys were born. Teddy doesn't know that, and the irony isn't lost on me that with so many albums to choose from, this is the one he filched.

Before I have time to add anything else to the conversation, I hear the loud warbling of the apartment phone and then Chip telling the doorman to go ahead and send up the visitors from the lobby.

"Come on." I stand and reach out a hand to Teddy, who holds tight to the baby book but grabs on to me with his free hand.

When Kai sees us walking toward him in the family room, his shoulders relax slightly, and he shoves the paper bag he was holding in between two of the sofa cushions—hiding it from Teddy, or our guests, or both.

"Here, let me." I yank the bag from where it's wedged in the couch. "Boys, come help," I call over my shoulder as I hurry back to the kitchen. They follow me in, and I hand Teddy the vegetable platter with the instruction, "Two hands."

As he heads dutifully back to the living room, I bend to eye level with Kai.

"We've got this, yeah?" I ask as his big eyes search mine. I've told him so many times already about how Maggie and Nick are kind-hearted, fun-loving people, how he should be proud that he shares genes with such smart, hard-working folks. I still haven't figured out what Kai is afraid of—whether it's a fear of disappointing his birth parents or impressing them so much that they want to take him from us. I wait for him to nod, but he only shrugs.

There's a knock on the front door and then I can hear Chip welcoming our guests.

"Here." I hand Kai the plate of colorful French macarons I picked up from the bakery, then place a hand on his back. "Come on."

I round the corner and see Maggie's familiar, smiling face as she greets Chip, and I can tell, even on first glance, that the smile is forced, that she is nervous. She sees me and her face transforms, the smile turning genuine for a moment, softening and reaching her eyes, and she opens her mouth to says something—but then her eyes drop down toward Kai and the color immediately drains from her face.

"Kai." She says it on a gasp of air, as if her voice has failed her. She steps toward him and then freezes, unsure. I give him a slight nudge, sending him forward to greet her properly.

"Hi," he says as he begins to study her.

"Hi," she repeats, her eyes glued to my son's face with reverence, as Nick steps up beside her and looks down at him too.

"Hello, Kai," Nick says. "I'm Nick." He holds out his hand to shake, and I'm grateful to him for trying to normalize this moment.

Kai shakes back, the expression on his face somber, earnest.

"Can I, would it be okay if I gave you a hug?" Maggie asks.

Kai doesn't look at me for guidance, like I expect him to; he simply lets go of Nick's hand and nods back like the sweet child that he is.

As she lowers herself to hug him, I try to imagine what this must be like for her, and I simply cannot. Those days after the Relativity test, when I thought we might have been given the wrong baby in the hospital, that our child could have been switched with another family's at birth, I ached for the son I thought we had sent to the wrong home. I see the same anguish in the quiver of Maggie's shoulders as she moves toward Kai, in the tightness of her jaw as she wraps her arms around him. Her eyes close, and it's as if she is trying inhale Kai back into her body, to breathe in his essence and find her own breath through his.

Kai is still holding the porcelain dish full of pastel macarons. He uses his free hand to gently hug back, a token gesture born of his polite nature. Just as I begin to wonder if I need to separate them, Maggie pulls back and looks up at me, her eyes wet. My eyes dart away from hers, and it's only then that

I notice Maggie and Nick are not alone: Wyatt is with them, lurking in the open doorway, a look of uncertainty on his face.

"Wyatt!" I exclaim too loudly, forgetting myself, as I take in this man-child who I last beheld when he was a messy toddler. He's grown into himself in a way you wouldn't expect of a thirteen-year-old. Rather than an awkward stage, Wyatt seems to be moving toward his golden age. His curls, once so wild and endearing, have been tamed into a closely cut style leaving only a hint of a wave to his rich brown hair. He's tall, like Nick, though lanky still, in the way of childhood. He turns to me, startled, when I call his name, and the look of surprise, of apprehension, renders his features so similar to Kai's that I have to catch my breath.

"Come in," I say, keeping my voice steady, trying to put us all at ease. "I haven't seen you since you were two, three?" I glance at Maggie, and she nods with pride about her grown boy. "Don't worry, I won't pinch your cheek," I joke. I don't say what I'm really thinking, which is that I thought Maggie and Nick were coming alone. As if this wasn't awkward enough.

Maggie looks over at Wyatt and holds out a hand.

"Come," she says softly. "Meet your brother."

My eyes dart immediately to Teddy, who is standing over by the sofa, dipping a carrot into the bowl of tzatziki. He doesn't look up, doesn't display any sign of having noticed Maggie's words, but I'm fairly certain he just felt a dagger in his solar plexus. Lord knows I did.

"Hey." Wyatt says, as he remains near the door but tips his chin up in greeting—a little too-cool-for-school, if you ask me.

"Hi," Kai says again.

"Can I get one of those cookies?" Wyatt asks, looking at the plate.

Kai lifts the platter a little higher up as he walks closer to him. "They're from L'Etoile," he boasts, mentioning my favorite French bakery.

"Which color is best?" Wyatt asks, and I'm heartened by the question, by Wyatt's aplomb in this moment. I know that when it comes to macarons, Kai has much to say about the pros and cons of each cookie, so I turn to Maggie and Nick.

"Drinks," I say, and motion them toward the wet bar.

I try to make small talk as I pour a glass of Perrier for Maggie and then an orange juice for Nick.

"Wait!" Maggie suddenly blurts, turning to Wyatt like she's just realized something. He stops with a chocolate macaron halfway to his mouth. "Nuts. They're macarons, right?" she asks me.

"Is he allergic? I'm so sorry; we should have checked." I grab a striped cocktail napkin from the counter. "Here, put it here." I hold out the napkin to Wyatt and hurry back to the kitchen, where I find an old package of Oreos in the cabinet and start piling cookies onto a plain white dinner plate. Kai was deathly allergic to eggs as a baby; I wonder now if allergies are a Wingate family trait.

When I return to the living room and hold the cookies out to Wyatt, Nick says, "Now you'll have a friend for life. Oreos are his favorite."

"Mine, too!" Kai says with excitement, his eyes opening wide. I see a new enthusiasm dawning in his face at the wonderment of similarity. "What else do you like?"

"Guys, come sit," I interrupt, and I shepherd everyone toward the sofa.

Kai sits down next to Teddy, so close he's almost on top of him, but Teddy doesn't scoot over to make room. Instead, he stays right where he is, his shoulder half-covered by Kai's, as if their bodies can simply meld into each other.

"Well," Wyatt starts as he sits on the chair catty corner to the sofa. "My favorites are pizza, lasagna, wings . . ."

Kai nods enthusiastically about Wyatt's impeccable taste as he continues his list. As we listen to the boys talk, I take the opportunity to size up Maggie and Nick. Nick looks the same as I remember—rugged and handsome in that devil-may-care kind of way. Maggie is different, though. Her curly hair is shorter, now reaching only to her shoulders, and she has lines around her eyes that weren't there the last time I saw her. She holds herself differently than she used to, as well, and I can't decide whether I'm detecting a posture of wisdom or resignation.

"That's the basics," Wyatt is saying, now that he has listed every comfort food known to man. "I also like a lot of fancier things," he adds, "like coq au vin and veal marsala. Did you know that my dad—*our* dad," he corrects with a self-conscious half smile, "is a chef?"

Even though no one else was speaking, the room suddenly gets much quieter.

"Wyatt," Nick says, and then he looks over at Chip uncertainly.

"No, that's okay," Chip says. "Wyatt, we haven't really figured out yet what Kai should call your mom and dad. We thought that after we got together today, maybe we could come up with something that made everyone comfortable."

Kai is looking at Teddy while Chip is talking.

Wyatt nods.

"Having two dads can be confusing enough. Three dads"— Chip shakes his head with a smile—"sounds like the beginning of a bad musical."

"And another brother," Wyatt adds with a small chuckle.

Kai smiles at that, his cheeks pinking up. Teddy leans forward and grabs three Oreos from the plate on the table before wiggling back into place, wedged against Kai.

"Teddy, why don't you show everyone the baby book?" I suggest. Now that the ice has been broken, we could use a little something to do.

Teddy seems hesitant, but he leans to the side and reaches to where the album has been hidden behind him. When he hands it to Maggie, she studies the cover for a moment and then turns to Nick.

"Wait, is this—this is the book that you sent, isn't it?"

Nick sits up to look over her shoulder.

"Huh. Yeah, I guess it is." His voice is clearly filled with wonder, as if he can't believe we kept it.

"You're sure it's okay?" Maggie looks over at me.

"Go ahead." I stand and walk behind the couch so I can see the pages of the book as they open it up.

"I remember you guys just like that," Maggie says to Kai and Teddy when she looks at the picture on the first page. It's a shot of the babies side by side, swaddled in their matching hospital blankets, knit caps on their tiny heads, just a few hours after they were born. There are some action shots from the delivery room, too—Chip cutting the cord, me reaching out to the doctor for Teddy. You can make out a corner of Maggie's hospital gown in a few of the pictures. I wonder if she notices the pieces of herself in the photos.

She begins turning the pages, reading the little notes I've written about each event. The first time the kids slept through the night, when they ate solid food, when first teeth grew in, a lock of hair from each boy taped into the book in tiny, clear plastic bags. We didn't cut Teddy's hair until he was eighteen months old, but Kai's hair grew like crazy and had to be cut when he was only seven months old. I watch as Maggie pores over the pages, smiling at intervals, running her hands appreciatively against the card stock.

I'm surprised that perusing this book with Maggie, Nick, and Wyatt feels so much more gratifying than showing it to friends, or even our parents. Maggie and Nick care about each milestone, each photo, in a way that friends or more distant relatives never would. I also feel such a strong sense of pride with each turn of a page, as we showcase for these people what an excellent job Chip and I have done raising our children.

Look how happy and secure we've made their upbringing, I want to say, what a loving home we've given them, how much we adore and nurture them.

When we finally finish flipping through the book, I'm feeling so much more at peace than I was when the day started. I'm glad now that Chip convinced me to allow the Wingates to visit, to tell Kai everything we know about his history. I get the sense that Maggie and Nick are feeling more relaxed, as well, as smiles and small talk are flowing easily now.

Nick finally glances at his watch and gives Maggie a pointed look. "We should get going," he says, looking over at Chip. "We're meeting Maggie's sister and her new husband for a late lunch."

"He's not new anymore, Dad." Wyatt says this like it's a statement he's made several times in the past, and then he glances at me. "My aunt and uncle. They've been married a year and a half already."

I begin formulating a sage statement about how time passes differently for adults and kids, but Wyatt's focus has already returned to Kai. "You have another aunt and uncle to meet," Wyatt says.

"Cool." Kai is noncommittal, and I'm glad the Wingates are readying themselves to leave.

"I forgot you had a sister in the city," Chip says as everyone rises from their seats.

Maggie reaches for the vegetable platter on the coffee table, where only a few spurned slices of red pepper remain. She lifts it like she's going to bring it into the kitchen for us.

"Leave it," I say. "Please."

She looks uncertainly toward the kitchen and then places the platter back on the table.

Nick shakes Teddy's hand and says how nice it was to meet him, at last, and Teddy seems to puff up under his praise. Nick then shifts his focus to Kai.

"Kai," he says, looking down at my boy. His boy. My boy. They look at each other for a long moment, and I wonder if there are silent messages passing between them, or if they are simply taking each other in. A boy and his father. But not *really* his father. "You ever need anything," Nick finally says, his voice unsteady, "there's nothing we wouldn't do for you."

Kai nods, solemnly, like he understands the weight of the words he's been told.

Maggie is standing beside Nick and she sighs loudly.

She puts her hand on Kai's shoulder, and we all look on, waiting to hear what she's going to say.

She opens her mouth to speak, and then closes it again. When she starts a second time, the words she blurts nearly stop my heart. "You could come live with us," she declares. "We're your family too, whatever the labels."

"Maggie," Nick says.

She ignores him and keeps speaking to Kai. "You're welcome with us, if that's where you think you should be."

"Maggie." Nick says it more forcefully this time.

"I'm just saying so he knows," she snaps at him. "Somebody has to say it!" She looks back at Kai. "We would have wanted you then if we had known. And we want you now."

Chapter 21

MAGGIE
AUGUST 2018

*I*t's only 11:00 a.m., but the humidity is already stifling as we walk the three blocks from the subway station to the Rigsdales' apartment. When we finally reach the chilled air of the lobby, I become more aware of the sweat that has accumulated beneath my hair, along my neckline, in the valley between my breasts. As we step into the elevator, I'm tempted to rub my forehead against Wyatt's shoulder, to dry my damp skin, transfer my nerves to his cotton T-shirt. I find a crumpled tissue in my purse and blot it against my face. It's not helping nearly enough.

"You're fine," Nick says, even as his own fingers tap nervously against his thigh. We are all on edge. I do not own this moment alone. I'm still unsure we were right to bring Wyatt here with us. Over dessert last night, Nick's parents convinced us that our firstborn son ought to be included in this historic family moment. With the sweet taste of cinnamon babka in my mouth, I agreed, but now, in the light of day, I'm wondering whether this would be easier if Nick and I were tackling the meeting alone. I realize now that I should have forewarned Donovan and Chip with a call or at least a text so that Kai would be prepared to meet not only his birth parents but also his biological brother. I was so wrapped up in making the right decision for Wyatt that I didn't think enough about Kai. Yet another way I have failed that boy.

When we reach the apartment and Chip opens the door, he's as bright and shiny as ever, as if he hasn't aged a day since he rolled his two babies out of the hospital at UCLA. I let him study me and digest the ways that I've aged, changes that make me proud; the wrinkles beginning to show at my eyes, signs of squinting at my schoolwork until late into the evenings. The laugh lines that have deepened in my cheeks, proof of the happy life I've been living as I've finally found my way into adulthood. Then he's wrapping his arms around me in a warm hug, and I remember how Chip's outsized personality always managed to make me relax, to quash whatever awkwardness could have arisen between us. Except today, I'm still nervous. I plaster a smile on my face and pull back, scanning the room for Donovan.

He emerges from behind a cutout to the kitchen, and for the briefest moment, I'm filled with genuine joy at seeing him, this man who's always felt like a kindred spirit. I take in his face—his skin still smooth, his dark eyes deep and round. He smiles back at me with that unassuming, almost tentative grin I remember, but then I'm distracted by the form that emerges beside him. My gaze shifts downward, and there, standing before me, is my son.

Our eyes meet, and it's as if someone has wrapped a fist around my vocal cords. I absorb his appearance all at once—his wispy dark hair, parted on the side, those slanted eyebrows, so long and dark above his wide eyes, the pointy chin, the thin lips. He is the spitting image of my mother. I've always thought Wyatt looked a lot like my mom, but seeing Kai standing in front of me, it's like my mother has just walked into the room, like she is standing beside me and whispering in my ear to go hug that precious boy.

"Kai." I finally manage to croak out the word. People always talk about the bond that parents feel when a child is born. Mothers worry that they won't feel the elusive "insta-bond," the sudden and intense love that supposedly materializes in delivery rooms everywhere. It happened for me with Wyatt. I wish I could say that I felt the same sudden love, the same connection when Kai was born, but I didn't. I felt relief and joy, and many wonderful emotions that I can no longer name precisely, but there was a degree of separation there, because I didn't believe the children I'd just given birth to were mine. Yet now, standing before this child who is so clearly of my own flesh and blood, so much more a part of my family than he even realizes, that insta-bond has come back at me with a vengeance. I want to inhale him, to wrap my body around this child whose first ten years I have missed, to devour him, to smother him in love, limb by limb and moment by moment.

I take a step toward him, bursting, but then I remember—he doesn't know me, not the way I know him. I carried him for nine months in my body, I share his DNA and know parts of his history he could never guess, but to him, I am a stranger, an intruder . . . so I stall.

Donovan gives Kai a slight nudge on the back, sending him forward toward me.

"Hi," he says.

"Hi," I repeat, desperate for more. Then Nick is beside me, and there's so much I want to say. Does Nick see it? Does he feel it?

"Hello, Kai," Nick says. "I'm Nick." He holds out his hand to shake, and I'm astounded by his ability to sound so calm, so regular.

"Can I, would it be okay if I gave you a hug?" I ask, my voice stilted. Kai nods back and it seems like he needs it too, for us to physically connect with each other.

I bend myself in half and wrap my arms around his slender

shoulders. He smells sweet, like vanilla and flowers. His bones feel delicate, unlike Wyatt's ever did. I'm careful not to squeeze as hard as I want to, not to snap this exquisite being into pieces. He's holding a dish full of cookies in one hand, but he wraps his free hand around me, and I squeeze my eyes shut to prevent the sudden tears from rushing out and frightening him. I want to run my hands all over his body and discover who this child is, to know him like I know my other one. But that is not my right, to touch and caress him the way I would a child who has lived with me since birth.

I try to pull a last bit of his core, his lifeblood, into myself before I let go. I think I've been holding on too long already, so I step back and look to Donovan, unsure how he might be reacting to all this.

His eyes only meet mine for a second, and then they careen to the doorway. "Wyatt!" he exclaims with what appears to be genuine enthusiasm. His eyes rove over Wyatt, taking in his grown-up form, and I feel a sense of pride in the handsome young man I've brought along today, the child Nick and I have raised. "Come in," Donovan says warmly, and I wonder how anyone can sound so smooth and steady in this moment when my own emotions are more frenetic, more tumultuous than I ever knew was possible. "I haven't seen you since you were two, three?" He smiles fondly at Wyatt. "Don't worry, I won't pinch your cheek."

It's difficult to drag my eyes away from Kai, but if my own feelings are any indication, Wyatt, too, must have a lot going through his head right now.

"Come." I reach for his hand. "Meet your brother."

The sweat on Wyatt's palm tells me that he's not as relaxed as he's trying to let on. His grip is tight, like he's afraid I might let go.

"Hey," he says as he looks over at Kai, not budging from where we stand.

"Hi," Kai says again.

I give Wyatt a discreet tug, prodding him farther into the apartment, closer to his brother. I hear him swallow loudly. It punctuates the moment.

"Can I get one of those cookies?" he finally asks, motioning to the plate in Kai's hand and walking toward him.

Kai looks at the platter as if he's forgotten he's holding it and then lifts the dish out toward Wyatt. "They're from Le Etoile," he boasts. I assume it's a fancy French bakery. I had wondered if his voice would be the same as Wyatt's, but so far, the timber seems to be all its own.

"Which color is best?" Wyatt asks, moving the conversation forward.

Donovan lets out a loud sigh and turns toward Nick and me. "Drinks," he says, motioning toward the wet bar. I assume he's trying to engage us so that Kai and Wyatt can talk for a minute without the adults breathing down their necks. I ask for a glass of Perrier and Nick says he's fine with nothing, but Donovan convinces him to try the juice he and the boys made earlier today from fresh Valencia oranges.

"Wait!" I suddenly blurt, turning to Wyatt as he lifts a cookie toward his mouth. "Nuts. They're macarons, right?" I ask Donovan. We are always so careful with Wyatt. Accidental exposure to hazelnuts or pistachios could send him straight into anaphylactic shock. How could I have allowed my distraction to lead to such carelessness?

"Is he allergic?" Donovan asks. He looks stricken with remorse—horrified, even—as he as he grabs a cocktail napkin from the counter. "I'm so sorry; we should have checked. Here, put it here." He holds out the napkin to Wyatt and then disappears with the offending pastries into the kitchen. I look over at Wyatt, who shoots me an eye roll, as if to say his allergy is no big deal, but I know how much it frustrates him to be singled out, limited.

Chip starts ushering us toward the large sectional sofa to sit down, and Donovan reappears with a new plate of cookies.

When Nicks sees the substituted offering, he smiles at Donovan. "Now you'll have a friend for life. Oreos are his favorite."

I wish I could be like Nick, pleasant and ostensibly laidback, even in the face of the intense emotions he must be feeling.

"Oreos are my favorite, too!" Kai says to Wyatt with excitement. He's clearly elated to see that he and his brother have something in common, even something as ubiquitous as Oreos. "What else do you like?"

"Guys, come sit." Donovan prods everyone toward the sofa. Kai sits next to Teddy, almost on top of him, and I realize I should introduce myself to the child who has grown up as my own son's brother. I tune out from Wyatt's enthusiastic list of favorite foods as I sit down on Teddy's other side.

"Hi Teddy," I say. He regards me warily and then says, "Hey," before reaching out and taking the Oreo out of Kai's hand. Kai doesn't bat an eye; he simply reaches forward to get himself another one. I can feel Donovan looking at me—wondering if I am a threat, perhaps. I notice that Wyatt has switched over from standard kid fare in his list of favorites to the more sophisticated food that Nick cooks.

" . . . like coq au vin and veal marsala. Did you know that my dad, *our* dad, is a chef?"

I smile, thinking of all the wonderful pieces of our family that I want to share with Kai, to relive with him.

"Wyatt," Nick says, and there is reproach in his voice, warning. Nick looks over at Chip hesitantly, and I realize that the concern is because Wyatt said "*our*" dad. Well, it's hardly a secret. Everyone knows why we're here, and it doesn't seem to me that we should be tip-toeing around the elephant in the room.

"No, that's okay," Chip says quietly to Nick. "Wyatt, we haven't really figured out yet what Kai should call your mom and dad. We thought that after we got together today, maybe we could come up with something that made everyone comfortable." I think he's going to ask Wyatt if he'd like to be involved in that decision, along with Kai and Teddy, but the question doesn't follow.

Wyatt nods into the silence, and Chip finally adds, "Having two dads can be confusing enough. Three dads"—he breaks into a smile worthy of a Crest commercial—"sounds like the beginning of a bad musical."

"And another brother," Wyatt adds, playing up to Chip.

I realize that I'm staring at Kai again, but I can't help myself. I want to memorize every detail, from his neatly trimmed fingernails to the faintest hint of a widow's peak at his forehead.

"Teddy," Donovan says, interrupting my thoughts, "why don't you show everyone the baby book?" I think this might be an attempt to get me to stop ogling, to distract me from the fact that I'm falling in love.

I look away, glancing down into my lap instead, and I notice I've placed a hand protectively over my own empty womb, as if there's anything left in there to safeguard. Teddy does as Donovan asks and pulls the album out from where it is wedged between his body and mine. Teddy hands it to me, and I take a minute to read the words on the cover.

"Wait, is this—this is the book that you sent, isn't it?" I realize the answer as I ask the question of Nick.

"Huh. Yeah, I guess it is." He sounds surprised.

"You're sure it's okay?" I ask Donovan, mainly to be polite.

"Go ahead," he says, standing from his seat. I wonder if he's leaving the room to let us study these pages in privacy, but then I realize he's coming to stand behind my seat on the couch so that he can look at the book along with us.

The first pictures are from the hospital, before I had even gone home. As I study the photos, I suddenly hear the voice of my old work friend, Bara, in my head. *You have to have taken at least one picture, right? Not even right after the delivery?*

This picture in front of me is the one I would have wanted. I'm surprised by the level of attachment I feel, not just to Kai but to Teddy too. We're all family, all related.

"I remember you guys like that," I say to the boys, careful to include Teddy, to make this day important for him too. I can see small pieces of myself in the pictures, an elbow in one, my toes in another. I hadn't wanted them to take any photos with me at the hospital. It was their moment, I had said.

I move slowly through the pages, glancing at Nick for confirmation each time I'm ready to flip the page. He nods solemnly in response, ready to confront the next section— more pages of moments we've missed, opportunities we've squandered. We're both reading all the little notes Chip and Donovan have written, papers they've glued inside to caption each event. This book is a scrapbooking tour de force. I would have expected no less from Donovan. As we meander through the boys' shared past, Nick and I get to see the photos of so many milestones—first steps, first solid food, the moment after a first word. And each time, it's Chip or Donovan hugging the boys and smiling for the camera. As I study the photos of Kai's pudgy baby cheeks, his toothless smiles, I wonder how Nick can ever possibly forgive me. We could have been a family of four. All these firsts we missed for our own child. A lifetime.

We reach the page from Kai's first haircut; his hair apparently grew long before Teddy even needed a trim. All that crazy hair, growing like weeds—just like mine, and like Wyatt's. There's a small plastic baggy taped to the page, a lock of Kai's downy baby hair inside it. It's all I can do not to rip the bag from the book and shove it deep into my pocket.

With each passing photo, I become more convinced how wrong I've been, how desperately important it is that we find a way to bring this child home, back to his family. As I hand the baby book back to Donovan, I squeeze Nick's hand, a symbol that we should go. We have so much to figure out, and it suddenly seems there isn't a moment to waste.

Nick pulls free of my hand, and when I glance over at him, he won't meet my eyes.

"We should get going," he announces to the room. "We're meeting Maggie's sister and her new husband for a late lunch."

"He's not new anymore, dad." Wyatt groans, looking at Chip and Donovan, performing for them. "My aunt and uncle. They've been married a year and a half already." He turns to Kai, who's still sitting on the couch, sort of flopped on top of Teddy and adds, "You have another aunt and uncle to meet."

"Cool." Kai smiles, his cheeks turning rosy again.

"I forgot you had a sister in the city." Chip stands too, but my focus is still on Kai, on those eyes that have been in my family for generations. I want to pick him up right this minute and run with him out of the apartment, extract him entirely from the life we accidentally dropped him in. We've lost so much time with him already. I want to pull him by the arm and start teaching him who he really is as we race to the elevator and out into the sunshine. All my schooling and experience instructing children his age tells me not to come on too strongly; I should wait, should move slowly and give him time. But as we prepare to leave, I feel like I'm abandoning him all over again.

"Leave it," Donovan says, and for a moment, I think he's talking about Kai, that I shouldn't mess with the situation as it is, but then I realize he means the vegetable platter I've just picked up.

I return the platter to its spot and try to hurry Nick along. The sooner we can talk through our next steps, the better. One thing is certain: I want to cancel our return plane ticket. There is no way I'm leaving this state without my *entire* family.

"Kai," Nick says, looking down at our boy, and I can hear a decade of regret filling that one word. In my mind's eye, a reel plays, and I wonder if Nick's seeing it too. All of those useless fertility treatments, the years of trying to conceive another baby, the tepid acceptances—it all could have been avoided.

They regard each other silently for a moment as the rest of us look on. For a flash, I think Nick is going to go for it, that he's going to ask Kai if he wants to leave with us this very second.

"You ever need anything," Nick finally says, his voice unsteady, "there's nothing we wouldn't do for you."

Kai nods, and I believe I see a flash of disappointment fill his eyes. That's all Nick can offer our son? I sigh loudly, not caring what message I'm sending to the room.

If Nick isn't going to do it, I sure as hell am. I put a hand on Kai's shoulder so he will look at me in the eye. "You could come live with us," I say. "We are your family too, whatever the labels."

"Maggie," Nick says.

"You are welcome with us, if that's where you think you should be." I keep going. He needs to know.

"Maggie." This time, Nick's word is a bite.

"I'm just saying, so he knows," I say. "Somebody has to say it." I hear the hysteria in my voice and try to rein it in as I turn back to Kai. "We would have wanted you then if we had known. And we want you now."

Kai looks back at me with those big saucer eyes, and I can't name the emotion I see in them. It could be hope or regret or confusion. As the adult in this relationship, I need to take control, to help him process and understand.

"You could come live with us." I start more gently, a conversation opener.

"Maggie, not now." Nick is moving closer to us.

"We are your family." I feel Nick's hand close around my wrist, an insistent squeeze trying to corral me before I go further. "This has all been such a horrible mistake," I persist. "Your dad knew it from the beginning, that you didn't belong here." Nick's fingers tighten on my wrist so forcefully that I shriek and my head snaps in his direction.

"We're leaving," he says, his eyes stone.

I try to escape his grip, but he pulls me toward the door without easing up on my wrist. Donovan and Chip look on with shell-shocked expressions as Nick propels Wyatt toward the open door with his free hand.

As we step into the hallway, he turns to me with a look I've never seen from him before. His expression has moved well beyond cold, beyond spent. "Go wait by the elevator," he commands, releasing my hand, and then he heads back inside the apartment, the door of which is still open.

I want to argue with him. That is *my kid* in there. How dare he get all up in my face like he owns this situation? But I'm frightened, and I tell myself that maybe waiting is best, that we can strategize while we let everyone's emotions settle.

"Come," I say forcing calm into my tone and looping an arm around Wyatt's back. Angry red bruises are forming already on my wrist where Nick's fingers cut into me. I don't know what he's saying to them now inside that apartment, but I don't wonder long before he's back in the dimly lit hallway, marching toward the elevator bank with a storm raging on his face.

He jabs at the elevator button and I wait for whatever he is about to say. Wyatt, thankfully, has the presence of mind not to insert himself into this situation; he stands a few paces apart from us, silent.

The elevator doors open, and we all file in. Images of Kai's chocolate eyes keep flashing through my mind. I want to press the red emergency button on the elevator panel, to stop this whole trajectory. If only there was a button on the panel to rewind, to send us back a decade in time, so I could make different choices from the beginning. I find the fresh bruises on my wrist, five dark smudges matching the placement of Nick's hand against my skin, and I fit my own fingers to their placement, pressing into the tender flesh with all the strength of my own, smaller hand.

Chapter 22

DONOVAN
AUGUST 2018

I keep a sharp eye on Teddy and Kai as they bodysurf in the waves on Sunday afternoon. Even though Chip is out in the water with them, I worry. A wave might catch them unaware and knock them too forcefully about while Chip's attention is momentarily elsewhere. An undertow could surprise them and pull one of them too far out to sea—away from me, out of reach. There's a kite in the air dancing high above the boys' position in the ocean, flapping and struggling against the wind in the perfectly blue sky. I try to enjoy the chorus of gulls and sea spray, the rhythmic tapping of a paddle ball somewhere down near the surf. As much as I want to luxuriate in this visit to Jones Beach, the campiness of crowded beach blankets and colorful umbrellas, everywhere I look, I see potential for disaster—distracted lifeguards, reckless jet skiers, broken beer bottles, sharks.

Fine, I don't see any sharks. But it could happen.

I've spent enough time in therapy to understand that my current state of hyper-anxiety is a reaction to the Wingates' visit yesterday.

Gina interrupts my thoughts from her chair, which is low to the ground in the sand beside my own, as she passes me an open bag of Lay's.

"Frito?" she offers.

"I don't know how you eat those things." I shake my head.

She shrugs and digs back into the bag. Gina looks terrific in her halter-top bikini and a pair of aviator sunglasses. She has her hair in one of those messy buns on top of her head, a few loose strands whipping around in the wind. Her sunblock-slicked legs are stretched out in front of her, crossed at the ankles, and she's rocking her feet from side to side in time with the country music wafting toward us from somewhere down the beach. She seems so happy and relaxed, so unlike her usual knackered self, and I assume Graham the Widower is the variable precipitating this positive change.

"Stop staring at me," she says without turning her head.

"Sorry." I laugh lightly. "You seem good, G." I turn back to the water, scanning the waves until I locate the boys again.

"I can hear the wistfulness riding on your voice like a freaking swan song. You got more to say about yesterday, say it." She emphasizes her statement by snapping into another chip.

I let a full minute go by without saying anything.

"It just doesn't sound so bad to me," Gina finally says. "So what that Kai knows his birth mother would have liked to raise him? It's better than feeling unwanted. He's big enough to understand that she feels regret."

"No." I am beginning to understand what has me so on edge. "It wasn't an apology or an expression of grief. She was full of intention." I can't even utter the next part of my thought because Gina's kids are weaving their way toward us through the patchwork of sunbathers. Both of them are licking at extralarge wafer cones as soft-serve ice cream melts onto their hands.

"Here," Miles says as he hands Gina change for the ice cream and the bottle of Diet Pepsi that she asked for.

"You two better eat fast," she says.

"Yeah." Flora licks a line of chocolate ice cream off the inside of her forearm in agreement. "Here, you want it?" She holds the cone out to her mother.

Gina cringes and leans away from it in her chair. "Don't pawn your trash off on me."

"Miles promised he'd come in the water," Flora says. "I don't want any more." She turns her head in a semi-circle until she spots a trash can in the sand and starts walking toward it.

When she's out of earshot, Miles tells us, "I am not coming back to the beach with you guys again without Ethan. She's like a suction cup."

Their brother Ethan isn't here because he was invited to go fishing with a friend from school and his family. Miles, accordingly, has become the primary object of his younger sister's affection today. In his defense, Flora *has* been following him everywhere since we got out of the car, the family dynamic dramatically altered by Ethan's absence. I noticed it from the moment we began rolling our beach gear through the tunnel from the parking lot onto the sand.

I watch Miles and Flora head in Teddy and Kai's direction. Flora giggles as Miles pretends to push her toward the water. How different would our family be without Kai? How different would Maggie and Nick's life have been if they'd had Kai with them from the beginning?

"I feel like I've stolen someone else's child. I *have* stolen someone else's child, but I'm not giving him back," I blurt to Gina, surprised I've confessed this aloud.

I keep my gaze on Flora and Miles as they make their way toward their cousins in the waves. When Chip sees them coming, he smiles and glances up in our direction from the water. He looks all GQ with his aviator sunglasses and toned abs. I can't tell from here, but I imagine his shoulders are beginning to burn. When he locates Gina and me, his expression changes—as if he knows what we're talking about, as if the only thing he can feel toward me lately is frustration. I glance at Gina, and I can tell she saw it too.

"You want to breathe into the bag?" She holds the package of Fritos out toward me again.

I push her hand away with a forced smile. I haven't mentioned to her how much Chip and I have still been arguing, but I can tell she knows. All those things I said about how he can't understand what I'm going through—well, I won't say I didn't mean them. We just haven't been able to find common ground. Every time I look at Teddy's face and see Chip's blue eyes staring back, I feel angry at Chip. Jealous.

"It helps to talk," Gina says gently.

A small plane flies low over the ocean, a long yellow sign for a local car dealership trailing from the back of it. I wait for the noise to settle before I answer.

"I think I'm going to get fired," I say, changing the subject.

"What?" She sits upright, startled. "They love you at your office."

"Yeah. They did. Before I lost our biggest client."

I tell her about how my junior associate, Erica, started meeting with our client, Wenzo, without me; about how the client loved her designs so much they decided to pursue an entirely different concept than the one I was advocating for; how they hired Erica away from us and then declined to engage our services.

"After all you've done to help develop her career. Doesn't she have a non-compete or something?" Gina asks.

"If we were in banking, maybe," I say. "Not in real estate. And honestly, I haven't done all that much to advance her career. My head hasn't been in the game since the beginning of the summer. I shouldn't be surprised." I run my fingers along the sand beside me, lifting a warm handful, then letting the grains drop slowly out from my closed fist.

"Well then you're going to have to bring in some other big fish to make up for this, aren't you?"

"That's exactly what the managing partner said to me." I look back at her and rub my palms together to get rid of the sand clinging to them. "He loves me, but they're trying to cut costs, and I'm expensive."

"Fish," she repeats.

I know she's right, I do have to recruit new business, but it's hard to focus on client development while I'm panicking about my family being ripped apart. I lean my head back and close my eyes, letting the sun warm my cheeks.

The next thing I know, I'm waking up from having dozed, and I can feel that a long stretch of time has passed. The air has cooled, and the sun is lower in the sky. I sit up with a jolt and look out to the waves, but Chip and the boys are no longer there.

"I'm here," Chip says from behind me, and I turn to see him sitting cross-legged on a towel in the sand. He's wearing a dry T-shirt and picking his way through a plastic container of grapes.

"Where is everyone?" I ask, noting that the crowd around us has thinned considerably.

"Gina took the kids back to her house to shower. I told them we'd meet them."

"Why didn't you wake me?" My tone is accusatory as I stand, and I don't even have the emotional energy to regret my shortness. I wipe the sand from the front of my swim trunks and glance around to assess what needs cleaning up before we can leave.

"Sit," Chip says, and there is a pleading note in his tone that stops me.

I look back at my beach chair.

"Here." He pats the space beside him on the oversize towel.

I sigh and sit across from him, crossing my legs like his and doing an internal eye roll as I brace for whatever vitriol is about to come my way.

"I'm sorry," he says.

Surprised, I wait for him to add more, but he seems to be waiting for me to say something in response.

"For?" I'm fully aware that I sound impatient, irritated, but we've barely said a kind word to each other in days. I don't feel like playing at romance right now.

Chip looks up at the sky, thinking. Instead of admiring the chords of his neck as he tilts his head backwards, I watch a seagull in the sand beside him pick and poke at a breadcrust.

"For tossing your breakfast into the disposal before you were finished, for slamming the car door at Gina's, for being a passive-aggressive, impatient prick."

"Well. At least you're honing your skills of self-description." I'm only half joking. A group of teenagers walks past us with all their beach gear and carts, heading toward the parking lot. I wait until they're out of earshot before adding, "I appreciate the effort. Can we go? I want to get the kids home before it gets late." I stand and start folding down the beach chair.

"What the fuck is your problem?" Chip demands as he, too, stands.

"If you have to ask, I don't even know where I would start."

He steps toward me so that his face is right in front of mine, close enough to kiss.

"He's my son, too," Chip says, punctuating each word with anger. "I'm scared, too." He's nearly growling at me. "You're the one who should be apologizing, not me. I'm doing everything I can here. You don't get sole possession of this moment just because you have anxiety issues, or because Kai looks more like you than me, or because your childhood was rougher than mine, or whatever the fuck other reason you think makes you the victim in this situation."

"I thought I had a biological son, Chip. My childhood? That's really what you want to talk about right now? We're adults now. What about *Kai's* childhood? What about the fact that we finally had it all, and now everything's going to shit? Everything is in jeopardy." I eye him from across the blanket for a moment. "You want to make this about childhood? Fine. You weren't there when I was panicking my way through adolescence. You don't get to judge me for trying to protect Kai from suffering the same kind of angst, the dread, even if for him it's for different reasons." I continue my tirade even though we both know I'm about to start careening off topic. I'm grabbing anger from everywhere I can, ranting away. "You don't know what it was like for me, in my neighborhood, while you were out there at your progressive prep school, owning your gaydom like a boss. You don't know," I repeat, driving the wedge of difference deeper. "How silly of me, how shameful that I believed anything would get better, that I could ever actually belong in a place. How foolish of me to think it had all worked out." I swallow hard. "I just want to go home."

I don't look at him as I bend down to lift the towel and shake out the sand. I can feel him glaring at me, but I keep moving, dismantling the remainder of our temporary camp, hurling items into our rolling cart with too much force. He's waiting for me to look at him, to say something, but I won't backpedal. I know I'm the asshole here, but I can't stop. Chip can't force me to be someone I'm not any more than I can force Kai to be my own flesh and blood.

Chapter 23

MAGGIE
AUGUST 2018

I roll over in the soft double bed at Nick's parents' house and find the back of Nick's head. I wonder if he's awake. The delicate white drapes in the room do little to keep out the morning sun, and I can see all the ways his hair has gotten out of line during the night.

"I can feel you looking at me," he says, his voice thick and warm with the morning, and I can't help but smile. It's reflexive, the small burst of joy I experience at the sound of his voice, but then I remember where we are, deep in the middle of our own war. Before I have time to wonder whether we will begin our argument afresh this morning or try to move toward some sort of detente, there's a soft knock at our door.

"Yeah?" Nick calls.

The door opens a crack and Wyatt pokes his head tentatively into the musty room. His eyes sweep over the scene before him—his parents, seemingly all cozied up in bed—and he asks, "Can I come in?"

"What's up?" Nick asks as he scoots over, even closer to me on the mattress, so Wyatt can have room to climb in. Wyatt only takes a small step into the room though, shifting his weight as though he's not sure he wants to stay. He's in a T-shirt and boxer briefs, which leads me to believe he hasn't been downstairs for breakfast yet.

"Mom, did you say something to Summer's mother?"

It takes me a moment to realize that he's asking about the situation with the tennis teacher.

"No. I promised you I wouldn't." I sit up in the bed, pulling the blanket with me. "Why?"

"Well, she's not talking to me, and Aiden York told me that she wasn't at work yesterday at the club. People are saying she quit." He squints slightly, trying to determine if I've betrayed him.

After I conferred with Nick on Friday night, we sat Wyatt down and I confessed to reading his texts. I explained my concern about Summer and her interest in the tennis coach, and he promised he would tell me if it ever seemed like she might be in danger. He was forthright with us, as far as I could tell. He complained about how Summer fawns over the guy, but he also said the coach has never shown one iota of interest in a young girl, Summer included, and Wyatt doesn't think she's going to lose her innocence to him. When I suggested that I should reach out to Summer's mom to prevent the situation from escalating, he freaked to such a degree that instead, I promised to hang back, as long as he agreed to keep talking sense into Summer and to come to me at the first sign of anything worrisome.

"I'm sorry, sweetie, but I don't know anything about why it's radio silence." I amble out of the bed, feeling thirsty for some fresh air. I push aside the drapes to open a window. "Maybe give her a couple of days to get over whatever's bothering her and then give it another try," I suggest.

"Maybe," he says halfheartedly before turning and leaving the room.

Nick gets out of bed then, too, and goes straight to the en suite bathroom to brush his teeth.

"I wonder what happened." I'm thinking out loud, putting my anger at Nick on hold as I focus on Wyatt's dismay.

"I know exactly what happened." Nick emerges from the bathroom with his toothbrush dangling from his mouth. "I called Bill."

"You called her father?" I demand. "After we promised Wyatt we wouldn't say anything?"

"I didn't promise a damn thing," Nick says before heading back into the bathroom to spit in the sink. He returns to the bedroom and points his toothbrush at me. "That crap with your high school teacher almost destroyed your whole life, and now you want to sit back and do nothing while another teenager risks turning her life to shit? So that your own teenage kid doesn't get mad at you? It's the height of selfishness." He goes into the bathroom again and turns on the faucet.

"Turning her life to shit? That's what you think happened to me, what I did?" I'm yelling as I follow him into the bathroom. "And yes, of course I care if Wyatt gets angry. He trusts us!" I throw my arms in the air in a gesture of frustration, defeat. Then I catch sight of the bruises on my wrist, darker today than they were yesterday, purple at their center, yellowing at the edge. The damage to my skin forces me to reckon with how much Nick must hate me, how much I hate myself. Maybe I did turn my life to shit.

"This isn't a pity party just for you. It's not all about you this time. It's never only about you. At some point you have to grow up and understand that." I'm not sure whether we are still arguing about Summer or if he's talking about Kai. My focus is on the latter now, and that's where I decide to stay.

"What I understand," I tell him, "is that we've both made mistakes over the years, starting with me giving away our child. I thought I could walk away, but I just can't. All this time, the child we thought we couldn't have was already out there. He has my mother's face!" I let him digest that for a moment before

I add more quietly, "I have to do everything in my power to get him back home. Even if it means losing you." I say it as an empty threat, no real intention behind it—but as the statement hangs in the air, I start to realize that I actually mean it. Despite what was once my burning love for the man in front of me, it will never compete with the responsibility I feel as a parent, or the sacrifices I'm willing to make for one of my children.

"Don't you think I want him, too?" Nick demands. "But it's too late. You gave him away. Gave him a new life. We can't just yank him out of that world because it'd be better for us to have him back now. It's not fair, and it's not right." His voice has somehow gotten calmer as he's been speaking, as if he's ready to have a rational discussion now.

"What happened to all the crap you spouted when I was pregnant with those boys about not giving babies to a gay couple to raise? Now you're just fine with it?"

"Yes!" he chirps, like he can't even believe I would suggest otherwise, like he never uttered a homophobic statement. "How many times do I have to say it? It was never about them being gay. I was jealous, and I was a bastard. But when you, Maggie Wingate, make a decision in your head that something is one way or another, you can't ever change your mind."

He's wrong, though. I've changed my mind a million times—about him, about my own life, and especially about Kai.

Chapter 24

DONOVAN
AUGUST 2018

I've just finished a call with John Rubes, the managing director of Bright Towers, a real estate investment trust that specializes in ownership of high-quality, net-leased restaurant properties. Like the last four groups I've spoken with, BT is fully leveraged at the moment and they're not interested in leasing any new space. It didn't matter how much I talked about the high-density population surrounding the properties I had in mind, the proximity to target demographics, the number of cars passing each of the spots on my list . . . these guys aren't buying what I'm selling, and my ass is toast if I don't figure out how to pull in another client.

I slide my desk chair closer to the computer screen and open another real estate firm's website. This one, though, I'm thinking of calling about employment. I've been wondering if a preemptive lateral move might be better than waiting until I've been canned to try finding another firm that wants to pick me up out of the ashes. I scroll through the photos on CREM's company pages, trying to be open-minded as I look at the different images the company uses to sell itself. There are photos of men and women in ultra-conservative business suits nearly glowering as they stand idly in conference rooms. Those shots are followed by pictures of skyscrapers captured from surprising perspectives, hard edges and angles photographed from vantage points that make them particularly intimidating. I feel myself making ugly faces as I ponder a career in any office that would find a website like this appealing.

I close the site and return to my contacts folder, wondering what else I might do to avoid losing my job so I don't have to subject myself to a place like CREM.

I'm scrolling through the different lists I've made over the years when a dialogue box appears on the screen. It's an email from Maggie. I brace myself and then click, somehow knowing exactly what bad news I'm about to read.

> *Donovan,*
>
> *Thank you for hosting us at your apartment on Saturday. It was nice to see you and Chip after all these years. You are clearly raising both Teddy and Kai as such little gentlemen already. I'm sending this email as a courtesy because I believe you deserve as much. Meeting Kai in person has changed everything for me. I realize now how much that child is a part of me, how his very existence screams my name. From the smallest details, like his fingers that are especially spindly, just like mine, to the more profound connections. Nick and I tried for so long to have a second child, Donovan. I never wanted you to feel guilty about the surrogacy and the impact it might have had on my ability to conceive again, but now, everything is different.*
>
> *Looking at Kai was like seeing a snapshot of myself as a kid and my whole family's history all at once. I need to know if he loves music*

like I did, if he's unpredictable like me or more dependable like my sister, his Aunt Tess. He has the same smile as his brother, who's been deprived of knowing him for too long already. I hope you can understand and that we might settle this quickly and amicably. I never agreed to hand over one of my own children to you and Chip. Of course, you should both stay involved in his life, but that sweet boy belongs with his real family. I have contacted an attorney, though I would much prefer to resolve this on our own. I am hoping for Kai to transition into sixth grade in Arizona while it's still early in the school year, so time is of the essence. I look forward to hearing from you.
Fondly,
Maggie

The taste of copper fills my mouth, and I realize I've bitten into my lip so deeply that I'm bleeding. I've been holding my breath since Maggie and Nick's visit, knowing this disaster would be coming, and it's almost a relief that the battle is finally on.

Rather than calling Chip, which might have been my first move a few months ago, I dial our attorney's office, thankful now that Dr. Pillar at the clinic advised me to retain someone. As the phone rings, I keep telling myself that Chip and I are Kai's legal guardians. Our names, not Maggie's, are listed on his birth certificate, thanks to the pre-birth order from California.

The call goes straight to voice mail, and I leave a hasty message asking for Lorraine to call me back the very second she hears the recording.

I re-read the message from Maggie, wondering if I'm supposed to respond, knowing that any attorney would tell me not to, that I should let the lawyers take over from here. I grab for my cell again and tap over to the screen listing my "favorite" contacts. My finger hovers over Chip's name. I need him now, we need each other, but I'm not sure if it's too late. He was so very wrong when he told me I was worrying too much, that we should let Maggie come meet Kai. But I was in the wrong, too, when I set this whole process in motion with those godawful Relativity tests, when I couldn't just leave everything alone after we got the results.

I move my finger away from the phone without calling. Instead, I simply forward the email to Chip without adding any sort of message. Right after I click "send," a knock sounds against my office door.

"It's open," I call out.

Paul, the managing partner, pokes his head in from the corridor. "Walter's here," he announces. "We're meeting in my office." He doesn't wait for me to follow, just moves on, and I assume he's heading toward the offices of the three other senior brokers at the firm to let them know that we're meeting in Paul's office instead of the conference room, like we usually do.

Since Walter has arrived earlier than scheduled, I take my time collecting myself. I close out of the email on my computer and gather supplies. Once I have the memo pad with my handwritten notes about cultivating new business, a couple of printouts tallying recent exclusive listings, and a fresh cup of hot coffee, I knock on Paul's door. I'm as ready as I can be to pretend I'm not completely distracted by the words of Maggie's email still pounding through my skull.

As I step into the corner office, I find only Paul and Walter Ruskin, the aging director of the board of our parent company.

"We might as well get straight to business," Walter says as he motions toward the small conference table in the corner of the room.

"Aren't we going to wait for the others?" I ask as I glance at Paul, who's still standing awkwardly near his desk, tapping a fountain pen absentmindedly against his palm.

"It's just the three of us," Paul answers without meeting my eyes.

I look back at Walter. His deep-set eyes are sympathetic beneath the massive lenses of his spectacles as he watches my understanding dawn. He motions again for me to sit. I do as he asks and place my coffee mug on top of my notes. We're obviously not going to be discussing those.

"We're letting you go." Paul's statement is firm, leaving no room to argue.

Even though I had been worried this might be coming down the pike, now that it's actually happening, it's still a shock. "For losing one client?" I half yelp.

"This isn't about Wenzo." Paul waves a hand dismissively. He shrugs out of his blazer and drapes it over the back of his chair without saying more.

"Well what then?" I ask, mentally cataloguing what else I could have done wrong, thinking of my distraction and the other deals I've worked on with perhaps less enthusiasm than usual in recent months.

"We're trying to take the firm in a new direction. You know we've been having trouble with the finances—it's hardly a secret. The biggest revenue generators have been the corporate clients. You don't want to be here finding space for big-box chain stores, clients with ready-made, derivative layouts. You know it as much as we do."

"So I'm being phased out?"

"With great regret," Paul answers, and I believe he means it.

~~~~~~~

I open my desk drawers one after another and conclude that most of their contents are items I will be leaving behind: paper clips, rubber bands, drafting paper. I have a few deal toys and framed pictures that I'd like to take with me, but it's not a lot to carry. I start stacking up my plaques and the little sculpture-like gadgets I've been gifted by various clients over the years. Then my eyes drift to the framed photos. I only have three: One of me with Gina and our cousin Noelle, goofy, nearly identical smiles on our faces. A shot of Teddy and Kai in their little league uniforms, Teddy's arm around Kai. And a picture of Chip and me, standing in the rain at the Cliffs of Moher.

I take a moment to study the photo. It was the first trip we took on our own after becoming dads. We booked a room at an old Irish castle, dined on potatoes in every possible incarnation, played a little golf in the rain, and managed to come home even more attached to each other than when we'd left. Funnily enough, it was Chip, not me, who missed our four-year-old boys the most, calling home so often that my mother had to scold him to chill out. I thought it was sweet, though—that for all his big talk about the importance of taking time for ourselves away from the kids, he was even more of a softie than I was.

I look now at our smiling faces in the photo, and I wonder if my relationship, just like my career, is all over too. I've pushed and shoved at Chip for so many weeks now, it's a wonder he can even stand to be in the same room as me. And yet, I can't make myself behave properly. I'm just so angry. Angry that Kai is not my biological son, angry that Chip got what he wanted in Teddy when I got robbed, angry that he can't understand how that makes me feel.

I don't see how we can ever work ourselves back from the antagonism I've injected into our relationship. I've made our entire dynamic so different from how we've ever related to each other in the past. I won't be surprised when he leaves me, nor when he tries to get primary custody of Teddy. Why wouldn't the court give the biological father primary rights to a child? I'm just the gay man who has been playing pretend for the last decade.

As I stare down at my own smile in the picture I'm holding, the grin a little too toothy, too happy, I ask myself: *How is it possible that in the span of a few months I've gone from having a fairy tale life, a great job, a handsome husband, and two wonderful children to a place where I stand to lose absolutely everything?*

Four hours later, I've deposited my office clutter on the floor of our entryway, eaten my way through several days' worth of leftovers, and taken an appallingly long shower. I'm now lying diagonally across the top of our bed, still wrapped in a towel, staring at the ceiling. Teddy and Kai are spending two nights with Chip's parents up in Greenwich so they can swim and sail and "summer" in the tradition of Rigsdales of yore. I now regret making these arrangements, as any time that I can spend with Kai, and Teddy too, has become so much more precious, precarious.

Tonight is the Trevor Prince annual dinner cruise, when everyone at Chip's investment bank gets all collegial and debauched. This is a plus-one event for the firm, and I'm supposed to meet him at Chelsea Piers in forty minutes, but I feel like I can't even get myself off the bed. I let my eyes fall shut as I ask myself why Chip would even want me there. I've become nothing but a nightmare lately, perma-stressed dead weight.

I finally heave myself off the duvet and head for the closet. After running my hands absently over several garments, I settle on cream-colored linen pants and a fitted teal green button-down shirt, an outfit that will set me apart from the bankers in their business attire and allow me to effectively play my part as Chip's fashionable, adorable husband. I wonder if this will be the last Trevor Prince event I attend, the last social outing of any sort I'll have with Chip. I feel my chest tighten, the air becoming hard to find, as I imagine a life without Chip.

Deep breaths, I remind myself. *In through the nose, out through the mouth. Now is not the time for a panic attack.*

I dress hastily and give the mirror one final glance. As the front door closes behind me, I realize I've left my wet towel lying on the bedroom floor. I can't even muster the energy to go back inside to pick it up. I must simply move forward.

When I arrive at Pier 61, it's almost 8:00 p.m., and the light in the sky has begun to soften to lavender. I walk myself through the large open space, the pungent scent of fresh fish enveloping me. As I reach the dock, I spot Chip waiting on a green Astroturf runner beside a large yacht bearing the name *Celestial Spirit of Liberty*.

He's looking at his phone and doesn't see me. I slow my stride and study him. With his long, narrow frame, fair skin, and light hair, I still often think of glistening icicles when I look at him.

As if he can sense the well of emotion swirling in his direction, Chip glances up and our gazes connect.

To my horror, I instantly erupt into tears. Big, loud, ugly tears. Chip doesn't hesitate; he dashes toward me before I even have a moment to contemplate what to do next. He wraps his arms around me and I cleave to him, burrowing my face into his shoulder, as my sobs grow even louder.

"Hey, what? What is it?" His complete surprise tells me that he hasn't seen the email I forwarded from Maggie. It's just like him to ignore personal emails during the day. I keep crying, barely able to suck air into my body between my sobs. I can feel my tears soaking into Chip's shirt, but I can't seem to get a hold of myself.

"What is it?" Chip asks again. "Donny! Come on, you're scaring me." He pushes me away so he can look into my face.

"Oh. God." I suddenly take in my surroundings, the random people passing us on all sides—tourists and teenagers, young women in business suits, couples holding hands, older men carrying coolers—and I pause in my hysteria, mortified.

When I finally bring my eyes back to Chip's, I tell him, "It's everything. Now, even this." I motion loosely into the air, indicating the spectacle I've made of myself.

"This way." He pulls me over to a covered stairwell where we're out of the way. I wipe the dampness from my face onto the back of my hand. "What happened?" he asks in a soft voice, using the "I'll fix this" tone I've been waiting to hear since we first got our Relativity results.

"Everything is going to shit," I declare on another sob, unable to articulate more eloquent sentiments at the moment.

"Stop it. Talk to me," he pleads, with the beautiful, beseeching kindness I've been pining for. Now, *now*, he's offering it up; now, when it's too late for everything.

"Well, Kai," I state flatly.

Chip looks back at me expectantly.

"You didn't see my email?" I don't know why I even bother to ask.

He shakes his head in confusion. "It's bad." I let him digest that for a brief moment before I add, "And I've destroyed our relationship."

He looks surprised, but now I'm ready to keep going, to berate myself, to punish myself for all I've done wrong.

"I've been petty, and jealous, and mean. I've walked all over you, and I know you've had enough. I got fired. And that was less than an hour after I got a letter from Maggie putting us on notice that she's going to petition for custody of Kai."

"No!" He shouts it. Now he's the one being loud and uncouth. I see genuine surprise on his face, as though he truly didn't expect her to challenge our son's guardianship. "What did she say?" He's aghast, his cheeks reddening, a vein in his neck pulsing in anger.

"That we'll be hearing from her lawyer, but that she'd rather settle the matter between ourselves. I don't know. I didn't write back. I was too busy getting laid off, I guess."

"She is *not* taking our kid," he says through gritted teeth as he looks up, behind me, like he's scanning the dock for something. Then his eyes are back on mine. "We are going to sic our lawyer on her, make her sorry she ever challenged us. She handed that child over to us free and clear and she can't come back here ten years later trying to take him back. We've been mother and father to that kid since the day he was born."

I just nod, relieved to finally have a teammate. If it's possible, I feel even more regret over how I've been pushing Chip away.

"I'm so sorry." I have to say it out loud. I can't help feeling like all of this is my fault. Well, because it is. The Relativity test was my idea. Following up on the cagey information, that was all me, too. Chip wanted to let it go, but I was the one who needed answers. Closure, I think I said. And now we're at risk of losing our child.

"No." He puts his hand on my cheek. "You don't get to blame yourself. Not for any of it. I don't want to hear you say that again. You've been shitty the last few weeks, fine. I concede that. But I don't know what you're talking about, 'destroying our relationship.'" He puts it in air quotes, says it like it's an impossibility, like I might as well have been talking about abduction by aliens. "We took vows. You are my person, the love of my life, no matter what obstacles we face. A couple of months of fighting isn't going to change that. I am not going anywhere, so shut up about that, and let's focus on how we're going to handle Maggie. Okay?" He wipes at a tear beneath my eye with his thumb. "What do you mean you got laid off?" he asks belatedly.

I fill him in quickly. A horn blasts from the yacht across the way, a warning that the boat will soon be departing. I finish with, "Maggie and Nick both have good jobs, and now we're fighting with one parent who is unemployed."

"Whatever." Chip waves a dismissive hand in the air. His own monthly take-home pay easily eclipses the annual salaries of most Americans.

I grab onto his bicep, holding his whole body close to mine. Then I step away and tug at him. "Come on. Let's not literally miss the boat."

He searches my eyes for a moment without budging.

"Fine," he finally says. "But no more catastrophizing, ok? We share our thoughts out loud? Like grown people?"

He waits until I finally give him a nod of assent, then lets me pull him toward the yacht.

We hold hands as we board the boat, and the relief I feel at the state of our relationship is so strong that it almost reduces the dread I'm carrying about Kai.

Almost.

Chapter 25

MAGGIE
AUGUST 2018

There are only two days remaining before we're supposed to fly back to Arizona, and I haven't told Nick that I'm feeling as if I can't possibly leave New York, not yet. Part of why I haven't mentioned anything to him is because we aren't speaking to each other. We're pretending that we're speaking, passing information back and forth by making comments to other people in the room, but really, we're just not talking. He knows how angry I am that he betrayed Wyatt by going to Summer's dad about her interest in the tennis coach. What I don't think he understands is my disappointment over his attitude toward my whole life. And none of this even scratches the surface of what happened at the Rigsdales'.

My dad finishes the last sip of wine in his glass, and I push back my chair so I can start clearing the plates from the table.

I stack Tess's dish on top of my own and then reach for Wyatt's while Tess pulls out her phone. She said she's overseeing a big case at work and it's been hard to get away, but I have a hunch she's checking for texts from Isaac, still acting like the newlywed that she is.

"Hang on," she says, then she stands and walks out of the room, typing away on her phone.

Wyatt, who's been unusually quiet all afternoon, watches me heading toward the kitchen with the pile of plates and wanders in behind me. "Is there dessert?" he asks.

Tess calls from the living room, "Why don't I take him downstairs to Frosty Delight for fro-yo?"

"I'm in!" Wyatt calls back to her as I turn on the faucet to start the washing up.

"But finish clearing the table first," I call over my shoulder.

Nick pokes his head into the galley kitchen, meeting my eyes directly for the first time tonight. "I'll go, too."

"Okay." I nod, as I scrub at a stubborn fragment of salmon skin.

There's a whirlwind of activity as the three of them make their way out of the apartment, and then it's just me and my dad left in the kitchen. I continue cleaning dishes, placing one after another into the dishwasher, while my dad leans against the doorframe, watching me.

"You want to talk about it?" he asks.

I look over at him. His thick hair has lost all its color and it's straighter now, so unlike the dark waves I remember from my childhood. I didn't witness the gradual transition as his hair went from brown to salt and pepper to blizzard white. By the time I was ready to behave as an adult, my parents had already gone through so many changes. That's on me, and I am trying to own it—first and foremost, by not repeating my past mistakes.

"I've already lost ten years with my son," I say as I close the dishwasher. "I don't want to lose another day, not another second." Looking into my father's weathered face is a surprising comfort in the turbulence that has invaded my life. "Don't you . . . aren't you curious to meet him?" I ask, wondering again what it's like to have a grandkid who's been effectively misplaced.

"One of the first things you taught me as a parent," he says, "was that I can't control what you do." He shrugs lightly and then crosses his arms against his chest, resting them on his shirt. The plaid flannel button-down he's wearing looks more appropriate for a ski vacation than a summer night in the city. I wonder if my mom used to help him choose his clothes, if he's now floundering and clueless about fashion choices without her. Another daughter would probably know something like that. There are doubtlessly several other ways in which he's been struggling since her death, but I'm ignorant of those as well.

"You've been pretty lucky," he says, "if your experience as a mother hasn't yet made your own powerlessness clear to you."

I wait for him to continue, not sure where this is going.

"Of course I want to meet him," he finally says. "A child of yours, a grandkid of mine. But he's not my son. I think the bigger question is, is he yours?"

"Are you saying he's not, that he's *not* mine?" I bristle, remembering immediately all the reasons I couldn't get along with my parents—how judgmental they've always been, all the snap decisions they always made before listening to my opinion on anything. My mom with her high-voltage, clipped words and then my father's passive agreement with whatever unreasonable, frenzied decision she grabbed.

"No." He holds up a hand in a defensive gesture. "I'm saying"—he pauses to choose his words—"that this is something you need to figure out. If he's yours, you don't back down until you bring the kid home. But first, you have to be certain you're not taking something that doesn't belong to you. Only you can decide. You and Nick."

I feel my lips turn down at the mention of Nick's name.

"What?" He walks closer to the counter and starts wiping at a wine glass with a dishrag. It's still jarring to see him do domestic work, tasks he never would have bothered with when my mother was well.

"I'm just thinking ten steps ahead, I guess. I told the lawyer we want to move forward, to send whatever it is they use to start the custody proceeding. I kind of failed to mention that to Nick, and when he finds out, I'm pretty sure he'll want to strangle me." I glance reflexively at the bruises on my wrist, faded now to a greenish yellow. I know my dad is about to say that I have to tell Nick, that it's wrong to be secretive, but I cut him off at the pass. "I'm thinking about leaving him." The words come out in a rush, like an ugly confession filling up the kitchen, scattering onto the counter, over the tile floor.

"Again?" he asks, a hint of irritation—or is it disbelief?—in his voice. I don't need to look up from the crystal glass I'm cleaning to know that his eyebrows are raised, his mouth a little twisty at the corner.

When I don't answer, he takes that as his cue to start lecturing.

"Marriages hit road bumps," he says. "You can't hightail it out of town every time you have a major disagreement with someone you love." I know he's talking about more than my relationship with Nick, and I'm hit with a fresh wave of guilt about all the time I lost with my mother, all those years I stayed away because I couldn't relate to her outlook on life, her goals, and the aggressive anger to which she so often surrendered when things didn't go her way. I will not be a parent like that, and I will not let space and time separate me from my child the way my own parents did.

"I'm not hightailing it anywhere," I shoot back. "I guess maybe we should go back to Sedona while we get the legalities sorted, but I think this case will have to be litigated in New York, which will require a lot of back and forth for me. Even though Kai was born in California, apparently the laws of New York govern since this state is his primary residence. I'd bet money that Nick won't come back to fight alongside me."

My dad doesn't say anything, and I can hear all his disappointment in the silence.

"I'm not saying I *want* to leave him," I hedge, "just that I feel strongly enough about fighting to bring Kai home that I'm doing it regardless of what it might cost my marriage. It's our only chance, Kai's and mine. And Wyatt's." I don't know if my father can possibly appreciate how badly I wanted another child, how crushing it was to try and fail, over and over again. And during all that time, with the repeated losses and the constant longing, my child was already out in the world—waiting to be found. I'm still struggling to wrap my head around it.

I grab for the rumpled dish towel on the counter, folding it in half once, twice, and then a third time before I drape it over the back of the full dish rack—just the way my mother used to, just the way I do in my own house.

"Seems to me," my dad says gently, "that you and Nick have some talking to do."

"Talking about what?" Nick asks, as we step into the main room of the apartment where he's standing in the open door with a paper bag in hand. At the expression of surprise on my face, he says, "Tess and Wyatt are lounging on one of those bean bag chairs while they eat, but I bought a couple of pints that I thought we could all share, so . . ." He trails off, waiting for me to fill him in on the conversation he's unwittingly joined.

My dad glances at me, and instead of seeing apology in his dark eyes, I see a command.

"I have to check a couple of things on the computer," he says before disappearing down the hallway.

I walk back into the kitchen, grab a couple of bowls and spoons, and bring them over to Nick where he has just taken a seat on the thirty-year-old sectional sofa. I retrieve the first container from the bag and begin scooping out coffee ice cream into one bowl, then the other.

"Here." I hand the larger serving to Nick.

"What did you need to tell me?" he asks, and his tone is kinder than it's been in the day and a half since our fight.

"I emailed Donovan this afternoon," I start, knowing I have to come clean.

"Okayyyy . . ." He draws out the word, making it a request for more information.

"I told him that we would be seeking custody of Kai." I brace for his reaction.

Nick blinks twice, hard, and then folds his lips over on themselves, like he's physically holding his words inside his mouth, restraining himself.

We stare at each other another moment and then Nick asks, "Did he write back?"

I shake my head, waiting for the inevitable eruption to follow.

"This is really what you want?" he asks. His tone is probing, curious, but not argumentative. "You think we should yank Kai out of his life, bring him across the country to live with us?"

"I think he was yanked out of his life already. All we'd be doing is bringing him back to where he belongs."

Instead of answering me, he stands and walks toward the window, and I notice that my hand is resting on my belly, as if I'm trying to contain the emptiness inside of me, to protect myself from it. He finally opens his mouth to say something in response, and I brace, but then he closes it again and turns his gaze back toward the evening lights outside the window.

"I don't think I disagree with you," he says, looking back at me and sounding as surprised as I feel.

"What do you mean?" I'm suspicious.

"I can't get his face out of my mind." He runs a hand over his own chin. "So many mannerisms just like Wyatt. You'd think that would be a nurture thing, not nature." He's talking to himself almost as much as me right now. "I thought that it was selfish, to come in like bandits and demand to take him home, but hearing you say that we're going for it, I just feel relieved, like it is actually the right choice. I don't want to devastate him, but ten-year-olds are resilient, right? He'll adjust to a new life eventually. We'll get a therapist. It'd probably be easier on him than knowing we didn't even fight for him, right?"

As Nick lets his thoughts spill forth, I berate myself for my own snap decisions, my knee-jerk judgments. It's time for me to confess the rest. "I called Tom Wellan, too." I scrunch my nose. "Told him to file the initial petition."

He lets out a long, slow breath and closes his eyes for a moment. The silence stretches as he pinches the bridge of his nose. While I wait, I catch sight of the bruises on my wrist and feel another self-righteous bubble of anger float up, but then he looks over at me, his eyes searching.

"Okay." He finally nods. "So, what happens next?"

I shake my head. "We wait for their response. Either Donovan will write back to me agreeing to settle outside of court, or, more likely, they'll lawyer up and fight this out against us."

"It would be pretty crazy to have another kid at home," Nick says almost wistfully as he lowers himself back onto the couch. "I guess we'd give him the guest room, unless Wyatt wanted to share. And we'd have to contact the school, obviously. That'll be a fun one to explain to Principal Willis." He smirks in that sheepish way of his, and I feel myself soften toward him.

I also find myself thinking about logistics in ways I haven't allowed myself to until this moment. "I wonder if he plays any sports?" I muse. "Or if he'd want to start?" I picture the Sedona Middle School soccer uniforms and an even crazier carpool schedule.

"So many of Wyatt's friends have siblings going into the sixth grade," Nick adds, probably pairing Kai with various kids in his head.

"For the record"—I hold up a finger—"I would never, ever, have named him Kai. He probably has to spell it every single time he's introduced to someone new."

"I think that's one detail we're going to have to live with."
Nick reaches out to squeeze my finger, and I marvel at how
quickly we've gone from the brink of destruction back to being
teammates. Maybe it's true what they say about how the secret
to a successful partnership is having a common enemy. I never
imagined that could apply to a marriage, and yet, here we are.

Chapter 26

DONOVAN
AUGUST 2018

Rather than having Chip's parents bring the kids back to the city after their two-night sleepover, I decide to use some of my newfound free time to drive out to Greenwich and pick them up myself.

I keep replaying the conversation with our lawyer in my head, looking for loopholes, anything else we can do. When I finally spoke with her on Tuesday morning, Lorraine explained that after the Wingates file their petition, we will be able to submit a response, and then there will be a period for discovery, for both sides to collect information about living situations, what Kai's needs are, and the like. If I had to guess, I'd wager that Maggie's hotshot lawyer sister has found her some sword-wielding shark of an attorney. Even so, Chip insists that we clearly have the stronger case and I shouldn't stress too much. Right.

I've learned that in custody cases in New York, the primary litmus test is to ask which outcome would most effectively serve the "best interests of the child." Apparently, all we have to do is prove that Kai is happy and thriving in his current life, with his brother, his friends, his school, camp, extracurriculars, so on and so on, and that removing him from his present living and guardianship situation would be detrimental to his mental health and well-being. Handing Kai over to a different set of parents to live in a totally new family would so clearly be counter to his best interests. It's not like he's a dress-shirt that was returned to the wrong customer from the dry cleaner. We can get testimony from his teachers, doctors, friends, grandparents, you name it.

The lawyer seems pretty confident about our case too, but she's forgetting about all the people out there who still think gay men don't belong raising children. Chip keeps reminding me that it's 2018, that families with same-sex parents are no big deal anymore, but what if we end up with some octogenarian homophobe judge? I take a few deep breaths as a I pull into my in-laws' sweeping semi-circular drive, the red brick of the home's exterior baking in the sun and beckoning me toward the extralong deep blue swimming pool that I know awaits in the backyard.

I try to put back on my regular face before I step out of the car, the one that is only subtly marred by my constant low-level anxiety, not the face I'm sure I'm wearing now, the one that is stunned and filled with terror.

I grab my tote bag from the passenger seat and make my way toward the back of the house. I can hear splashing and laughter before I even reach the wrought iron gate.

Teddy sees me first and shouts in delight.

"Papa! Watch!" he demands as he runs from the grass onto the stone patio surrounding the pool and then propels himself into the deep end, cannonball style. I offer up a two-fingered whistle in appreciation, like my dad would have done for me as a kid, if we'd had access to a pool like this. My mother-in-law, Lynn, is sitting at the stone table on the other side of the patio, and she laughs good naturedly as she rises from her seat.

"Now me!" Kai shouts, water dripping from his hair, as

he climbs the ladder. He runs to the spot where Teddy started. "Teddy, the ball!"

"Go!" Teddy shouts, and Kai runs toward the pool. Teddy throws the football and Kai jumps and catches the ball seconds before he plunges into the water, swells of pool water erupting into the hot air as he disappears triumphantly below the surface. It's something I've watched them do nearly a hundred times before, but suddenly, I see this as a beautiful, choreographed moment—the epitome of a child's "best interests."

"Again!" I demand. "I'll tape it." I drop my bag on the grass where I'm standing and begin fishing for my phone in my shorts pocket.

"Oh, stop," Lynn says warmly, coming in for a hug and then a wet kiss on my cheek. "Film them later. They've been at it all morning. Rosie's just bringing out lunch."

I glance toward the French doors that lead to the kitchen, and they open on cue. Rather than Rosie, Chip's dad, Chris, emerges, wearing a pink polo shirt and a pair of his signature madras Bermuda shorts. I imagine he's just returned from a round of golf at the country club. As the semi-retired chairman of the board at Tryptum Industries, he doesn't demean himself with trips into the office on beautiful summer days.

"Donny!" He shouts the greeting like we're old football buddies. After making a beeline across the grass and giving me the requisite "man hug," a couple of strong whacks of his palm against my shoulder blade, he picks up my bag and starts back across the lawn, assuming Lynn and I will follow, which we do.

"You brought a suit? Go for a dip with the boys?" He's being overly cheerful, the way you do in a crisis.

"Lunch first," Lynn declares, and now Rosie does appear from the kitchen, a tray full of white melamine bowls in her arms. She sets it down on the long table and rushes back inside, leaving me to marvel, as I do every time I'm here, what a different childhood Chip had from my own.

I glance again at the boys, who are now wrestling in the pool, and I try not to think about the different childhood they each might have had if we had known the facts from the beginning.

"Let the boys keep swimming," Lynn says, motioning to the chair across from her at the table. "I want to hear how you're holding up."

Chris gives Lynn a quick look, like he doesn't think we should talk about "the situation," but Lynn shrugs and says, "They need to know we're on their side, that we will do whatever it takes, whatever you need." She looks at me again. I think she's offering financial help at this moment, but luckily, we have the resources we need in that department.

"Best interests of the child," I say. Maybe saying it over and over again will help me process, push me to start thinking more about logistics and strategy. "That's the standard in these cases," I explain. "What's in the best interests of the child."

"Well if anyone would say that removing a happy boy from his home is in a child's best interests, our court system is even more troubled than I realized," Chris says.

A squeal from Teddy interrupts us as Kai takes a hose from the pool sweeper and starts squirting it at Teddy's head.

I open my mouth to reprimand him—playing with the sweeper like that has always been against the rules—but Lynn holds up a hand.

"Let them," she says, glancing at the boys and then back at me, and that's when I notice the sadness around her eyes. It's not just concern for me, or for the kids, but for herself, as well. If Maggie and Nick take Kai from us, so many people will suffer.

"I've been researching custody cases in New York—adoption law, surrogacy law. I feel like I've earned half a law degree in the past twenty-four hours."

"Maybe I should grab the gin," Chris offers, but I shake my head.

"I still have to drive the kids back into the city and then have a sit-down with them to discuss all this."

"You're going to tell Kai?" Lynn is incredulous; the tuna wrap she's holding paused halfway to her mouth.

"Maybe not." Chip and I haven't reached a decision about this. "I suppose it's not necessary yet, but eventually there's going to be evidence collection, court visits, maybe home visits, God knows what else."

"Couldn't we just pay her off?" Chris asks. "She sold the kid once before. How much do you think it'd take for her to do it again? We'll double it." He pats at his pocket, like he's ready to write out a check at this very moment.

I open my mouth to tell him that no, I don't think Maggie can be bought this time around, but Kai is out of the pool, walking toward us with Teddy only a few steps behind him, so I change the subject.

"In other news . . ." I decide to come clean, even with Teddy and Kai filling their plates within earshot. "I've been let go from Hopper."

"You got fired?" Teddy demands as all eyes land on me.

"Well, yes and no." Can't I save face a little at least? "The firm is moving in a direction that doesn't exactly gel with my skill set, so we decided to part ways."

"Do you need me to make some calls?" Chris's voice is warm and full of assuredness. I imagine he feels relieved to be back in familiar territory, as finagling employment through nepotism is more within his comfort zone than the particulars of buying and selling children.

"I don't think so." I shake my head as I continue to ponder my options. "I hadn't realized it until now, but I don't think I've been passionate about the real estate game for quite some time. I think maybe this is a blessing in disguise, time to choose a new direction."

"Why don't you just not work, then?" Kai asks as he puts two pieces of corn on the cob on his plate and sits down next to his grandmother. "Like Aldo and Zack's moms? And doesn't Xander's dad stay home, too?"

I study Kai as I try to figure out how that would play in court. Would it look better if Kai has two working parents? Or will it cut in our favor if one parent has more time to devote to the kids? I could even spin the situation for a judge's benefit and say I decided to focus on the kids because of how confusing current circumstances have become, show how I'm always putting them first. As I'm thinking it through, I realize that maybe this isn't just about pretending that Kai and Teddy need me around more. Maybe they actually *will* need me around more. Maybe this case is going to require so much focus that it's best if I'm just as present as possible.

And then the worst thought of all hits me, which is that I better make the most of the time I have left with the family we've created. It could all be over soon.

⸻

After another hour of cannonballs and pencil dives, the boys have finally tired themselves out, and, and they are now sitting quietly in the backseat of the Range Rover with damp hair and fresh clothes. As I navigate through the tree-lined streets of Greenwich toward the highway, the phone rings and Chip's number appears on the car's dash screen.

"Hey," I answer with genuine cheer in my voice. It's such a relief to have returned to a place of affection with him, a sliver of sunlight in the otherwise bleak family drama we're suffering through at the moment.

"I just got fucking served with court papers!" His angry voice fills the car at high volume.

I swerve to the side of the road and take the phone off speaker as I move the gearshift into park.

"Jesus, Chip, I'm in the car with boys." I glance in the backseat and quickly add, "The language on you," as if that is the reason I didn't want the kids to hear what he said. "You're not on speaker anymore."

"Shit," he says, but pauses for only a moment before he continues. "A process server, this shady guy with a beat-up messenger bag and a ratty suit—he came to my office, to my desk."

I want to ask if Chip has read the papers, what they say, if he's called Lorraine, our lawyer, if we're going to survive this. A lone car appears in my rearview mirror, making its way down the winding suburban road where I've stopped, slowing as it approaches us. I roll down the window and wave the car past us.

"I can't now," I say, glancing in the rearview again. I see Teddy pulling down the TV screen in the backseat. I shake my head no, and he rolls his eyes at me but flips it back into the closed position.

"Ok," Chip says, the timbre of his voice so much higher than I'm accustomed to. He's breathless and panicked in a way I don't think I've ever heard him. "I'll go through these and talk to Lorraine. Call me as soon as you're home."

As I pull the car back onto the road, Kai asks, "What's he so upset about?"

"Just something that happened at his office this morning. You know how he gets worked up sometimes," I add, trying to play it off. Except that Chip almost never gets worked up. Histrionics are my thing, not his. And damn their little ten-year-old brains, but the squinty eyes and tight lips I see in the mirror tell me they're not buying it one bit.

"It's about the Wingates." Teddy says this as a statement, but I know it's really just a question in disguise. He's acting like he already knows the scoop so that I won't try lying.

"Look," I say, "let's just talk about something else. It's not important right now."

"About the Wingates?" Kai asks, looking at Teddy. "About them how?"

Teddy opens his mouth, but I shut him down before he can say something to frighten Kai.

Or rather, frighten him *more*. There's no reason that innocent boy needs to feel the abject terror that I'm suffering at this moment. "It *is* about the Wingates," I confess. "They want to be able to spend more time with you, Kai, and we're just figuring out how to handle it in a way where everyone can feel the most comfortable."

"More time how?" Kai asks, and I can't read his voice. He almost sounds excited.

"We're not sure yet," I say as I merge the car onto the highway. The clanking sound of a truck barreling past us punctuates my statement.

"What if they want him to go live with them in Arizona?" asks Teddy.

So much for hiding the ball.

"Way to cut to the chase, kid," I answer. "We don't know exactly what they're asking yet, but there's no reason to jump straight to that scenario."

Tell that to my blood pressure, I think as I glance in the mirror again. Kai is looking out the window, while Teddy has his gaze on me. I give a small shake of my head. His lips tighten in surrender, an understanding that he needs to put his brother's emotional comfort above his own at this moment. He blinks at me a couple of times and then he trains his gaze out the window, just like his brother beside him.

⁓⁓⁓⁓⁓⁓

After we get back to the apartment, Kai and Teddy begin unpacking their overnight bags and I call Chip, as he instructed, but the call goes straight to voicemail.

We've only been home about twenty minutes when I get a

call from Rory, the doorman. There is a man named Antonio Sharp in the lobby, Rory tells me, who has a package he'd like to hand deliver. I know exactly what this is about, and I'm not interested in having the guy come up here. I contemplate asking Rory to send him away, to tell him I'm not at home, but I've seen how these things shake out on TV. Eventually, the guy will find me; I might as well succumb to the inevitable. I tell Rory that I'll come down to accept the delivery, and then I shout to the boys that I'm running to the lobby for a minute. They holler back a muffled, unified response, and I hurry down to face my fear.

When the elevator doors open into the brightly lit lobby, I'm surprised to find Chip there already, engaged in conversation with a middle-aged man in a hellacious brown blazer and mismatched yellow necktie. Chip catches sight of me and gives an almost imperceptible shake of his head, like I should either stay back or walk on by. I suppose the custody battle can't begin in earnest until both of us have been served with the court papers—but what is the end game here? Am I going to spend the next eight years dodging the process server, running around in disguises or never setting foot outside the apartment? As much as I'd prefer to avoid this guy and his combover, I think this is a moment for ripping off the Band-Aid.

I walk up to where they're standing, alongside rows of mailboxes. "I'm Donovan Gallo-Rigsdale," I say. "Lay it on me." I hold out my hand for the manila envelope he's clutching.

"Have a good day," he says with a curt nod as he hands me the folder, and then he pivots toward the building's revolving door without finishing whatever he had been saying to Chip.

Chip and I stand underneath the lobby's art deco chandelier in silence for a moment, watching the man's departure, and then we look back at each other.

"Why are you home so early?" I ask, not that the sight of his chiseled face doesn't bring me instant comfort.

"I just needed to be here."

I try not to think about the fact that Chip would only leave the office early in the direst of circumstances. "Come," I say. "The boys are upstairs. They were asking in the car about your outburst."

"We should tell them," Chip says. When we step into the elevator, he presses the button for our floor and then leans against the brass railing on the wall as if he can't bear to hold his own weight up for another moment.

"But not until after we read the papers," I say. "Because"— I perk up with a sudden hope—"maybe it's not even what we think."

"I already read them. It's exactly what we think. A total shitshow." He shakes his head in anger.

I blink once, twice, devastated all over again. The elevator opens to release us, and I follow Chip toward the apartment, but when he opens the door, I hover outside.

"You go in," I tell him. "Give me a few minutes out here to read these for myself." I hold up the envelope. "I need to know exactly what we're up against."

Chip nods and kisses my temple before stepping over the threshold and closing the door behind himself.

I sink down beside the door and take one long, deep breath before tearing the top off the envelope. I'm expecting to see a lengthy legal memorandum or at least a complaint, but instead I find two short documents. The first is a pro forma summons, literally a fill-in-the-blank kind of form, demanding that Christopher Latham Rigsdale III and Donovan Gallo-Rigsdale appear at New York County Family Court on a date in September that is approximately three weeks from today. I flip to the second document, which bears the title "PETITION FOR CUSTODY" in big, shouty capitals, as if the simple fact of this document is not terrorizing enough. I read quickly through the paragraphs, most of which also seem to be written in stock language for filings like this, talking about "Petitioners this" and "Respondents that," but mainly making clear that Petitioners want to wrench custody of Kai away from Respondents, post-haste.

I scan the paper quickly, taking in where they've entered names, the relief they are seeking, and so on, until I reach the paragraph numbered 13. The document asks the person filling it out to complete a statement: *It would be in the best interest of the child for the Petitioners to have custody for the following reasons*, the form states, and then it leaves a blank space. The Wingates—or, more likely, their lawyer—filled in a list of seven answers.

1. *Petitioners are the child's biological parents;*
2. *Petitioners reside with the child's biological sibling;*
3. *Custody was granted to Respondents under erroneous information;*
4. *Due to the surrogacy arrangement and fertility interventions, Petitioners were unaware this child was their biological offspring;*
5. *Petitioners believe child will thrive more in traditional family setting with parents to whom he is biologically related than with two men to whom he bears no genetic relationship.*

I gasp as I read number five. For some reason, I didn't imagine Maggie and Nick would bring up our sexuality. I mean, that's dirty pool. Our orientation didn't matter to her when we entered into the surrogacy contract eleven years ago. Though it did matter to Nick, I remind myself, remembering their long-ago breakup. How foolish of me to believe that people could truly evolve. I brace myself for the remaining two points:

6. *Petitioners believe the child would flourish in a suburban environment instead of a crowded city;*

7. *Petitioner Margaret Wingate is a trained educator who possesses the necessary expertise for rehoming the minor child and orienting him to the painful reality of his biological history.*

I shove the papers back inside the ripped envelope and rest my head back against the wall. *Orienting him. Yeah, I'd like to orient her about the real meaning of family.* My chest begins to feel tight as I realize that a judge, someone who doesn't know any of us from Adam, might consider these reasons compelling, might truly grant custody to the Wingates. I close my eyes and follow the breathing exercises that I learned as a teenager, a tactic I've resorted to with increasing frequency lately.

As I take in a deep breath and hold it, I shock myself by wondering if we're in the wrong here. Have we really and truly stolen a child who doesn't belong to us?

Chapter 27

MAGGIE
SEPTEMBER 2018

Nick and I are sitting at the kitchen table brainstorming all the ways in which our home would be a better environment than the Rigsdales' city apartment for Kai to finish out the remaining portion of his childhood. After the petition for custody was served, we were given an appearance date, an actual time and day when we will stand in front of a New York City Family Court judge to plead for custody of our son. Our lawyer says this hearing will just be pro forma, a prerequisite to setting the actual trial date, but you never know what might come up at this first hearing. Chip and Donovan will obviously attempt to refute each of the claims we proffered in the initial petition, so our lawyer wants us to stockpile additional arguments to have on deck. The more ways we can show that we would out-parent the Rigsdales, the better.

The sky has begun to darken outside the kitchen windows, and I know that any minute, Nick will declare his intention to return to the restaurant. I'm about to flip the page on the yellow notepad, hoping to eke out one or two last ideas before he goes, but then he releases another deep sigh. It's the third one in an hour.

"What?" I finally ask as I try, but fail, to read the meaning behind the pinched lines on his face. "What are you not saying?"

He drops his pen onto the table and leans back in his chair to stretch. His gray T-shirt pulls taut across his chest as he interlocks his fingers and extends his arms behind his head. He's quiet for a moment as he straightens and looks down at our notes about our flexible work hours, our large yard, the fresh mountain air we breathe here, information about Kai's religious heritage, his older brother, his grandparents, and more. There is a shadow of stubble along Nick's chin that has returned since the morning, but I don't point out that he's running low on time to shave before returning to work.

"I'm starting to second-guess this again," he says, motioning to the notebook. His eyes meet mine and then shift to the ceiling, as if he's looking for answers up there among the high-hats, seeking out any opinions other than mine.

"What do you mean?" I'm cautious, hoping he's focused on a micro issue. "Something on the list?"

He's quiet, his eyes still focused on the paper in front of us. His reluctance is telling me everything I need to know.

"Or do you mean attempting to get custody at all?"

He's so slow to react that I begin to feel like we're on a long-distance call and there's a delay each time I speak before he hears me.

"The second thing," he finally says, his lips tightening in defiance.

I'm immediately livid. Now? After two weeks of prepping, after telling our parents, our son, that we are going after Kai, that we're going to bring him into our family and get him back where he belongs—*now* he's having second thoughts?

"I think it's a little late for that." I'm careful to keep my tone measured, not to explode and prove to Nick yet again that I too often lead with emotion over logic, even though the man is damn near killing me at the moment.

He's watching me, waiting for the inevitable outburst. I can see preemptive agitation written in the upward protrusion of his chin, like he's ready to take whatever I've got. I shove my hands into the pockets of my denim shorts so he won't see the fists I'm making, the nails digging little half-moons into my palms. I don't want to admit that I've been having thoughts similar to his, wondering what is best for Kai, for Wyatt, for our marriage. But even with my doubts, I keep arriving at the same conclusion.

"We've already set everything in motion," I continue, still using my indoor voice. "Filing with the court, telling the Rigsdales. Look, everyone is already miserable about this on both sides. We're not saving anyone grief by backing out at this point. I mean, not Kai. What message would that send to him, that his birth parents wanted him back, but actually not that badly?"

Nick blinks a couple of times at that, a slight acknowledgment that maybe I've made a fair point, that it might be more hurtful to Kai if we stopped fighting for him at this stage of the proceedings.

"We could throw the case," he offers. "Like a sports game. Lose on purpose."

The ridiculousness of his words set off an intense visceral reaction in my gut. Suddenly, I can't take the sight of his face, like I literally might vomit if I have to look into his questioning eyes for one second longer. I toss my pen onto the table, beeline toward the back door, slide it open, and storm into the night.

The fresh air quells the nausea, but not the anger, the disgust. I stand in the backyard with my hands on my hips, glad that Nick hasn't followed me, and I stare up at the Sedona sky. Even though there is still a hint of light in the atmosphere, the stars are plain to see. It's a whole different sky than what I grew up with in Manhattan—another reminder that I'm so many miles away from home, from my dad and Tess.

I can just make out the constellation Lyra above me; its brightest star, Vega, catches my attention. Wyatt once learned in school that the Earth wobbles on its axis, and the direction that was north thousands of years ago is no longer north today. That star, Vega, used to be the North Star, and apparently, as the wobbling continues, in many thousands of years, Vega will eventually be the North Star again. Wyatt kept mentioning this fact long after they finished the astronomy unit in school, fascinated by the idea that there could be a new North Star, a different beacon to follow.

A thought ripples through my mind, something that's been subtly niggling at me for days already. I take a deep breath and walk back into the kitchen. Nick is still sitting where I left him, watching me.

"Maybe we should move to New York," I declare.

"What?" His mouth remains slightly agape as he tries to grasp the many implications of my statement.

"Come on, Nick. Keep up, here." I snap my fingers like I'm trying to wake him.

"We can't just move to New York," he scoffs. "And what, you'd want to withdraw the custody petition then?"

"No." I'm not entirely sure what my plan would be. "But I think it would strengthen our case, showing how much we're willing to do for Kai. And he'd probably be more comfortable coming to live with us if it didn't also entail being shipped across the country. He could see Chip and Donovan whenever he wanted. We've both said we don't want to cut them out. So."

Nick is silent, his lips now pursed in thought as he processes my statement, probably parsing through the different possibilities—what would happen to his job, to Wyatt. My thoughts follow the same path.

"No," I say before he speaks. I've changed my mind already. Just like my mother, it seems I'm chock full of big ideas that I have no intention of carrying out. "I think it'd be too much for Wyatt. Getting a new brother and also having to relocate all at once? Definitely too much. Forget that suggestion." I walk back to my chair and slump down. "I could never live in that city again, either." I don't want to admit to Nick that I'm grasping at straws, that I'm so far out of my depth. Whether I meant to or not, I gave Kai up. It's my fault. So, is it fair now if I just rip him away from everything he's known, from the men he thought were his fathers, from Teddy, who isn't even the half-brother he's always believed him to be? But even with all my questions, I just can't shake the feeling that Kai belongs with us, with his real parents and his real brother, under the beautiful, starry, Arizona sky.

"Maybe there's some reason it's been just us three?" Nick asks, and I can hear the wistfulness in his voice. "Maybe we just weren't meant to have another child. Certainly not like this."

"You really want to back out? To let it go, like this was some inane idea we dallied with and now we should move on to something else? Nick. He's our son."

"I know." His voice is stronger now, his own anger rising. "Which is why I think we have to make the choice that's best for him. You just said you wouldn't do it to Wyatt, that moving to New York and adjusting to a new brother would be too much—but you'll do it to Kai? We have to put *him* first, too, before our own wants and needs."

"That *is* what we're doing!" My voice is growing louder too, shrill and incensed. "He's not some toy, some pet that I want to add to our collection. Is that what you think of me?"

"Jesus, Maggie. For once, just once, can you realize that not every goddamned thing is about you?" He pushes back from the table and walks off toward our bedroom, leaving me alone with my anger.

Of course this isn't about me. Is it? I mean, it's about all of us, isn't it? As I try to contain the rage inside me, the boiling anger I feel toward Nick, I wonder if he's right, if I should simply be thankful for the family we've created and let Kai remain where he is. But then I think of Kai—what he might feel knowing that I didn't fight for him, that just I let him go.

All I know for certain is that the air in the kitchen feels easier to breathe without my husband in it. I hear him coming back toward the front door, and I don't turn to watch him as he leaves the house for his evening shift.

As I stare down at the notes on the yellow pad in front of me, my thoughts drift to the pet my family had when I was a kid, a yappy little terrier named Penchant who lived to be nearly fourteen years old. We called her Penny. An older couple from three floors up used to watch her for us whenever our family traveled. I always worried when Penny went to stay with that couple—Gloria and her husband, whose name I can't recall— because I was afraid the dog wouldn't know which home was temporary and which people were her "real" family. If she lived with Gloria for a week while we were in the Bahamas, how did she know it wasn't we who were the babysitters watching her only temporarily, that she wasn't just waiting for Gloria and the husband to get home so she could go back to her real life? My dad used to tell me that Penny would just know—that dogs know their family, no matter the vacations their owners take. I chose to believe him back then because I liked his version of the truth better than the possibility that we didn't mean any more to Penny than our upstairs neighbors, whom she only saw a couple of weeks a year.

I wonder if the same logic could apply to Kai—that he will just know where he belongs, that he might feel something different because we are his real parents, his real family. Like there's some sort of sixth sense for genetic bonding.

As I continue to mull this over, I hear Wyatt's key in the door. I glance toward the clock on the microwave and see that it's 9:58, meaning he's made it home just in time for curfew.

"Cutting it close tonight," I say lightly as I walk into the foyer to meet him.

He stands on the terracotta floor in his cargo shorts and an untucked button-down shirt, the sleeves rolled up to the elbows. I can't help but admire how handsome he looks when he upgrades from his usual athletic attire. I would tell him so, but he's been giving me attitude for days, so I hold my tongue.

"Yeah, but I'm still on time." He puts his key back in his pocket. "I'm tired." He looks toward his bedroom, seemingly unsure whether he's free to go. He meets my eyes with that same unreadable expression he's been wearing since we got back from New York.

"What?" I ask him, tired of his reticence. "What is it?"

He shakes his head. "Nothing."

"How was Chester's?" I ask, trying to engage him, to ferret out the issue we are having—or rather, the issue he is having with me.

"Fine." He adds a half shrug. "Summer's not mad at me anymore." His phone buzzes with a notification in his shorts pocket, but he ignores it.

"That's good." I nod, relieved that Nick's meddling won't have long-term side effects for Wyatt's relationship with Summer. "So . . . you want to tell me what's on your mind, then?"

He walks past me back toward the kitchen and goes to the cabinet for a juice glass. I can't see his face, but I can tell that he's deciding whether he wants to share anything with me. He fills his cup with water from the sink as I wait, and then turns to face me.

"Summer forgave me because she likes Bennet, and she wanted me to talk to him for her." As he looks at me from across the kitchen, there's a pleading look in his eyes, as though there is something I can do to redirect Summer's affections. He's never confessed his crush on her, but he seems more in need of comfort than privacy at this moment, so I assume we are taking the infatuation as a given from here on out.

"What'd you say?" I ask.

"What could I say? I talked to him, and then he asked her to the movies for next weekend."

"Well, then, you're a good friend to her, and maybe she'll eventually realize that you could be more."

He looks unconvinced.

"In the meantime," I say, squeezing past him to access the freezer, "a snack." I pull out a large container of chocolate chip ice cream and glance back at him. When he nods, I collect a few more supplies—a bottle of whipped cream, rainbow sprinkles, bowls, and spoons.

"You know what my friends and I used to do when boys got us down? This." I open my mouth and spray the Reddi-wip directly onto my tongue while Wyatt looks at me in disbelief.

"Now you." I move toward him with the can. He laughs and opens his mouth, which I promptly begin filling to the brim with clouds of whipped cream, keeping at it until he starts waving a hand like a white flag.

He swallows a couple of times and smiles. "That is so wrong." He laughs as he wipes his mouth with the back of his hand. "Again." He opens his mouth up to me like a baby bird.

This time, instead of spraying the Reddi-wip into his mouth, I intentionally spray the whipped cream directly onto his nose.

"Hey!" he protests, wiping at the white fluff. He looks down at his hand to see what he's collected and then rubs a big glob right onto my cheek with whoop of victory. "Ha!"

"You are dead meat, Wyatt Wingate." I smile and step toward him, the can poised in the air.

"Don't shoot." He raises his hands in mock surrender and steps back, a sheepish smile on his face.

I lower the whipped cream. "You're lucky you're cute," I tell him as I grab a paper towel and wipe my cheek

———————

After assembling our sundaes, we drop down on the sofa in the family room and turn on an old Jim Carrey movie. I watch Wyatt laughing over and again at the slapstick humor. Instead of giving myself a pat on the back for knowing exactly how to cheer up my lovelorn son, my mind shifts again to Kai, and to Nick's doubts about taking him away from Chip and Donovan. If Kai came home upset, pining over a girl or a tough day at school, would I know what to do to put a smile back on his face? For a moment, I think that Nick might be right, that Kai should stay with his adoptive fathers, but then Wyatt laughs again, and when I look at him, I see all the parts of his face that resemble Kai, who is just as much my son as Wyatt is.

In spite of everything, I want to bring my child home to his family. This is where he belongs.

Chapter 28

DONOVAN
SEPTEMBER 2018

"Let's look at this logically," Lorraine is saying. We've been sitting in her office on the thirty-second floor of a Midtown skyscraper for the past ninety minutes, prepping for our court appearance on Monday and running through a host of possible scenarios. Lorraine insists that the initial hearing will be administrative only. We'll show up, and the judge will assign us a trial date. The court will likely appoint a lawyer for Kai as well.

Thankfully, he doesn't have to be present at the first appearance. He's struggling enough already just coming to grips with the fact that he's not genetically related to any of us. We haven't told him yet that his birth parents are trying to take him away from us completely. Even though we won't participate in substantive arguments in court next week, all three of us—Chip, Lorraine the Lawyer, and I—will feel better if we've hashed out various possibilities, and the main points to be argued at trial, in advance.

"Obviously we need to list a host of reasons why Kai's continued residency in his current home is in his best interest," Lorraine says, "but we also need to anticipate the other side's arguments so that we can be prepared to rebut them."

Lorraine has already informed us of various factors the court will consider in its examination of this case. There is the age of the parents, which is basically a wash, as there are only a few years' difference between us and the Wingates. Other considerations could include family finances, the overall home environment, the mental and emotional stability of potential guardians, existing custodial arrangements, siblings, religion, substance abuse, availability of the parents, and preferences of the child.

Lorraine explained that guardianship cases are different than most court cases because when the question is custody, the judge has to use the evidence to make guesses about the future. So instead of looking backward, like most other cases do, where the judge or jury tries to determine what actually happened in a given scenario—like, did the defendant really steal the bread, or was it Mrs. Peacock with the lead pipe?—in custody cases, the court has to try to predict what will happen going forward. There's never been a case exactly like ours, so the best we can do is try to find situations that are somewhat parallel and then draw comparisons. For example, we've been looking at cases where children were placed with adoptive families and then, several years later, the birth parents wanted their biological child returned to them and filed for custody.

Chip starts reiterating all the grounds we've listed already to attest that Kai is living in a stable home.

"Look," Lorraine interrupts him. She puts her palms flat against the small conference table where the three of us are sitting and leans forward like she's got a secret. "Courts generally don't like to undo adoption agreements years after the fact unless one of the birth parents didn't receive notice of the adoption or there's been an error of fact or law."

"But there was clearly an error of fact in this case." My words come out in near-falsetto as my panic rises.

"Right." Lorraine looks down at the pile of papers in front of her, searching for something, and I notice that her russet curls are greying at the roots. "But the court will still look at the best interests of the child before making any changes to his guardianship. Plus, aha!" She holds up the paper she'd been digging for. "The keystone. The California pre-birth order."

She's referring to the document we obtained prior to the boys' birth, when Maggie was living in LA. Thanks to the generous surrogacy laws in California, we were able to obtain a court order before the boys were even born stating that, pursuant to our gestational surrogacy arrangement, both Chip and I would be listed as the parents of record on the babies' birth certificates from the time of birth, rather than having to amend the birth certificate at a later time.

"But New York doesn't recognize surrogacy contracts, so doesn't that negate the impact of the pre-birth order?" Chip asks as his eyes roam over the paper Lorraine is holding.

"Nope." She says it triumphantly, and I feel a flicker of hope. "There was a case. A gay couple that had twins in 2001. Like you, they obtained a pre-birth order from California listing them each as the parents. In 2010, after the couple split up, they got involved in a dispute over child support, and Dad Number Two sought to escape support obligations by challenging the validity of the California parentage ruling. The court said that the Full Faith and Credit Clause of the Constitution trumps New York's surrogacy ban and that the California order would stand. See, here it is." She hands a printout to Chip. "The case of D.P. versus R.M."

I cringe hearing another one of these family court cases designated by the parties' initials only, protecting their identities because something about all this family drama is considered shameful. I never want Kai, or Teddy, for that matter, to feel embarrassed about their family structure or the conflicts that have arisen in this situation.

"Still, isn't there some validity to the 'error of fact' argument?" I push. "I mean, Maggie didn't know she and the baby were biologically related when she agreed to issuance of the birth order. That's got to sway a judge, no?"

Lorraine shimmies the pen she's holding between her thumb and index finger back and forth as she considers my question. "If they take that argument seriously, our response is that by entering into the surrogacy arrangement, Maggie Wingate assumed the risk. Clearly, surrogacy is still an evolving field, and there was no guarantee that some sort of medical error wouldn't be made. Additionally, there were any number of safeguards she could have put in place to ensure this didn't happen, and by failing to do so, she relinquished her rights to seek custody a decade after the fact. She could have tested the babies' DNA at the time of birth, or even in utero through amniocentesis. Or she simply could have kept her legs crossed for the duration of the pregnancy."

I find myself nodding along with Lorraine the Lawyer. The points she is making seem logical, and maybe even persuasive.

"So, let's get back to the best interests of the child, shall we?" She pulls her laptop closer and positions her hands, poised to type.

As Chip tells her about the state of our finances, my mind drifts back to what happened last night. We were sitting at the kitchen table, eating takeout with the boys, when Kai started up again about computers. He and Teddy are both still navigating several of the logistical adjustments attendant to becoming middle schoolers, and the big topic at dinner was how so many kids at school are now using laptops instead of paper and notebooks in class.

"I just don't understand how that's productive," I said. "Isn't everyone going to just tune out and surf the internet?"

"You can't do that," Kai argued, maintaining his position as the leader of the crusade for two new laptops in the house. "The teachers walk around the room so they can see what's on all the open screens." His comment reminded me of the way classmates in my architecture program would play solitaire and

Tetris on their laptops until someone inevitably got busted by an instructor. I always credited my pen-and-paper approach with my higher class ranking throughout grad school.

"Why don't you guys focus on getting used to middle school for the time being, and we can revisit this discussion in seventh grade," Chip offered as he lifted another chunk of ahi tuna from his poke bowl.

"That's so unfair," Teddy piped up. "Everyone else has them. Aiden just got one today."

"Yeah, but Aiden's parents buy him whatever he wants ever since they got divorced," Kai said. "It's, like, gifts for messing up his life or whatever."

"Maybe you should ask Maggie Wingate," Teddy said, brightening up at his new idea. "Maybe she'd get them for both of us out of guilt for messing up *our* lives."

"Messing up your lives?" I echoed. "What's messed up with your lives?"

"Well, she does sort of owe us because she made us think we were brothers, and since it turns out we're not, maybe she needs to make it up to us," Teddy postured. When he looked next to him and saw Kai's stricken expression, his smile disappeared. "Not that we're not brothers now," he hedged, his usual sensitivity to his brother's feelings arriving on a delay. "It's just that we had to do all the work ourselves instead of just relying on our genes, like other people can. So . . . laptop from Maggie?" He raised his eyes hopefully at the rest of us.

Whatever tension had started to build in Kai was apparently alleviated by the latter half of Teddy's argument. He started nodding along.

"Maggie did say if I ever needed anything, I should call her."

"You don't *need* a laptop!" I bellowed, surrendering to my rage and shocking us all into silence.

Kai didn't know that Chip and I would be spending the morning with Lorraine, dealing with Maggie and Nick's decision to seek full custody. He didn't know that they're trying to snatch him from us and drop him into a whole new life.

As I sit in Lorraine's office now, remembering my reaction, I think back to all the years I regarded Maggie as a godsend. I wish I could send a letter to *that* Maggie, the one who called us each week when she was pregnant to tell us about every last kick and punch from the babies. That woman would never want to cause the kind of stress and anxiety that's now rippling through my family, unsettling everyone—us, the boys, their grandparents, their cousins, my sister. This isn't just about the parents and the child. We've built a whole, large life for Kai over the last decade.

"Now let's talk about witnesses," Lorraine is saying. "Other family members, parents of Kai's friends who can attest to the positive impacts of the home environment, perhaps a teacher or coach?" She looks at us hopefully.

I run a mental tally through the many family members and friends I'm sure would be more than happy to testify on our behalf.

"Yeah, sure, that's no problem, but what about us being gay? Isn't that a big issue?"

"Yes and no." She closes her laptop. "A judge is not permitted to consider your sexual orientation in a custody case. Plus, modern families are old news, especially in New York. That said, there's nothing we can do about unconscious bias."

"So, we're just at the mercy of the judge's emotional response to our lifestyle choices?" Chip asks.

"Not entirely. If you present the more compelling case as to why you're providing Kai with a better home environment overall, even a bigoted judge might see past his personal prejudices. The laws are clear."

Might. I let that word settle into me, and suddenly I know we are going to lose. Maggie and Nick are the birth parents. They never intended to give up their biological child. Kai has a natural sibling and a traditional, intact family ready to take him back. What judge would say no to that?

Lorraine must see something on my face, because she leans across the table and covers my hand with her own. "Look," she says softly, "one thing at a time. First, we respond to the petition. We'll go to the initial appearance, see who our judge is. Maybe we'll get a nice young man who's a father himself and an adamant champion of LGBQT rights. There's no reason to panic, not yet."

Chapter 29

MAGGIE
SEPTEMBER 2018

*W*hen I emerge from Penn Station into the bright sunshine and the swell of the Manhattan streets, I still have two hours to squander before lunch. The midmorning air is so warm and humid that I feel like I'm walking through a swamp. On impulse, I head toward the air conditioning of Macy's flagship store, a behemoth retail establishment that attracts tourists from around the world, and which was once a favorite shopping destination of my mother's.

The doors have only just opened for the day, and the store has yet to fill with the sort of crowds I remember. I wander past the makeup counters and perfume sellers who are dabbing fresh scents onto paper samples to hand to passing customers. It occurs to me that I could pick up a couple of things for my dad, like my mom would have done. Or some souvenirs to bring home for Wyatt. Instead, I ride the escalator toward the higher floors, stepping on and then off at each landing until I reach the fifth floor, where I make my way toward ladies' dresses. I packed a long, floral skirt to wear to court, hoping to project my most wholesome, upstanding schoolteacher/mom vibe, but now I wonder if I would do better in something more serious or sophisticated. I'm not sure which look would encourage a judge to favor us over the Rigsdales. Logically, I understand that a judge shouldn't be making decisions based on my fashion sense, but emotionally, I feel desperate to get this all completely right.

I make my way past sparkly party frocks and sales racks full of flouncy, patterned beach rompers until I reach an area that looks like workwear. The dresses here are serious, sharp. These are dresses with agendas. My eyes land on a cobalt blue fitted sheath. The design is bold and unapologetic. I lift the hanger and picture the thick fabric of the dress hugging my curves and making me brave.

A saleswoman appears and helps me to a fitting room. As she hangs the dress on the back of the door, she asks where I'm visiting from. I'm about to answer that I'm not a tourist, that this is my hometown, but then I'm jolted by the realization that I don't actually consider myself much of a New Yorker anymore. The sense of attachment I feel to Arizona is something I never experienced living here. I offer her a few details about the wonders of Sedona before she goes, and then I take a seat on the fabric-covered bench behind me to rummage in my tote for my phone.

Tiffany Thompson picks up after two rings.

"Hey," she says, sounding slightly out of breath. "The boys just left."

I glance down at my watch and adjust for the time difference. It's only 7:20 a.m. in Sedona.

"Oh. I thought I'd just check in, but . . ." I feel a need to apologize. It's the first time we've left Wyatt like this to go out of town. We didn't want him missing school, and he swore that he'd be fine staying with his friend Chester's family. Chester's mom, Tiffany, works as a concierge at the biggest resort in town, so she's particularly comfortable with company coming and going.

"We're all good over here," she says. "Don't you worry. You just enjoy your time with Nick's folks, and we'll see you when you're back." We haven't told her the true reason we're in New York. "You could try his cell," she adds, "but I'd let him just get on and start his day. There's nothing he needs you for."

"Oh. Right. Okay. Okay, good." I thank her again and end the call.

The dress stares back at me from the hanger, and I'm suddenly too weary to try it on, to put in the effort required for curating my best self. Tiffany's comments have my mind on overdrive. Do I need Wyatt more than he needs me? Does Kai need me at all?

As I leave the store and wander down Seventh Avenue, I wonder if it's always the parents who need their children more than vice versa, if parenting is a more selfish endeavor than any of us really let on. I pull my phone from bag again, and this time, I dial my dad.

———

Twenty minutes later, I walk into the Starbucks near my parents' apartment to find my father standing at the counter, collecting two blended drinks from the barista.

"Just in time," he says. He hands me an icy Frappucino, then leans in for a quick peck on the cheek.

He looks different from when I saw him just a few weeks ago. His weathered skin is tan, and his thick white hair seems recently cut. The cornflower blue golf shirt he's wearing is tucked neatly into a pair of navy-blue Bermuda shorts.

"Walk and talk?" He looks toward the street.

"Really?" I grimace at the idea of returning to the muggy streets.

"I have to do my steps." He taps the digital watch on his wrist. "Ten thousand a day doesn't just happen."

I roll my eyes and motion for him to lead the way.

As we walk out and head toward Seventy-Eighth Street, I find myself heartened to be with my dad, nostalgic, and delightfully needy. A child who still needs her parent, even as an adult.

"You look good," I tell him. "I was a little worried last time we were here."

He furrows his brow as we both step around a UPS delivery man and the large stack of boxes he's creating on a dolly on the sidewalk. The man is scanning each box with a handheld device and doesn't look up as we pass.

"You seemed . . ." I don't want to tell him that he had appeared suddenly so much older, lonely, abandoned. "Tired?"

He lets out a small chuckle and takes a sip from his green straw.

"What?"

He gives me a sheepish look before stepping into the crosswalk and waiting for me to follow him across Second Avenue. "Dare I admit that I might have been hung over?"

"Hung over?" There are many names I might have called Gail and Leon Fisher over the years, but "drunks" was never one of them.

"I've gotten into this card game," he starts to explain, "with Paul Witzler and Jerry Stein. A few other guys. Poker."

I stop walking and turn to face him head-on. "Poker?" My head tilts as I say it.

He points again to the step counter on his wrist and turns back toward First Avenue. "Let's make that traffic light." I know that when we reach First Avenue, we'll turn left and continue north toward Carl Schurz Park. This walk, at least, is familiar to me.

"Look," my dad says with a long sigh as he tosses his empty cup into a metal trash basket and continues walking. "Ever since your mother . . . Well, as much as I miss her, all that time taking care of someone—it was an eternity sometimes. And now that I don't have the responsibility, I like to blow off steam now and again."

"All that time?" I bristle. "Relative to most cancers, I think hers moved pretty quick, Dad."

"Not the cancer. No, of course that was too fast. Way too fast. I meant the manic depression." He stops at the corner of Eighty-First Street as the light changes and traffic moves into our path.

"The . . ." My voice seems to stall, and then it fails me completely as a window begins to open in my brain. The window becomes a door, then a long hallway that continues into an enormous stadium, an arena, filled with evidence to support what my father has just said. I grab on to my father's forearm as I process his words. It's something that's so incredibly obvious yet has never, not once, crossed my mind.

A small crowd of pedestrians is building around us as we all wait for the light to change. People are making their way about their daily business. Heading out for midday appointments, a bite to eat.

My father studies me for a moment and then a look of surprise flashes across his features.

"You didn't know?" He sounds stunned.

"Know?" My voice is rising. "How would I know?"

The traffic light changes but we stay where we are.

"The mood swings," he says. "The highs, the way she'd keep you up into the middle of the night baking batch after batch of cupcakes for a bake sale or when she'd start reorganizing the living room at four in the morning?"

"I was a child! I was supposed to start making a clinical diagnosis?"

"Not then. But you're not a child now—haven't been one for years. I assumed you'd have figured it out."

"Was she on medication?"

"Sometimes." He nods. "A lot of the time." He starts walking again, and I follow.

"Does Tess know?" I ask, even though I'm sure she must.

"Your mother loved you girls more than anything. If she made any mistakes, it was only in loving you too hard sometimes. You don't need to hash it out with Tess. There's nothing your mother would hate more than the two of you sitting around dissecting her mental fragility. Anyhow." He says this last word like a punctuation mark, a signal that we, too, are finished discussing my mom's mental health.

We continue toward the park in silence, and I'm grateful for a moment to digest the information he's shared with me. I'm not sure whether I feel increased responsibility for the strife in our relationship, for my lack of understanding of her illness, or outrage that I was kept in the dark for so long.

After my father and I say good-bye, I realize that if I don't hurry, I'm going to be late to meet my sister for lunch. At least the cab I land in for the journey back to Midtown is air-conditioned.

When I arrive at the restaurant, it takes a moment for my eyes to adjust to the dim lighting. Tess is waiting at the bar, her attention focused on the viewing screen of her small digital camera. She's wearing a bone-colored pencil skirt and a matching short-sleeved blouse. Her blond hair is loose and youthful, and it falls over the camera as she studies the screen. Even with all the hours she spends at her desk doing lawyerly things, she can't seem to surrender her passion for photography. I keep encouraging her to participate in a couple of exhibitions, or even to try selling her work online, but she's happy just to look at the beautiful photos and know that she was responsible for creating them. At least, that's what she claims.

"That's stunning," I say, looking over her shoulder at the black-and-white photo of large male hands covered in some sort of chalk or powder, maybe a gymnast or some other athlete preparing.

"You're here!" she exclaims with typical Tess exuberance as

she half-stands and extends her long arms, beckoning me for a hug. I breathe in her familiar flowery scent and squeeze tightly, letting my big sister hold me up for just a moment before I let go.

I'm bursting to discuss the conversation with my father, but in a rare effort to respect my mother, I hold my tongue.

Once we're settled in a booth, I ask about the photo Tess was studying.

"Oh, it's an old one. I took it just a few minutes before I met Isaac for the first time, actually," she says wistfully, referring to her biomedical engineer husband of the past fourteen months.

I'm jealous of the way she says this, how her eyes get all big and dreamy at the mention of Isaac's name. He has Tess totally smitten. Maybe it's the fact that she was the last one in her group of friends to get married, so he became all the more valuable to her, or maybe being soul mates is sometimes a real thing. I try not to roll my eyes at the thought. Either way, she won't credit a bad word about him. As I think back, I can't remember if I ever felt so positively about Nick, if he ever made my face go all pink and moony like hers is right now.

"I was just killing time because my client meeting ended earlier than I expected. Can you please update me, though? Are you ready for tomorrow?"

"Tom's been very patient with us," I tell her, referring to the lawyer she found for us. "He thinks we have a legit shot of winning this. I don't know, I'm less confident." I open the menu and start scanning the choices, feeling uncomfortable for reasons I can't quite articulate.

"What is it?" Tess asks, and her perceptiveness annoys me.

"What? Nothing." I motion to her menu with my eyes. "What are you going to get?"

"Maggie." She waits. It's just like our mom used to do.

"What? Stop it."

She raises her eyebrows at me, and I know she's not going to let me off the hook until I open up.

"Nick wants to drop the case," I finally confess.

She gasps slightly and then releases her breath in a loud sigh.

"I'm not sure what this case is going to do to our marriage," I add.

"Is there ever a moment where you and Nick actually want the same thing?" she asks.

I know where this is going. It's not the first time we've had one of these conversations.

"I'm not divorcing him," I say, exasperated, trying to get to the end of where these discussions always land. We've skipped the in-between, where I tell her all the things Nick does wrong, but then I defend him and the life we've built together. Then she tells me how I deserve more.

"You could be so much happier," she says, but I already hear the defeat in her voice. She knows that she is not winning this debate.

"You used to be Nick's biggest cheerleader," I remind her, thinking of how she lobbied in his favor after I moved to LA on my own so many years ago, when I tried to leave him.

"Because I knew you loved him back then. Now . . ." She studies my face for a moment. "I'm just not so sure anymore."

I let out a deep breath before I answer. "Look, I won't say I haven't been thinking about it," I admit. "But I've come to the conclusion that I just don't want to be a divorced person, and I don't want Wyatt to suffer through whatever fallout it would create." She opens her mouth to say something, but I continue. "This one custody battle is enough. I don't want to get involved in custody questions about Wyatt, too, the whole 'weekends and every other Wednesday' thing. I'd rather just stay in my mediocre marriage and have an intact family, keep raising Wyatt as we are, socializing with other couples. Unraveling the whole thing just seems like more trouble than it's worth. My marriage doesn't have to be my main priority. Wyatt's good, I love what I do for a living, and things with Nick are fine. Sometimes it's even affirmatively good with him, like really good. But when it's not, well, fine is good enough for me. It's fine. It's all fine."

The waitress arrives to take our order, and I'm saved from whatever response was waiting on Tess's lips. As soon as she's gone, I steer us back toward the topic of Kai.

"Anyway, I think Nick is just nervous about losing."

Tess nods, her eyes shifting to the side a little, like she's thinking, strategizing. "You should start figuring out who's going to testify on your behalf at the hearing. Besides me, obviously." She smiles. "I wonder if you'll also want the doctors from the fertility clinic, and that surrogacy matchmaker you used, just to show what your original intention was here."

I shake my head. "Tom said the other side would probably stipulate that we all thought both babies were genetically linked to the Rigsdales. The real issue now is just what's best for Kai going forward."

"And you think that what's best for him is coming to live in your house with your mediocre marriage?" she asks.

"Now you suddenly think I'm making the wrong choice?"

"No." She shakes her head. "I'm just trying to help you see the big picture here."

"I don't even know what that means."

The waitress is back, sliding our glasses of iced tea into place on the table as Tess and I pause our conversation.

"Look," Tess says when the waitress disappears, "let's not fight. I want what you want, okay? Whatever you want to do, I will support you."

I take the olive branch she's offering, and instead of fighting about Nick, we talk about what it would be like to have two boys in the house, which bedroom would become Kai's, how they'd get along.

I don't tell her that I'm a little overwhelmed by the thought of integrating an additional child into our daily lives, especially one who's already ten years old. I worry that he'll have trouble acclimating, that he won't have the same tastes or hobbies as the rest of us, that his presence will change everything. But I worry more that if we give up on him, we might break his innocent little heart and also my own bigger, bruised one.

As we work our way through our salads, Tess fills me in on the latest with Isaac—recent improvements he's devised for the prosthetic hands he builds day and night in a lab. As cool as it is to hear about technological advancements in the medical field, it's hard for me to get fired up about something that keeps him stuck at work during almost every social event Tess tries to get him to attend. She is so overcome with his genius and doesn't seem to mind, but I mind on her behalf.

"You know," she says, getting suddenly serious, "no one would judge you if you dropped the case."

I pause with my near-empty iced tea halfway to my mouth. "Why would I drop the case? I'm not dropping the case."

"I'm just saying," she offers lightly, like she's pointing out the weather. "Regardless of what I think, or what Nick thinks, or anyone else, you shouldn't feel trapped."

"I don't know why you would say that. I'm not going to abandon him again. Not when it would be intentional this time."

"You're the only one who would see it that way."

I don't answer.

She glances at her watch and pushes her chair back from the table. "I've got to get back. Give Wyatt a hug for me when you get home, okay?"

We both stand and she leans forward to kiss me quickly on the cheek—breezy, like we might see each other again in twenty minutes, when in fact it will likely be several weeks until I'm back in town for the next court appearance.

After I leave the restaurant, I begin to wander on the city streets, aimless except for my reluctance to head back to Jersey, back to Nick. The thought of his clenched jaw and clipped remarks has me turning east again, away from Penn Station. As I make me way over to Lexington, glancing into the various storefronts, I replay Tess's words in my head, her bold assertions that I can just change any of my circumstances at will—my marriage, my pursuit of custody, my satisfaction with my life. Until she has kids of her own, I'm not sure she's qualified to be doling out so much advice.

The mid-afternoon streets are growing increasingly crowded. Teenagers zigzag past me, shouting at each other, their knapsacks flailing behind them. I wander past a few repetitive coffee shops and candy stores, trying to decide how long I can stall, and then I notice a music store across the street that I've never seen before.

The sign over the store reads MAINE STREET MUSIC. Back when I was a kid, I could have located every instrument vendor in Manhattan with my eyes closed. I cross the street and stop outside the shop, studying the window display. There are several instruments visible on a platform behind the glass, arranged for pedestrians to admire as they happen past the store, including one Stratocaster that's the exact same shade of powder blue as the only guitar I've ever owned.

I haven't thought about that guitar in more than a decade, probably longer. After I turned thirteen and celebrated with a big bat mitzvah party, I was allowed to use a small portion of the gift money I received to buy myself one special present, any item of my choosing. My parents made me put the remainder into a savings account, but I was permitted the one indulgence, and what I wanted more than anything was to make music. I found a not-so-gently used Fender down at Sam Ash, its body a shocking icy blue, and I was smitten. My small hands turned out to be a bad fit for guitar playing, however, and it wasn't very long before I sold that guitar back to the store in exchange for my first saxophone.

As I push open the door and step inside the shop, a bell jingles overhead. The store is surprisingly busy, and also larger than it appeared from the outside. Several patrons are milling about in the different areas, sampling instruments and chatting with salespeople.

An older man is standing just inside the door, a ring of keys hanging from his hand. "Let us know if you need any help," he says casually as he rounds a glass display case and unlocks it.

I nod and let my eyes wander over the expanse of the store as the clerk begins arranging microphones in the case. There are several other glass display cases throughout the store, many filled with recording equipment and electronic instrument tuners. A platform running the length of the store displays drum sets of various sizes, their glittering purple and red shells calling to mind rock bands of the 1970s. The other side of the store is dedicated entirely to guitars, the true king of music stores. Various styles of electric and acoustic guitars hang on the wall, amplifiers and other equipment artfully arranged beneath them. There are also cases filled with guitar accessories, wah wah pedals, capos, humidifiers, shoulder strap clips. I keep scanning the store, my eyes moving past the shiny brass section of tubas and trombones, until I find the section for woodwinds.

As I make my way toward the saxophones, past the instrument cases and music stands, I'm filled with such nostalgia that I suddenly can't believe I ran away from it all. I squeeze past a cramped display of baritones and sopranos until I locate an alto sax. My eyes land on a Yamaha. It's brand-spanking-new, not long-used like the only one I was able to afford after my guitar trade-in. I run my hands over the keys, remembering the hours I used to practice, the spittle that dripped from the instrument onto my jeans, baptizing me each day as a musician, a badge of honor, just like the red indentation from the shoulder strap that was a constant presence on my neck. In retrospect, I wonder for a moment if I loved the music or if I was simply delighted that I was good at something, that I possessed a natural skill. I've hardly been pining endlessly for my sax over the years. Maybe if I'd had more time as an adult before becoming a mother, I might have thought to pick one up again. I lift the instrument off its display stand and hold it like I used too. It feels awkward, like I've forgotten the basics.

"Maggie Fisher?"

I look up to see a man in a baseball cap emerging from behind a rotatable rack full of sheet music. He takes the cap off, and I recognize him instantly. Of course. Naturally I would bump into my old music teacher on my very first trip into a music store since the day he derailed my entire musical career.

I notice two things about Trent immediately. He's not nearly as handsome as I remembered him, and he also seems very close to my own age. His light hair is shorter now, cut close to his head, but his wide, angular face is the same. He seems to be aging well, his angled cheekbones still pronounced in a way that makes me think of Johnny Depp. He's wearing small, round spectacles that soften his entire appearance. I had allowed him to achieve some sort of mythic monstrous status in my mind, but seeing him in person again, I remember that he was just a regular guy, someone I even admired.

"Trent." It's all I can think to say.

We stare at each other for a moment—in the way of long-lost friends, I think.

"You're still playing?" He motions with his chin to the saxophone I'm holding.

"Not one note since high school." If the comment sounds pointed, well, good. I place the instrument back on the stand. "I was just walking by, and I don't know. I never saw this store before." I shove my hands into the back pockets of my jeans, trying not to appear as awkward as I feel.

"You're all grown up." It's a little skeevy, the way he says it, and I wonder how he ever made me swoon.

"A married mom and everything." I hope the reference to a husband isn't lost on him.

"Look . . ." His eyes dart around the store and then back to me. "Maybe it's too late to say it, but as long as we've bumped into each other like this . . ." He swallows. "I'm so sorry."

I hold up my hand, trying to stop him. I don't want to go wherever he is trying to take this conversation.

But he's building momentum.

"I never should have changed your schedule after everything that went down. I was trying to do the right thing. I was trying to do what I thought was best for you. Not being one of my students anymore, I thought. I just—I didn't know nearly as much about what you needed as I believed I did back then, and I'm sorry."

I thought he was going to apologize for encouraging my feelings for him, for crossing the line and toying with the emotions of a student when he was in the position of teacher. Instead, he's gone straight to the big picture, and to my surprise, this apology actually matters more.

"It was a long time ago," I answer, glancing behind him at an older couple who are just walking into the store. I'm unwilling to go deeper with him.

He looks like he wants to say something else, but instead he just lets out a long breath and considers me. "I'm glad to see everything's going so well for you. Take care." He walks toward the register with his stack of music booklets.

I watch him for a moment as he pulls his wallet out from the back pocket of his jeans. I'm digging around inside myself, trying to tap into the anger I once felt for him, or to find relief in his apology. Instead, I feel only defeat. I blink hard and then leave the store.

———————

Nick is quietly snoring beside me. It's late, but I can't sleep. I'm wired, thinking about our day in court tomorrow, wondering about everything that could occur. Unlike Tess, who parades around courthouses all the time, I don't think I've ever actually been inside a real courtroom before. I'm basing all my expectations of tomorrow on the scenarios I've seen on television and movie screens. I keep picturing crazy situations arising, like Donovan slapping me across the face or Chip storming out in an angry rage. I don't think they will bring Kai to the hearing. Our attorney explained that there's no need for him to be present, and I'm sure it would only be stressful for him.

After I bumped into Trent, I went directly to Penn Station and hopped onto the next train to Jersey. As I turn onto my side now and push my back up against Nick's for warmth, I gaze toward the window, where a faint sliver of moonlight creeps around the edges of the guest room's gauzy curtains. I wonder if I shouldn't have felt better to hear Trent finally apologize, to know that he wasn't trying to be vindictive when he kicked me out of honors band. Instead, all I keep wondering is, *What good is the apology now?* The decision he made was the catalyst that led me to drop out of school, to waste years of my life trying to find myself, and ultimately to enter into a gestational surrogacy arrangement.

Would it all have happened anyway? Maybe. I was itching to get away from home, to make some sort of point to my parents, to punish them for never understanding who I was or who I wanted to be. Maybe I was being punished by the Universe for never understanding who my parents were—my mom, especially.

I suppose it's nice to know now that Trent thought he was looking out for me. It strikes me as very similar to the way my parents thought they were looking out for me when they cut me off. After I left home and quit school, they didn't chase me down; instead, they gave me the space they thought I needed. What I actually needed was so entirely different. I needed more attention and support. I needed them to stand up and bring me home. But space was all they gave me then, and I ended up losing years with my mother that I can't get back. My heartrate speeds up as the anger—the frustration that I was so woefully misunderstood, to my own detriment, time and again—rises inside me.

With a start, I wonder if I'm doing the same thing to Kai. What if I'm superimposing my own ideas and completely failing to understand what that child needs? I think about the loving home he's grown up in since the day he was born. He's been raised for over a decade alongside a boy he believed to be his brother, and relying for everything on fathers who clearly love him more than words can express. What if trying to do what's best for him isn't the same as *actually* doing what's best for him?

Chapter 30

DONOVAN
SEPTEMBER 2018

As we approach the boxy white exterior of the courthouse, I can't get my emotions in check. I know that this morning is only supposed to be an administrative hearing, but it's also the beginning of so much more. Chip is climbing up the stone steps beside me, and somehow, maybe because it's finally go-time, he seems so much calmer, eerily composed. He's also astonishingly handsome in his crisp dark suit and shiny silver tie, and I'm sorry he's not dressed up for some other, happier, occasion.

Lorraine the Lawyer is waiting for us inside the lobby, standing next to the metal detector with a frustrated expression on her face.

"I missed three calls from Tom Wellan this morning," she says by way of greeting, referring to the Wingates' attorney. "He's not answering now."

Chip and I both speak at once.

"He better not be requesting an adjournment," Chip says.

"This is bad, isn't it?" I ask, but my words are drowned out by Chip's louder ones.

"Well, we'd better just go up and see," she says, motioning us toward the metal detector.

When we get upstairs, we read the signs beside the various courtrooms until we find Room 222a. Just before we push open the doors, I see Maggie and Nick rounding the corner at the far end of the hallway with a portly, middle-aged man who I assume is the illustrious Mr. Wellan.

"They're here," I say quietly, pushing the words out of the corner of my mouth toward Lorraine.

She lets go of the door handle.

"Give me one second." She points us toward a bench on the opposite wall.

After glancing at each other uncertainly, Chip and I do as we're told and settle onto the bench.

When Lorraine reaches the Wingates, she speaks with them in hushed tones. Whatever she says results in Maggie and Nick nodding and turning to walk back the way they came. Nick glances back over his shoulder at Chip and me before they disappear from view.

Lorraine and the other attorney continue to confer as he props his briefcase against his thigh, opens it halfway, and removes a document. When he hands it to her, she scans it, nods, and then points to a part of the paper and asks him something.

"We're just supposed to sit here?" Chip nearly spits.

"Shhh," I warn, afraid to make any of this worse than it already is.

But now Lorraine is walking back toward us, her heels clicking purposefully against the shiny floor.

"They're requesting an adjournment," she says when she reaches us.

Chip shoots out from his seat. "What? No. No way. Why? This has taken long enough already."

I stand too and realize that I'm just as anxious to move forward as Chip is.

"The birth mother is requesting a meeting with the child to see if the matter can be resolved."

"With Kai? Why?" I ask, reluctant as ever to subject Kai to any portion of what's happening here.

"I think this could work in your favor," Lorraine says, glancing back at where she was just speaking with the other attorney. He's no longer there, and I imagine he's gone to find Maggie and Nick. "It sounds as though the birth parents are having second thoughts. Tom didn't spell it out so completely, but he implied that moving forward, the Wingates would like to base their actions on what Kai tells them he wants."

My heart speeds up at the idea that we could get through this case so easily, that a simple meeting with Kai could resolve all of this.

"No," Chip declares. "We've waited long enough. We're not dragging Kai down here and freaking him out just to pick up where we left off, except on a later timeline."

Lorraine holds up a manicured finger. "We can set the meeting for tomorrow morning. I'll suggest we use a conference room at my office. I agree there's no reason to distress Kai by bringing him to family court. I think this is worthwhile, though, Chip. If everything goes well, the matter could be resolved by the end of the day tomorrow."

Chip looks from Lorraine to me, and I nod vigorously.

"We'll be in the room with them, right?" I ask her.

"Well, in this particular instance . . ." she begins slowly, and I know I'm not going to like her answer. "They want to meet with him alone."

"No," Chip says again, and this time I agree with him. Kai does not have the emotional constitution to attend a meeting like this on his own.

"There's an argument that he might feel pressure to adjust his answers to your liking if either of you is in the room with him." She purses her lips as her eyes dart to the side with a new thought. "I can be there, though. I can make it a condition of our acceptance of this proposal—that at least your attorney should be present in the room."

"He's going to be so nervous," I say, looking at Chip. "What will we even tell him is happening?"

We're all quiet for a moment, which Lorraine correctly interprets as cautious acceptance of this development.

"I'll go tell the attorney that we consent to the adjournment, provided that the meeting with Kai occurs tomorrow, at my office, and in my presence."

As she walks away, I turn to Chip. "What will we even tell him?" I ask again, picturing Kai's confusion, his fright, when he realizes that Maggie and Nick want to remove him from our custody.

Chip rubs his hands together slowly, the way he does when he's thinking. "We just tell him that the Wingates would like to get to know him a little better, that Maggie and Nick want to talk with him some more. We'll say that you and I made Maggie nervous, that's why she got weird at the end of their visit to our apartment, so we agreed to wait outside the next time they talk. I don't think we even have to get into the fact of Lorraine being our lawyer or any of that." He shrugs, as though everything he's said is obvious. When I don't respond, he continues, "Look, I know we don't want to upset Kai. He's . . ." He pauses, as if he's struggling with how to craft his thought into words. "I know he takes things to heart. But if a meeting between Maggie, Nick, and Kai is all it will take to resolve this situation, we have to go for it. Kai's going to have to take one for the team on this."

He's right. Of course he is. But my chest tightens as I think of what Kai will feel. I wish I could sit in that meeting for him. I would do any number of highly unpleasant tasks in lieu of sending him into that room on his own tomorrow.

Lorraine is back. "That's it," she says, and motions for us to head back toward the elevators. "Tom's going to call me later to firm up the details on timing and so on, but we will see you in the morning at my office."

"Will there be rules?" I ask. "Things they can and can't ask, so Kai doesn't get upset?"

Chip and Lorraine glance at each other before Lorraine looks back at me and puts a conciliatory hand on my forearm. "I think you have to let them ask their questions. If you really want to get this matter put to bed."

Chip nods, and I know they're probably right.

I don't argue. The goal is to keep our son with our family. This will hardly be the first time I've had to sit on pins and needles waiting to find out if I get to be a dad.

At dinner that night, Chip does as I've asked and tells Kai about the meeting tomorrow. I was worried that if I started the conversation, I'd get awkward, like I do, and it might be a tip-off that the stakes are higher than we're letting on.

"Kai's going to be a little late to school tomorrow," Chip begins, addressing Teddy rather than Kai. He has just enough regret in his voice to create the impression that he's nearly apologizing to Teddy for whatever Kai will get to do.

"Why?" Kai asks, looking up from his baked ziti.

"Maggie and Nick Wingate are in town—"

"No fair," Teddy says. "Can't I go late, too? I have Latin first period." He makes a gagging face.

Chip rolls his eyes good-naturedly at Teddy and continues to explain that Nick and Maggie want to have a conversation with Kai, give him a chance to get to know them, so he can decide if he wants to have a relationship with them going forward. It's not exactly what Chip and I discussed as the cover story, but I suppose it's close enough.

"Okay," Kai says easily. I catch a glint of something in his eye, which I think is excitement at the opportunity to spend time with his birth parents. I try not to feel the sting of that. "Will Wyatt be there?"

"Not this time," I say, "but I'm sure you could ask to see him in the future. If you want."

Kai glances at Teddy. "Maybe," he says noncommittally.

Chip hasn't mentioned anything about us not being in the room when they talk, but maybe that's the right call, downplaying it like this. When we finish dinner, it's Kai's turn to do the dishes, so I follow Teddy back to his room.

"Latin's really not your favorite, huh?" I ask as he sits at his small desk and opens a science textbook.

"I don't understand why they make the whole sixth grade take it," he says. "I mean, when am I ever going to use it? It's not even a real language anymore."

Rather than engage on the topic of useful middle school courses and the importance of word roots in building new vocabulary, I change the subject. "Are you doing okay?" I stare him down a little in an attempt to convey that he can't hide his feelings from me. When he shrugs in response and turns his face toward the homework on his desk, I push. "I'll wait, you know."

"There's more, isn't there?" he asks. "About why Kai has to meet with those people tomorrow morning?"

I can't come clean to Teddy without risking that he'll say something to Kai.

"Not really." I shrug, trying to appear casual, like it's no big deal, like the fate of our family isn't hanging in the balance.

"I wish we never did that Relativity test." He looks at me almost hopefully, like there's anything I could possibly do to make this all go away, to allow us to un-know everything we've learned since taking those DNA tests at the beginning of the summer.

"I know, sweetie. Me, too."

"Not Kai, though," Teddy says.

"What do you mean?" I'm unsure of the point he is making.

"Kai's all excited," he says, "knowing about his birth parents, his *real* brother." He makes little jazz hands, underscoring Kai's excitement, or his own agitation.

"He's allowed to be excited," I say.

"I guess." Teddy shrugs, sounding very far from actual agreement. "He doesn't see any of the bad stuff that could come from this, though. He only sees all the good possibilities."

I should probably ask what Teddy means by "bad stuff," but I'm not sure I have the strength to handle any of the answers right now.

"Well maybe the rest of us should take a lesson from him on that, don't you think?" I ask. "It's nice to see him looking for the positives in a situation, and we should try to do the same." If only I could follow my own advice and see anything other than the potential for disaster.

Chapter 31

MAGGIE
SEPTEMBER 2018

I wish their lawyer didn't have to be in the room. It makes everything about this conversation feel so contrived, the way she's stationed at one end of the lengthy conference table, observing Nick and me, as we sit with Kai at the other. If she's trying to intimidate me with her rigid posture and her crisp black skirt suit, well, it's working.

Nick and I are both dressed more casually because we wanted to come across to Kai as approachable. Nick's in his standard uniform of dark jeans and a solid black T-shirt, and I'm wearing wide-leg linen pants with a fitted white T-shirt. The lawyer's whole ballbuster routine has me so busy wondering if she's making mental notes about everything we're saying and doing wrong—tidbits she'll use against us in court—that I'm having trouble focusing on the conversation with Kai. Luckily, Nick seems to be especially on top of his game today.

Kai just finished telling us about how all the kids in fifth grade had to choose an instrument to play during school last year. Kai chose the trombone, and it was a debacle because he could barely carry the thing. Well, any band teacher worth his or her stripes should have told him to choose an instrument more suited to his smaller size.

Nick chuckles lightly, smooth as ever. "So that's it?" he asks. "Music is over for you?" His cell phone begins ringing, and he reaches a hand into his pocket to silence it.

"Yeah, I guess it's just never been my thing," Kai says as he fiddles with a rope bracelet on his wrist. Wyatt never gravitated toward music either, but for some reason, the lack of musical inclination is more of a disappointment to me coming from Kai. At least I had an opportunity to work with Wyatt, to explain the joy of music from my perspective. Or maybe I'm still looking for evidence of a connection to this boy, some pastime we both enjoy, a link beyond the physical. I open my mouth to ask another question about the trombone, but Nick's already changing the subject.

"What about cooking?" he asks. "Is that something you ever do?"

Kai smiles and nods, his round cheeks pinking up. "Teddy and I bake almost every Saturday night. When our dads go out, Gemma, our babysitter, helps us. We make brownies or cookies for them to have when they get home."

"Lucky guys," Nick says, and he's smiling even with his eyes.

"Do they go out a lot?" I ask, wondering how much time Kai spends with sitters. I glance over at the lawyer as I finish the question, her pen poised in midair.

"Usually only Saturdays," Kai says, "and not if there's something special going on with my brother or me. Teddy," he clarifies before turning his attention back to the worn bracelet on his wrist.

"So, what are some of your favorite things to do together when your dads don't go out?" Nick asks. "Or when you're all together?"

Kai thinks silently for a moment and then perks up. "They took us kayaking on the Hudson River a couple of months ago," he offers with a slight shrug. "That was pretty cool."

"Cool indeed," I say, happy to hear that Kai has the opportunity to enjoy some outdoorsy activities despite being a city kid. "There are some pretty awesome places to go kayaking in Arizona, too, near where we live." I glance at Nick, who smiles back at me as though we're the happiest couple you've ever stumbled upon.

I turn back to Kai, getting excited to tell him more about Sedona, but something in his face has changed, making his features suddenly slack. I can't figure what is causing the sudden fear I see in his eyes, and rather than put him on the spot to question him, I keep talking.

"There are a lot of places to hike out by us, too. People travel to Sedona from all over the world to hike some of the trails our town offers. I don't know if you've heard of the red rocks, but the scenery is just amazing—colors you wouldn't believe unless you saw them with your own eyes."

Kai looks even less relaxed as I ramble on, his eyes darting furiously from side to side, as though he's looking for escape.

"Is something wrong?" I finally ask, realizing how little I know about this boy.

"Teddy said you guys were going to try to make me go live with you. I didn't believe him before." It's an accusation.

"I'm sorry," Lorraine announces from across the table. "We're going to have to change the topic."

Kai looks from Lorraine to us and back to Lorraine again, and his face drains of color.

"It's okay," I say to Kai, "You didn't do anything wrong."

He nods, but his breathing is becoming shallow. He's making these audible huffs that are increasing in speed, as if he's been exerting himself.

"Why don't you tell us about camp?" Nick says, trying to move our conversation back to the easier place it was in before. "Maggie's been working at a summer camp," he says, "so I'm sure she'd love to compare notes with you."

I feel him look over at me, but my attention is still on Kai, who's really starting to huff and puff.

"Kai, do you have asthma?" I ask, my concern growing.

He shakes his head quickly, but he has a frantic look about him.

"Okay—can you slow down, then? Just take a deep breath?" I reach out to touch his leg, but then I think the better of it and draw my hand back before we make contact.

His eyes seem to lose focus as he shakes his head again and pushes his chair out from the table so he can drop his head between his knees.

Now Lorraine is on her feet, and she and I are talking over each other, trying to help Kai.

"Kai, it's all right," she says, rubbing a hand on his back. "Everybody who's here is just looking out for your best interests."

But now Kai's breaths are coming in these raspy gulps that sound like whooping cough, like suffocation.

"It's asthma!" I shout to Nick over the sound of Kai's wheezing. "He can't breathe!"

Nick shoots out of his chair and runs from the room. A moment later, Donovan is there.

"Kai!" Donovan says, crouching beside Kai and putting a hand on his leg. "Kai," he repeats it, calmer this time, like he has all the time in the world. "I'm here, buddy. Let's find a focus object, okay?"

Kai just keeps on gasping for air, his head still folded into his lap.

"I see a tree," Donovan says, and Nick and I share a confused glance. Donovan is looking at a potted plant in the corner of the room. "It's a green leafy thing," he says. "In a tall white pot." He's speaking slowly, calmly, and to my surprise, Kai's breathing sounds like it may be slowing down slightly. "The pot has some interesting etchings on it." He waits a moment.

"They're like geometric shapes." He pauses again. "Can you look for me?"

Kai lifts his head and looks at Donovan. He's still panting, his eyes wide, stunned. But then his gaze lands on the plant.

"Good," Donovan says. "Do you see the plant?"

Kai nods as his rasping begins to abate.

"Do you see the pot?"

He nods again.

"The etchings?"

He nods one more time, quieting a little more.

"I find that shape appealing," Donovan's voice is smooth, unhurried. "It reminds me of geometry."

We all wait as Kai stares at the pot. He seems to be catching his breath, slowing down in increments. "They're hexagons," he finally says, and his breathing sounds almost normal.

"Yes," Donovan says, leaning down to kiss the top of Kai's head. "Yes, they are."

Kai keeps his eyes focused on the plant while Donovan looks up at Nick and me.

"Maybe we should call it a day?" His voice is bland, but his eyes are firm.

"Of course," I answer, still reeling from the fright of watching Kai struggle for air.

The attorney is there suddenly, standing between us, pushing Donovan out of the room. "You and Kai go ahead," she tells him. "Get some lunch or something. We'll finish up here. Don't worry about us." She sounds more chipper than she has all morning, and I understand that she's just putting on a show for Kai.

As soon as the door has closed behind Kai, she turns back toward Nick and me, all traces of smiles absent. She raises her eyebrows at the two of us before finally speaking.

"Best interests of the child? I don't think so."

Chapter 32

DONOVAN
SEPTEMBER 2018

*K*ai and I are in the backseat of a taxi heading toward the middle school before I say anything about what happened in that conference room. To Nick and Maggie's credit, at least they didn't complain about ending the meeting early. I'm sure they can't stay in New York indefinitely to wait for another chance to talk, so this was a subpar outcome for them.

"You want to talk about it?" I take a chance with the question, knowing that sometimes he prefers to process for a while before talking with me about whatever might have made him anxious. He often seems more comfortable having time alone with Teddy when he needs to regroup, but Teddy is at school right now, probably still suffering through a lecture about prefixes in Latin class.

Kai's looking out the window, watching the crowded streets of midtown, as our cab hurtles from one traffic light to the next. He doesn't turn toward me as he shakes his head.

I let out a long breath as I try to choose my words properly. "We don't have to. I just want to apologize, that's all," I tell him. Now he looks over at me to listen. "You seemed so relaxed about all of this—excited, even. I should have realized that you run deeper, that you were churning through scenarios all on your own." We're both quiet for a moment before I add, "You don't always have to try to put on a brave face for Dad and me. You're not even eleven years old yet. You're allowed to have feelings. And fears."

His eyes begin to glisten, as though he's about to cry, but no tears fall.

"We're all just doing our best to get through this. It's okay." I rub my hand between his shoulders in concentric circles.

He turns back toward the window, but I also feel him relax into my touch. "I didn't want to make it worse for you and Dad," he says without turning to face me. "I thought if I just seemed excited about everything, then you'd be happy for me instead of scared."

"But why—"

Kai whips around to face me. "They want to take me back, don't they?" His eyes are wide. "To make me live with them in Arizona. That's why they're here, why they wanted to meet with me?"

"Did Teddy tell you that?" I ask, wondering if Kai's known all along.

"That day when you picked us up from Grandma and Gramps's, when Dad called and cursed on the phone." He swallows hard as he finishes.

I suppose the ruse is up. There's no reason to continue trying to protect him from what he already knows, so I say, "You're right that they want you. Who wouldn't? How could you blame them, right? But the fact that they made a mistake when they gave you to us ten years ago doesn't mean we have to give you back now. Family is about so much more than blood and DNA, and we are doing everything we can to make them understand that."

"I don't want to live with them."

I slide closer to him on the worn seat of the cab and pull him toward me so that we're shoulder to shoulder. I rest my head down against his in solidarity as I try to think of something comforting to say that won't be a lie.

"Do you want me to take you to the nurse when we get to school? I can stay there with you until you're ready to go to class."

"No, I'm okay now," he says.

For a moment, I think his voice has gone back to its normal timbre, but then I realize this is the same tone he's been using for the past several weeks. It's the sound of Kai putting on a brave face.

"Excuse me, sir?" I lean forward toward our Eastern European driver. "Change of plans. Could you please turn around and take us to the Bronx Zoo?"

The driver glances at me in the rearview mirror, looks down at the meter, and shrugs. "No problem," he says.

"What? Why?" Kai demands, his eyes growing bright with excitement.

"I don't know. No big deal. Just seems like a nice day for the zoo." I try to act casual, like this kind of spontaneity is part of my usual MO, but I can't stop the smile from breaking onto my face.

"What about school?" Kai asks. He's smiling now too.

"You can go tomorrow," I offer.

"Awesome!" He's getting into the spirit of it now. "Hot dogs and the carousel?"

"Hot dogs and the carousel," I agree.

I don't know what's going to happen going forward. I'm concerned that Maggie and Nick are going to read Kai's panic attack as a symptom of an unhappy home life, a suboptimal childhood that they want to rectify—or maybe they'll see it as they should, an indication that they are upsetting him and should back the fuck off. What I do know for certain is that it's a beautiful day in New York City, and I'm lucky enough to be sitting here with my sweet, sweet boy.

I suppose we've been living on borrowed time for the last ten years as it is. I don't know whether I will get much more—but I'm sure as hell going to make the most of the time we have left.

⁓⁓⁓⁓⁓⁓

We're just walking uphill to the giraffe enclosure when my phone lights up with Lorraine's number. I don't want to get into any of the details with her while Kai is standing right beside me, so I let the call go to voicemail.

As Kai points out the giraffe's black tongue, the phone starts buzzing again. One of Lorraine's best qualities as a lawyer is probably the fact that she's persistent, but right now, it's irritating as all hell. I turn the phone completely off, reasoning that in the unlikely event an emergency comes up for Teddy, the school will call Chip too.

As we walk the paved path at the zoo, stopping at every exhibit along the route to Jungle World, which is Kai's favorite part of the zoo, I am overcome with so much love for this boy that it's physically painful. I don't know what I'll do if Nick and Maggie decide to move forward with the lawsuit—or, worse, if they win. My mind starts to run through all the possibilities again, and I begin to wonder if we should just take the boys and leave the country. It might be illegal at this point, but if it's the best thing for our child, maybe we should do it anyway. An image of Kai in the conference room flashes through my mind, when he was sitting beside Maggie and gasping for air. In all the time he's struggled with anxiety, he's never had a full-on panic attack like that before. How can I stand back and risk allowing him to land in a situation where he feels that way all the time—trapped with the wrong parents, unable to breathe?

We could go to Sicily. Change our names. Start over. Or maybe a place where it'd be even harder to trace us, like Bali or the most remote part of New Zealand.

Kai reaches into his pocket for his phone, and I'm about to tell him to put it away and enjoy the zoo when he shows me the screen, which is displaying an incoming call from Chip.

"Go ahead," I say, realizing only now that I never called my husband to let him know how the meeting went.

"Hi Dad," Kai says into the phone. "Yeah . . . yeah . . . We're at the zoo." He glances at me as he says this, like he's unsure he was allowed to tell.

I nod to let him know it was no secret.

"He wants to talk to you." Kai holds out the phone.

"Hey. Sorry I didn't call sooner," I say as I put the phone up to my ear.

"Why aren't you answering your phone?" he cries in a near shout. "I've been trying to reach you like crazy!" He sounds frantic, and I'm sure he's about to tell me that the case is back on, that we have to be in court this afternoon or tomorrow. I brace for the worst, flinching before he even says the words.

Chapter 33

MAGGIE
SEPTEMBER 2018

"Why don't you two take a moment to discuss how you'd like to proceed," Lorraine says. "You can find me in my office, three doors down the hall, when you're ready to talk." She motions with a hand that we should sit back at the conference table.

"I'm not sure we'll be able to resolve anything in the next few minutes," Nick says curtly. "It's kind of a big decision."

"No rush," she says, all breezy and accommodating. She picks up her notepad and leaves the room.

After the door clicks closed, Nick looks over at me and sighs dramatically. "Well that complicates things," he says.

"It does? I thought it settled the matter."

"Yeah, I guess." He pulls out his phone and starts swiping at the screen. "But now we probably have to stay in the city longer to get the case going again. It's going to be a real shit-show getting more coverage at the restaurant."

"Get the case going?" I ask. "No—I meant settled it, like, ended it."

Nick's head snaps back in surprise. "What do you mean? How can we leave our kid in a situation that's given him some sort of anxiety disorder? How can *that* be in his best interest?" His face is turning redder with each question.

"His living situation didn't give him an anxiety disorder. He probably inherited it."

"Inherited it?" Nick parrots my words back to me. "We don't have anxiety disorders. Wyatt doesn't have it. What are you talking about?"

"I'm talking about my mother," I explain.

"Again with your mother." Nick throws his hands up in the air. "Not everything in this world has to revolve around you and your mother."

"Nick."

"What?" he barks without looking at me.

"My mother had mental illness."

"I know she drove you crazy, but that doesn't mean we would create a kid with a real problem."

"No," I explain, "she was legit, diagnosable, bipolar. Like, medicated and everything."

He looks over at me and eyes me up and down, like he's trying to figure out whether I'm being serious. He blinks a few times and then asks, "Why would you keep that a secret? Jesus, Maggie. You don't keep something like that from the person you're going to create a family with."

I hate the way Nick always assumes the worst of me, as though I'm out to get him, constantly ferreting away little secrets and personal infractions.

"I only just found out." I say it quietly, hoping my calm demeanor will highlight his own irritability, his inappropriate reaction. "The other day with my dad."

"Your dad didn't think it was relevant for me to know this information when we decided to make babies together?"

"First of all, we didn't *decide* to make Wyatt, and I wasn't even talking to my parents back then. As for all the ones we tried and failed to make, a bipolar grandparent is not generally considered a cause for concern when having children."

I don't add that ever since my dad enlightened me, I've been tallying so many of my mother's symptoms in myself—the impulsivity, the oversize emotions, the way I cling to anger and feel pain so deeply. As for any of my mom's imbalances trickling down to Kai, I've learned enough about anxiety disorders over the years to know that while trauma or other stressful events can cause the symptoms, genetic predisposition is often a major contributing factor.

"You say there was no cause for concern," Nick nearly growls, "and yet we seem to have produced a child who can't breathe when he gets worried."

"Yeah." I'm nearly shouting. "And it looks like his *real* dad knew just how to handle it."

I've shocked Nick into silence. I'm worried I've finally pushed him too far.

"Right," he finally says, and I brace for whatever's coming next, but the intensity of his expression starts to mellow and he asks, "So that's it? You really want to just drop the case now?"

He's not going to fight me. He knows I'm right. Nobody could argue with the bond that we just saw between Kai and Donovan. To remove Kai from that security, to take an anxious child and drop him into a whole new family—that would be the very opposite of acting in his best interests. As much as it pains me to let go, I have to accept this. For Kai's sake.

"I want to drop it," I confirm.

Nick stares at me for a long moment and then runs both his hands over his face, rubbing at his eyes and swallowing hard. And then, finally, he nods.

As we stare at each other, I keep seeing images of Kai gasping for breath in my mind's eye—reliving the sense of helplessness I felt, the uselessness of my presence. Only when I backed away from Kai was he able to breathe, only when I gave him space was he able to get what he needed. I can't help thinking of my mom when I consider the idea of giving a child space. I may have had my bumps along the way, but perhaps my parents' decision to pull back and give me space is what eventually allowed me to develop the blessings I now have in life. Maybe it's time I stop focusing on what I don't have, and start doing a better job of appreciating those things that I do.

I can almost feel my mom here, standing beside me and nodding, proud that I am finally, at long last, starting to get it.

We make our way down the carpeted hallway to Lorraine's office and tell her the news. She is gracious in her acceptance, suggesting that we have our attorney make a proposal about our visitation rights with Kai going forward, telling us to have our lawyer send it along to her. Based on this act of good faith by us, she says she'll put in a good word for us with her clients.

As we walk back to the elevator, Nick puts his arm around me, and my first instinct is to shrug it off and push him away. But I don't. Instead, I clasp his hand and pull him a little closer.

"What?" he asks, clearly surprised by my reaction.

So many potential responses run through my mind. I could explain how letting go of Kai makes me think of all the other areas of life where we could try harder to be empathetic, to be generous. I could say something about wanting to do something to make our marriage stronger, about how I'm sorry for so much, about how I miss what we used to have. But I don't want to say any of it. I just want to move forward and do the best we can. So I just shake my head and rest it sadly against Nick's shoulder.

"He's my son too, you know," Nick says with a kindness to his tone, I suppose to show me that we can suffer together, that we can lean on each other. The elevator doors open and we step inside. Nick presses the button for the lobby.

"No." I turn to face him as I realize the truth of what I'm saying. I hold my hand to his stubbly cheek to soften my words before I say them. "He's not your son. He's not my son, either. He's been theirs all along."

Chapter 34

DONOVAN
SEPTEMBER 2018

The crowds at the zoo disappear into a fog as all my focus goes toward whatever Chip is about to reveal from the other end of the line.

"They're dropping the case," he says.

"Wait, what?" I was certain that Maggie and Nick would be motivated to move forward at a furious pace after witnessing Kai's panic attack. Chip must have misunderstood. "What do you mean?"

"The Wingates. It's over. Lorraine called me. She said she couldn't reach you."

"It's over?" I hear the words but somehow can't grasp the concept.

"Over," Chip repeats. "All of it."

I look toward Kai, who has wandered over to a souvenir seller's cart at the opposite side of the path and is running his hand along a brightly colored stuffed monkey. He's studying the Velcro patches on the animal's hands and is uninterested in my call.

"Are you sure? Did Lorraine tell you what happened?" I prod, afraid to get my hopes up.

"She told me. She said we couldn't have scripted the morning better if we'd planned the panic attack. Whatever you did in there to calm him down, I guess it proved something to the Wingates."

It takes me a moment to digest Chip's words, to understand that the way Kai came out of his panic was of more relevance in the meeting than the fact that he panicked in the first place. I try for a moment to imagine how I would have felt in Maggie's shoes, or Nick's, in a room with a child who was struggling in ways I didn't understand. I suppose I did prove some sort of capability as a father, or as Kai's father specifically, when I brought him out of his attack. Who knew Kai's anxiety would end up being such a gift to our family?

"I can't believe it," I pant into the phone, breathless from excitement. "So, what does it mean? Now what?"

"Now nothing," he says. Even though I can't see him, I know he's smiling all the way up to his hairline right now. "Lorraine said they might request some visitation rights, but they won't be challenging our parental rights or custody."

I glance around for a bench, feeling literally weak in the knees from the relief coursing through my body. When I don't find one, I simply lower myself onto the pavement on the side of the path. "So that's it," I say, still processing, as the warmth of the concrete below me seeps through my pants. "I had us halfway to Malaysia already." I confess to my plans of taking the family on the run.

Chip laughs. "I'm pretty sure my passport expired a few months ago."

"We'd have gotten you a fake if we had to," I declare.

"Sure."

"What? There must be a way."

"Okay, Houdini. Well, I'm glad we won't have to put your disappearing skills to the test just yet." This may be the longest phone call I've ever had with Chip while he's at work, but it's clearly worth the time to him.

Kai looks over and his brow furrows when he notices me sitting on the ground.

"Papa, what are you doing?" he asks, walking back over to me.

I wave my hand to indicate it's nothing, that I'm all good, as I say to Chip, "We're at the zoo," even though he knows that already.

"Yeah, okay," he answers. "See you at home."

"See you at home," I say, and that word, *home*, fills me up, runs through my veins and makes me strong.

I hang up as Kai reaches me and then I pull him onto my lap.

"Pa, stop." He tries to wriggle away from me, clearly too old to sit on his dad's lap in public. I plant one hard kiss against the back of his head and then release him.

"Help me up," I say, reaching out to him and letting him pull. "Dad called to tell us that Maggie and Nick want you to stay exactly where you are. They don't want to mess with your life."

"They don't?" His eyes grow big as he looks back at me.

"They must care about you a whole lot," I tell him as I put a hand on his back and start walking toward all the funny little monkeys that await us in Jungle World. "They just want you to be wherever is best for you."

"With you is best for me."

"Yeah." I scruff up his hair a little, trying not to get too sappy. He hates it when I'm all tears and emotions—but come on, if there was ever a time for it, right? "With you is best for me too."

I glance at the sky to prevent any happy tears from spilling out and then I open the door to Jungle World and stand back, letting Kai lead the way.

Chapter 35

KAI
TEN YEARS LATER

*T*hat bell. If Darla doesn't stop ringing that freaking bell, I may actually call campus security on her. All I wanted was a ten-minute break to relax in front of the Celtics game before returning to my massive study guides.

When I can't stand it for a single second longer, I pause the game and march over to the intercom. "Jesus, Darla, give it a rest!"

"It's not your psycho ex-girlfriend, fucker," my brother's voice says through the speaker on the wall. "Let me in."

"Teddy? Why didn't you call me?" I pat down my pants and realize I must have left my phone in the bedroom.

"I did, bro. Let me in before I freeze my nuts off out here."

I jog down the stairwell, where I can see my brother waiting on the stoop on the other side of the glass door. He's wearing a red puffer jacket and a black wool beanie, and he's bouncing up and down on the balls of his feet as he blows clouds of steam into his hands. I push the door open for him and a burst of cold air follows him inside.

"Just a little advice, man," he says. "If you don't want Darla to know when you're home, maybe park your car down the block or something."

"Yeah, happy birthday to you, too," I say as we give each other a quick hug, pounding each other on the back for a moment, open-handed, before turning to climb the three flights to my apartment.

"How was dinner with Brynn?" I ask as Teddy follows behind me.

"Good, good." He says it noncommittally, but he's got it bad for this girl, and I know there's no other way he would have wanted to spend his birthday. "The pub crawl was fun?" he asks in return. The question sounds casual, but I know he's looking for reassurance that I'm not sore at him for choosing Brynn over me.

"There's no other way I would have wanted to spend my birthday." I shrug as I push open the door to the two-bedroom apartment I share with my friend Ron. "Really," I add. "Just a few friends drinking our way through several Bostonian establishments of questionable repute. It was good, promise."

This apartment isn't much, but compared to the Tufts University campus housing, where there was never a moment's peace, landing in this grimy apartment after sophomore year felt like a serious upgrade. My roommate spends most of his time in the library, and I often feel like the whole place belongs to me alone.

"Here." Teddy reaches into his pocket and removes a small square of paper that's been folded over itself several times. He hands it to me and then starts taking off his jacket. As he pulls off one sleeve and then the other, I see that he's wearing only a T-shirt underneath.

"No wonder you were freezing out there. Doesn't the crew team have any long-sleeve shirts to give their rowers? Maybe a sweatshirt?"

Teddy pulls at his shirt, stretching the logo of the Boston University bulldog on it into a distorted, alien shape until he releases the hem. "Will you just open the paper?" He's got his eyes on my hands.

"What is it?" I ask as I unfold the printout and see the words *Relativity Logins* written across the top.

"Pa sent it to me last night. If I want to search for any half-siblings from the egg donor, I guess he thinks I'm of age to make that choice on my own now."

"And here I thought becoming legal drinkers was the best part of yesterday," I deadpan.

He winces slightly at my words, and I realize I've been too flip. "That's what you want to do?" I ask, changing gears. "You're sure you want to go there?" As if it wasn't enough of a mindfuck the last time our family started investigating our roots.

"I don't know." He drops down onto my sofa and starts tapping one foot against the floor at a furious, repetitive pace. "Will you just look for me? Tell me what it says? No." He stands up again. "Don't."

I wait for him to make up his mind, the creased paper still in my outstretched hand. He reaches out to reclaim the paper but then pulls back quickly, as if he's been burned. I know better than to rush him as he struggles, so I just stand opposite him and wait. His eyes shift back and forth as he puzzles out one piece or another of this dilemma, and then he takes a deep breath and looks around the apartment, his eyes roving over a half-eaten buttered bagel that's been sitting on the coffee table since lunch and a pile of charging cords stacked in a corner on the floor, waiting to be untangled.

Finally, he looks back at me with his eyes wide. "That's why I came all the way out here." He rubs a hand over his chin. "I think . . . I think I want to know. But I feel like I can't look. Can you just do it for me, tell me what you see?"

As usual, the helplessness in his voice, the fear, pulls at my heart, just like it has ever since we were kids. I wish I could be a dick and tell him to grow some balls, but that's just not how we roll. I'm the one who watches over him.

I walk over to the small computer desk and flatten out the folded sheet he handed me.

"There are two different logins here," I say, looking back to Teddy for guidance.

He lowers himself onto the couch again and starts chewing on his thumbnail. "I know. Pa couldn't remember whose was whose, so he just gave me both. Just try both of them."

I type in the first username, *rigsdale123*, and follow it up with the long list of numbers that constitute the password. The screen updates and it's my name that appears at the top, not Teddy's. I reach for the paper to look at the other username, but an insistent icon flashing in the corner of the screen catches my eye. I move the mouse over to the icon, and a pop-up message tells me I have a new 25 percent genealogy match with the birth year 2010.

"Well?" Teddy asks from his spot on the sofa behind me. He's literally covering his eyes with his hands, like a toddler watching a scary movie.

"No, nothing. I signed into mine by mistake. Hang on." I click back to the login page while my mind tries to process what I just learned. A 25 percent match. I'm pretty sure a cousin is only a 12.5 percent match. A parent or sibling would be a 50 percent match. So 25 percent has to mean a half-sibling. But Wyatt would have already been five years old by 2010, and he's a full biological sibling for me anyway.

"Here we go," I say as the page for Teddy's results loads on the screen. He's got three new matches, but when I click around, I see that they are all distant cousins of Chip's, names I vaguely recognize hearing throughout my childhood. No matches for a half-sibling or a mom.

"Sorry, man, looks like there's nothing." I glance behind me to Teddy, who finally begins lowering his hands from his face. Small red circles show on his cheeks where he must have pushing in with the heels of his hands.

"Nothing?" He blinks a few times and then stands to come stare at the screen alongside me. "But basically everyone's in this database." He takes the mouse and starts navigating up and down the screen, but there's nothing else to see.

"Maybe she just donated the one time," I conjecture. "Maybe you were her only offspring."

He doesn't answer as he steps away from the computer desk.

"Maybe she got hit by a car right after she left the clinic and couldn't donate any other eggs." I keep listing possibilities. "Or maybe she became one of those survivalists and moved completely off the grid. She could be living in the woods of West Virginia, stockpiling canned goods as we speak."

He looks so crestfallen that I try to backpedal.

"She probably just did the one donation to earn money during school or something. Some gorgeous young girl from Princeton or Yale who wanted any babies that came from her eggs to be able to have happy lives on their own, without her interfering. What do you need her for now, anyway?"

All these years, Teddy has always been the one making these type of comments, insisting that I don't need a relationship with my birth family, that our little family of four should be enough.

He flops back onto the end of the sofa and pulls a face.

I swivel all the way around in my chair so we're facing each other head on. "You could try that Sibling Donor Registry," I offer. We've talked about this website in the past, but Teddy has always shot the idea down.

"Nah." He shakes his head. "This is probably for the best. Brynn got it in my head that we should know more about my history, but this is better. Who needs another can of worms like the last time?" He says it lightly, like that was just a blip in our past, and I can't help but feel the littlest bit surprised at how cavalier he is. He seems to have forgotten everything I went through back then, the emotions I rode out in order to protect our family. But that's Teddy for you, always rewriting history to see just what he wants to see.

"Want to go get burgers?" he asks, and I guess we've finished with this investigation. "Belated birthday dinner?"

"Midterms," I say, motioning toward the stack of textbooks on the floor beside my desk.

"Right." He nods, having to be reminded, yet again, that his schedule at BU isn't exactly in sync with the Tufts calendar.

He looks downcast, so I say, "Okay, burgers. We'll make it quick."

Who am I to deny Teddy anything at all?

I grab my coat and follow him down the stairs.

———————

When I finally get back to my apartment two hours later, I shake the snow off my parka, toss it on the couch, and beeline for my computer.

I let the cursor hover over the link on my Relativity page for a few seconds. Do I really want to know whatever revelation is waiting on the other side of this URL? After all the years I've denied myself a relationship with my birth family, all the information I might have had access to if they were a part of my life—yeah, I guess I do want to know.

As I click the link, I find an entirely unfamiliar family tree, a page filled primarily with people bearing the last name Westlake. I search the screen until I see that the name Clyde Westlake is highlighted with a little icon above his name showing that he's my 25 percent match. I follow the lines of the tree and see that his mother, Brianna Westlake, lives in Phoenix and was born in 1980. I don't seem to have any other matches along the tree, and I've never heard of Brianna Westlake. Clyde doesn't have any siblings listed either. Someone has, however, uploaded a picture of Clyde.

I click on the photo and my mouth drops open. A younger version of Nick Wingate's face is staring back at me. I feel a rush of adrenaline as I process this new information. It seems that my biological father had a kid in 2010, during a time when he was supposedly happily married to Maggie.

Back when I was in middle school, I told my dads that I didn't want a relationship with the Wingates, that it would be easier for me that way—but what I meant was that it would be easier for Teddy, and for them. Since then, I've done my share of research from afar. I've tried to live vicariously through the pages of their social media accounts, imagining reunions that I knew wouldn't come to pass. I've never once seen anything about Nick having another son other than Wyatt. And yet it would appear that my bio dad had his dalliances, and I have yet another brother out there in the world. This one, I guess, is only a half-brother, unlike Wyatt, the brother I gave up long ago in favor of Teddy.

Teddy wouldn't have been able to handle it, me having a relationship with my birth parents, possibly going to spend extended time with them. I don't regret faking the panic attack that day in the lawyer's conference room. I knew as soon as Maggie started talking about Arizona during that meeting that they were trying to get custody of me, and I couldn't let that happen to Teddy. Even though he and I don't share DNA, I guess sharing a womb was enough. We're that close and always have been. That day in the lawyer's office was just one more time that I had to play the role of the anxious twin in order to protect my fragile brother. Luckily, all those other times I stepped up for Teddy had Pa telling me over and again about the panic attacks he had as a teenager. The nights when I asked Pa to stay in the room because of the thunder, or when I claimed one or another movie was too scary for me, or when I peppered him and Dad with the questions Teddy was too afraid to ask, all those moments led Pa to tell me all about what panic attacks look like. I knew just what to do to make it seem real. And it was a good thing, too, because Teddy would have been devastated if I had moved away.

I look back at the screen, digesting the fact that my bio dad was probably unfaithful and wondering what I should do about it. I could reach out to Maggie or to Wyatt and tell them what I've found. But from the tidbits I pick up online, it seems like they're living as a happy family out in Arizona. They don't need me crawling out of the woodwork to mess everything up again.

All those years ago, I made a choice. I opted to relinquish my biological family in order to protect Teddy, the brother I love beyond measure, and our fathers, the men who've given us everything. I was willing to sacrifice for the person who still feels like a part of my own soul and for the family that we've always been so proud of.

Now it's time for me to protect my other brother and the life he's lived.

When I move the mouse over to the X in the corner of the screen and close out of Relativity, I feel only relief. I shut down the computer and let the screen go dark.

Acknowledgments

I love being a writer. As much as I enjoy dreaming up plots and transferring them to the page, nothing I do happens in a vacuum. There are endless behind-the-scenes moments and herculean efforts by people other than myself that go into creating and distributing a finished book, and I owe many people a deep debt of gratitude.

First, I would like to thank all the inspiring women at SparkPress and She Writes Press for believing in my work and helping me bring it to its fullest potential. Brooke Warner, Crystal Patriarch, Lauren Wise, Samantha Strom, Shannon Green, and Krissa Lagos. I am blessed to work with you all. I'm also in constant awe of my publicity team at BookSparks: Crystal Patriarche, Taylor Brightwell, and Hanna Lindsley. Your creativity and commitment inure to the benefit of all around you. I owe a special thanks to Nicola Kraus, as well, for bringing her unparalleled editing skills to bear on this work.

There were several people who were kind enough to consider the complex issues in this book and weigh in on varying topics. In particular, I would like to thank Dr. Jamie Cohen Knopman and Dr. Janice Marks for taking the time to talk through several medical questions. A special shout-out to Melissa Brisman at Reproductive Possibilities for offering her insights and expertise on issues I might never have considered without her guidance. To Lisa Wippler at Growing Generations, thank you for your incredible generosity. The time you spent talking to me and educating me about surrogacy and family building was crucial to the success of this book, and I cannot thank you enough. To Dr. Kim Bergman at Growing Generations for being supportive of the ideas for this book, and especially for connecting me with Lisa Wippler. To Dan Ziskin, attorney extraordinaire, for helping me with the intricacies of surrogacy and adoption law in the magnificent state of Arizona. Each of the experts listed above brought invaluable information and wisdom to my attention. Any errors within the text are mine alone.

Many of my friends and beta readers have also stepped up, yet again, to support my work. First and foremost, I would like to thank the beautiful and talented Amy Blumenfeld for talking with me at length at the beginning of this project to help make sure I was looking at the plot from many critical angles. Your ongoing support, insights, and cheer mean the world to me. Thank you to Rick Bettan for an especially careful beta read. Thank you to David Yanks for providing me a thorough tour of your offices in Manhattan and informing more parts of the story than you might guess. Thank you to Aliya Sahai for consistently cheering me on, for always knowing how to be such an incredibly supportive friend, and for introducing me to Dr. Bergman.

Thank you to the friends who continue to read my drafts and support me through thick and thin: Marci Cohen, Ali Isaacs, Nancy Mayerfield, Ari Mayerfield, Daria Mikhailov, Jenna Myers, Robyn Pecarsky, Michele Sloane, and Amy Tunick. Thank you to Bree Schonbrun Dumain for introducing me to ranunculus flowers. Thank you also to the friends who always go above and beyond to spread the word about my books: Jenny Brown, Jocelyn Burton, Alissa Butterfass, Lissy Carr, Reena Glick, Michal Plancey, Julie Schanzer, Stacey Wechsler, and Mimi Sager Yoskowitz.

One of the best parts of being a writer has been getting to know many fabulous members of the writing community. It's a delight to have found inspiration and kindred spirits in so many of these friends, especially Lisa Barr, Jenna Blum, Laura Dave, Fiona Davis, Camille Di Maio, Elyssa Friedland, Reyna Marder Gentin, Nicola Harrison, Susan Kleinman, Lynda Cohen Loigman, Annabel Monaghan, Amy Poepell, Marylin Simon Rothstein, Ines Rodriguez, Susie Schnall, Meredith Schorr, Courtney Sheinmel, Jonathan Tropper, Rochelle Weinstein, and Kitty Zeldis.

These acknowledgments would not be complete without an extra-special thanks to all the book bloggers, podcasters, and bookstagrammers who do so much to promote the work of authors. I've been lucky to work with and get to know Barbara Bos, Robin Kall Homonoff, Lauren Blank Margolin, Brad King, Sue Peterson, Ashley Spivey, and Renee Weiss Weingarten. I am especially grateful for the friendships I have developed with Zibby Owens, Jamie Rosenblit, Suzy Weinstein Leopold, and Andrea Peskind Katz.

Finally, I offer the deepest thanks to my wonderful family: Sheila, Bob, Allison, Ben, Samantha, and Mike, for their unceasing support. My father, who offers endless grammatical advice and knows which airports have revolving doors. Seymour, who brings me so much joy and keeps me laughing through everything. Kelly, who listens closely and offers the very best advice, and Harry, who takes care of us all. Dorothy, who brings calm and consistency to everyone around her and allows me to get my work done. To my mother—it is my great honor to be able to make you proud, and I love you so much. Abe, Asher, Shep, and Nava, who run plots with me around the dinner table and run circles around me everywhere else. You guys are my whole world. And Jason, whose heart is actually bigger than his biceps—you are my loudest champion, my greatest love, and I am so lucky you're mine.

About the Author

*J*acqueline Friedland is the author of the award-winning
novels *Trouble the Water* and *That's Not a Thing*. She
holds a BA from the University of Pennsylvania and a JD
from NYU Law School. She practiced as an attorney in New
York for a hot second before transitioning to writing full time.
She lives in New York with her husband, four children, and
two very bossy dogs.

Author photo © Rebecca Weiss

SELECTED TITLES FROM SPARKPRESS

SparkPress is an independent boutique publisher delivering high-quality, entertaining, and engaging content that enhances readers' lives, with a special focus on female-driven work. www.gosparkpress.com

Attachments: A Novel, Jeff Arch, $16.95, 978-1-68463-081-3. What happens when the mistakes we make in the past don't stay in the past? When no amount of running from the things we've done can keep them from catching up to us? When everything depends on what we do next?

Goodbye, Lark Lovejoy: A Novel, Kris Clink, $16.95, 978-1-68463-073-8. A spontaneous offer on her house prompts grief-stricken Lark to retreat to her hometown, smack in the middle of the Texas Hill Country Wine Trail—but it will take more than a change of address to heal her broken family.

That's Not a Thing: A Novel, Jacqueline Friedland. $16.95, 978-1-68463-030-1. When a recently engaged Manhattanite learns that her first great love has been diagnosed with ALS, she is faced with the impossible decision of whether a few final months with her ex might be worth risking her entire future. A fast-paced emotional journey that explores whether it's possible to be equally in love with two men at once.

Trouble the Water: A Novel, Jacqueline Friedland. $16.95, 978-1-943006-54-0. When a young woman travels from a British factory town to South Carolina in the 1840s, she becomes involved with a vigilante abolitionist and the Underground Railroad while trying to navigate the complexities of Charleston high society and falling in love.

About SparkPress

$\int$parkPress is an independent, hybrid imprint focused on merging the best of the traditional publishing model with new and innovative strategies. We deliver high-quality, entertaining, and engaging content that enhances readers' lives. We are proud to bring to market a list of *New York Times* best-selling, award-winning, and debut authors who represent a wide array of genres, as well as our established, industry-wide reputation for creative, results-driven success in working with authors. SparkPress, a BookSparks imprint, is a division of SparkPoint Studio LLC.

Learn more at GoSparkPress.com